Straight White Male

WESTERN LITERATURE SERIES

Straight White Male

Gerald W. Haslam

UNIVERSITY OF NEVADA PRESS

Reno & Las Vegas

WESTERN LITERATURE SERIES

University of Nevada Press, Reno, Nevada 89557 USA
Copyright © 2000 by Gerald W. Haslam
Manufactured in the United States of America

Library of Congress Cataloging-in-Publication Data
Haslam, Gerald W.
    Straight white male / Gerald W. Haslam
        p.   cm. — (Western literature series)
    ISBN 0-87417-354-x (alk. paper)
    1. Parent and child—Fiction.   2. Middle aged men—
Fiction.   3. Adult children—Fiction.   4. Aging
parents—Fiction.   I. Title.   II. Series.
    PS3558.A724 S77 2000
    813'.54—dc21   00-008598

The paper used in this book meets the requirements of
American National Standard for Information Sciences—
Permanence of Paper for Printed Library Materials, ANSI
Z39.48-1984. Binding materials were selected for strength
and durability.

09 08 07 06 05 04 03 02 01
5 4 3 2

For Chuck and Carol Brandner
—special pals

Straight White Male

1

The Hall of Justice that summer morning was sticky hot. A sluggish wooden fan whirled above, and flyspecks dotted the large light globes like acne. Everyone in the office seemed rushed and uncomfortable.

I stood in suit and tie next to Yvonne Trumaine, the pregnant girl I would marry, and glanced about warily. I didn't want my buddies to see me with her. Only Travis and Juanita Plumley, who barely knew Yvonne, and Jess and Marge Soto, who didn't know her at all, were there, along with one of my bride's roommates.

My parents stood behind us—Pop, tall and weathered, unflinching in his lone white shirt with an inexpertly knotted tie at his neck; Mom in a dull pink dress, damp-eyed and leaning on his shoulder. Yvonne's father wore a cheap suit with a dark shirt and light tie, his pencil-thin mustache twitched into a smirk. His wife had red henna hair, her eyebrows appearing to have been drawn by the same pencil that produced her husband's mustache; she snapped chewing gum and seemed totally disinterested. I had told only Pop why I was marrying Yvonne.

My father was nothing if not a realist. "Your momma's gonna give you more grief than a little bit, but you do what you need to," he had counseled me when I told him our plans. Then he added something: "I bought me plenty a beer off of Yvonne's momma at the bar where she works, and I know her good. I know the old man too. He's a prick. You can bet them two never give her too good a start in life. You can bet that girl's had a tough row to hoe."

I started to turn away, but he grasped one of my arms and added, "And, Leroy, don't go into this with no stars in your eyes. Ever'body's been fuckin' somebody—just you remember that. Ever'body." That comment jolted me like a punch; he knew about her. "If you and her can get along," he added, "get to be pardners, that's what matters. You can start buildin' somethin' together."

Despite his words, I remained embarrassed to care about this girl, embarrassed even to be here with her, embarrassed that I didn't know if I was really the father of her baby. But I was relieved that she was pregnant, because that allowed me to tell my old pals if asked that I'd been forced to marry her. They could accept that and so could I: nobody would marry a whore unless he had to ("... there's plenty guys coulda knocked that honey up, but ol' Leroy got nailed").

But it wasn't true. I couldn't discard her and live with myself, and I could no longer stand sharing her. Increasingly, our sex was becoming an intimacy I felt in my heart as well as my genitals. I couldn't fathom this, but I couldn't deny it either.

I couldn't let her go.

The sweating justice of the peace hurried through the ceremony— several other awkward-looking couples were waiting in the next room—and his words rushed past me. Yvonne's hand was damp in mine, and her face was innocent and hopeful. I scanned the room as the magistrate spoke, gazed out a window at a hot sky faded to the color of Swiss cheese, and pretended I was someone else somewhere else ... watching this like a movie.

But I managed to focus long enough to hear the justice mumble, "... for better or for worse, till death do you part?"

Then I said, "I do," but I wasn't sure I did.

2

A thick, balding man slips through the French doors onto the deck, then lights a cigarette, smoke obscuring his face for a moment. His remaining gray hair is burred into a neat flattop, and like me, he wears pressed jeans, polished boots, and a pearl-buttoned western shirt. When he notices me, his face jolts.

So does mine.

After a moment of hesitation, he manages a rough smile and slowly approaches. "Hey, Leroy," he nods. "I shoulda figured you to be here. You still coachin'?"

"Hello, Floyd." My body is alert, fists suddenly clenched.

We both quiet, standing three feet apart. He holds his cigarette between his teeth, lips parted, and nods at the house. "Ol' Trav's sure done good, hadn't he? This place must be worth a mint."

An antique rage has risen in me, and I can only croak, "We can't both stay here, Floyd, you know that."

Silence hangs between us like fresh tripe. What can we say?

"I see ol' J.D. ever' oncet 'n awhile," Floyd ventures. "Me and him, we get to talkin' sometimes 'bout some of the ol' shit us guys used to do. He'd be here today himself but he's a-workin' daylights. He's a grandpa now, ya know."

"Floyd . . . ," I choke, and he at last seems to realize how close he is to being hit. We see each other rarely, so perhaps he's forgotten.

Our eyes meet, and I notice that his face, like mine, is filigreed by tiny creases: too much sun too young. Then his lips seem to tug slightly at their corners as he says, "About all that stuff between us way back when— me and you and your wife, I mean—I surely wisht it never happened. I know I shouldn't've said what I did, but we all talked about that stuff then . . . you too. I never meant to hurt nobody any more than you did, you know that. Besides, how could I know you'd marry her someday?" His voice deepens. "I surely wisht it'd never happened. I'd give anything to take it all back, Roy"—the name only my closest pals use. "Me and you been buddies a long, long time."

"Since kindergarten," I manage to say, ready to strike, not talk. Floyd, the great cocksman, has come to represent all the guys, all the stories, all the fears that I've never been able to escape.

Floyd slumps. "I surely wisht it never happened. We was best buds."

"Me too, Floyd. I wish it all hadn't happened." My eyes are warming as I speak. "If some guy was whipping you, he'd have me to whip too."

"I 'ppreciate that, Roy."

"But some things just don't heal."

He gazes beyond my shoulder for a moment, then sighs. "I appreciate that too."

My hands have begun to shake; I'm close to losing it, on a cusp of rage and tears, memories of one evening in particular bludgeoning me . . .

Full of beer, the three of us were, of course, talking about our favorite subject.

J.D. raised his bottle like he was making a grand pronouncement, and said, "You guys know what I figured out. We don't screw women because of how we feel—that's always the same—we screw 'em because of how they act—that's always different." He raised his eyebrows fast like Groucho Marx, causing Floyd and me to chuckle.

Then J.D. added, "Take ol' Earlene. Whenever I first stuck it to her, she got all stiff and closed her eyes and just kinda panted. I mean she done that ever' time I fucked her, and, boys, I fucked her crossed-eyed." He closed his own eyes, stiffened, and panted, looking like a quavering fence post.

That broke Floyd and me up. When the wave of guffaws passed, I said, "How about good old Cherry, with all that 'Ohhh, big boy! Gimme all you got!' stuff."

Floyd, who was also quite familiar with Cherry, was nodding and laughing when he said, "Yeah, she's somethin'. But I'll tell you guys the best one I ever got into is that Yvonne, the real pretty gal that works in the drugstore." He winked, then said, "When her mouth wasn't full"—J.D. and I burst into laughter and exchanged punches on the shoulder—"she kept carryin' on—'Ohhhhhh, lover! Ohhhhhh, God!'—buckin' like a damn bronco. She flat wore me out. I'll tell ya, boys, I never seen nothin' like it before. She even had me fuck her tits. You two oughta give that honey a try. I guarn-damn-tee she'll be game and plenty good . . . not that any pussy's bad."

We all laughed again, then Floyd added, "I b'lieve ol' J.D.'s right for a change. It really is how they act that makes it fun. If it wasn't for that, I'd just buy me one of them jack-off vibrators. It'd be cheaper than payin' for dates and easier than sweet-talkin' gals." He raised his eyebrows then and added, "Except maybe for that Yvonne. Boy howdy! For that ride I'd pay and sweet-talk both any ol' time."

I am focused on injuring Floyd. "Don't make me say it again: We can't both stay today."

"As long as it's straight between us, I can leave, Roy. I know you and your wife come a long ways to be here, and I live just over yonder. I can see Travis any ol' day."

"Do that."

He extends his right hand, but I ignore it, saying, "Go, Floyd," needing to jerk him close and to pound, to pound, to pound him until bad memories burst like boils.

It's far too late in our lives to build friendships like the one we once had, but it's also far too late to reconcile: I'll never forget and I'll never forgive. We can never be pals again.

Floyd turns and slumps away, but his cigarette smoke hangs in front of me, blue in the heavy air.

And I think, then, of J.D., who had teased shortly after learning I would marry Yvonne, "*Looks like maybe ol' Floyd put that dough in the oven, and you're gonna end up payin' for the biscuit.*" He had still been grinning when that punch bounced off his jaw.

As J.D. had staggered away that day, he'd threatened, "*You big bastard, I'll get you back someday.*"

"*Stay away from me . . . from us,*" was all I'd said then. And for twenty-five years he has wisely done that. But the possibility he mentioned hasn't stayed away, not in my deepest dreams or memories, though I've never talked about it. I guess J.D. really won the fight.

All I want now is for the past to stay away. Yvonne and I have built a life for ourselves far away from here, both of us better together than we had ever been separately. We return only selectively, and if I have to threaten or even injure old friends to protect us from the past, I will; they know I'm not kidding. For every moment of psychological pain they cause my wife or me, I'll return physical damage . . . and probably be sorry afterwards, but I'll whip them from asshole to appetite. There will be no winners if anyone starts that.

My hands are still shaking when I grasp the deck's railing, my face is unsteady, tears nearly spilling. I raise my eyes, gasp for breath, and gaze into the past. To the north below this slope trickles what's left of the Kern River. Beyond it, low beige hills—barely more than mounds—waver and bulge in light bent by heat. The land itself appears to sweat—hot, so hot. Those brown California hills, creased and rounded like supine hips, sprout not trees but wealth: oil pipes, oil pumps, oil wells, and strands of metallic pipes like luminous linguine. Plumes of steam erupt over there as though hell has sprung a leak, vapors escaping from an elaborate mechanism that dissolves the dense petroleum deep beneath those slopes: a simmering, vaporous scene that appears unreal to non-natives. To me, however, born and blooded here, it is as genuine as breath.

Now that Floyd has departed, I can't seem to stop memories from sweeping me. The high bluff on which I stand was itself once treeless, but now it is lush and landscaped, property of the wealthy who have colonized it. Here at the southern end of the state's Great Central Valley, I stand on the deck of Travis and Juanita Plumley's luxurious residence.

Below me, the dammed and diminished river is still marked by the remains of a riparian forest, a thin lane of green winding from a distant slash in those brown hills.

For more than forty years, my father had toiled among the oil pumps on those beige mounds. As a young buck I had too, and hunted rabbits there, and rutted with girlfriends. Later, on visits to my folks, I'd driven my own children there to seek trapdoor spiders or to enjoy the brief splendor of spring wildflowers. I exhale deeply, take a sip from the beer I'm holding, then someone squeezes my left biceps and a breast is suddenly soft against it.

"Remember when we used to park over there, Roy?" sighs Yvonne.

"Sure." I can't manage a smile, because I remember too much. My wife and I had indeed parked there together, as well as with others, folded our tan and youthful bodies as the hills still fold . . . with those others as with one another. This place where we both came of age still troubles and excites me. I can't seem to let go of events that occurred here so long ago, although we have lived elsewhere for nearly a quarter century.

We stand silently, her breast warm against me, a breast Floyd had once touched, once tasted, once titillated with his engorged penis, and I hear behind us the mingled voices of other guests clustering in the air-conditioned comfort of our old friends' large home.

After gazing at me for a moment, Yvonne kisses my cheek and asks, "What's wrong, hon'? Worried about your dad?"

I nod. It's easier than explaining who I saw and why I'm tense.

Yvonne's voice is pleasant: "He had a lot of good times over there with his cronies." She nods toward the section of town where we were both raised.

"Yeah," I agree, "Pop has some tales to tell."

"Don't be low." She squeezes my arm again, kisses my cheek, and I immediately wish we were alone over there on those hot slopes sweating together in bold daylight as we did many times before our marriage, then she says, "I'm going to go help Juanita and Marge with the hors d'oeuvres."

She kisses me again and departs, and I once more sip at my beer, flat and flavorless now. We are celebrating Travis and Juanita's silver wedding anniversary, so we are back in Bakersfield among old chums and some new ones.

By leaning around the pear tree that shades the western edge of the deck, I can study the panorama of my old neighborhood: it is below where I now stand, a distant sprawl of houses surrounded by those oil pumps, by those steam plumes, and by bright metallic tank farms—what Pop called "the oil patch." Somehow, it looks drier than the other sections of town visible from here.

"Aren't you *hot*?"

I turn and face a young woman I don't know. "A little," I reply.

"I'm Dolores Patterson," she extends her right hand and I shake it. "My husband works for Travis. So you're Leroy. I just met your wife—she's so *cute*."

"Thanks," I mumble, thinking, Beautiful, yes. Cute, no.

"You're one of the old boys, I hear."

"Getting older all the time."

"And you live *where*?"

"Mill Valley."

"Oh, really! Right at Mount Tamalpais. Bob—that's my husband—Bob and I went up there for the Harmonic Convergence. It's a *real* mystical power point, don't you think? You can just *feel* the psychic energy there."

I suppress a smile. "Some of us used to do a little harmonic converging right down there by the river."

"You *did*?"

"Ask Travis and Juanita if they ever converged down there."

She catches on, chuckles perfunctorily but appears unamused. "Juanita mentioned that your parents are living up north with you and that your father is . . . ah . . . failing."

I keep my tone neutral when I respond, "We're taking care of things."

"Was your family dysfunctional?"

What business is this of hers? "It was imperfect, but it worked fine."

"How do you *feel* about that? Have you gotten in touch with your anger? You have to take care of yourself, you know."

She is about to get in touch with my anger, but doesn't seem to realize it. Her right hand reaches like a tentative lover's, then lightly rests on my left one, where I so long ago tattooed L-O-V-E at the base of each finger, the letters childish and fading today.

"Isn't that interesting," the woman remarks. Then she continues, "We were at Esalen just last weekend for an aging-and-dying workshop. Death is *beautiful*," she confides.

"No shit?"

Her eyes blink, and she quickly removes that intimate hand from L-O-V-E. "It's a *natural* thing," she asserts, her chin thrust slightly forward.

"*No shit!*"

This time she flinches, stares at my unsmiling face, then sputters, "I've got to help Juanita," and is gone.

3

I'm settling into a troubled mood—those simmering hills, those seething memories—when Travis punches my shoulder. "Hey, big guy," he grins, "what'd you say to little ol' Dolores?"

"I praised her wisdom." Seeing him lightens my mood.

His grin widens. "I'll *bet*. She's a good little gal, but a space cadet, into everything. Right now it's Adult Children of Alcoholics, but—get this—her husband told me that neither of her folks were drinkers. I asked her about that the other day, and she said she thought her momma *might've* used too many prescription drugs. It's a good thing you stopped her or she'd've been tellin' you about crystals and channelin' and astrology . . . even *angels*." He flutters his arms like wings and adds, "All that stuff you Bay Area types're into."

"You mean the stuff people think *all* Californians are into?" I say, shaking my head. That reminds me of a story, and I can't resist grinning. "My second cousin Booger Scarborough—that's really his name—came out from Texas a couple of years ago. He wanted to see where my dad had lived and worked, so I brought him into the Valley here, and showed him the farms and the oil fields. Ol' Booger said something like, 'Hell, this ain't California. Where's them palm trees, them beaches, them movie stars?'

"I said, 'Hey, Boog', this is the *real* deal, the heart of the state, the richest agricultural area in the whole history of the world. This Valley produces more oil than some OPEC nations. . . .' I was into my sermon, but old Booger cut me off. 'Farms in California? Oil in California? You smoked too much of that wacky tobaccy, Leroy. Where're them damn movie stars at?'

"That got me to laughing, and I figured he was happier with the stereotype than with reality. I said we'd hunt some up, but we didn't find any."

Travis is chuckling. "Yeah, I've got kin in Oklahoma who won't come out here because of the beatniks and the earthquakes and the gays hoverin' around to give folks AIDS. They believe that stuff."

"Anyway," I say, "it sounds like your friend Dolores is about a year behind the nutty fringe up on the coast."

Travis's chuckle has turned into a laugh. He nods. "You know, last fall she told Juanita that we oughta go to a Marriage Encounter deal up at Esalen. Juanita said we were happy. Dolores said, 'You only *think* you're happy. You have to get in touch with that.' You know Juanita—she laughed at her and said we'd just keep on foolin' ourselves, thanks. Dolores wasn't all that pleased. She avoided Juanita for a while. Just as well, because my little bride can be . . . ah . . . somewhat outspoken."

"No shit? I hadn't noticed."

"Anyways, ol' Dolores, she doesn't think Bakersfield's very progressive. She wants Bob to move up there to where all you New Age types hang out."

I grin and make a V with two fingers of my left hand, saying, "Peace and love, brother."

"Kiss off," he grins.

I add, "Tell the airhead's old man I said to forget the crystals and play a little hide-the-wienie at home."

"Bob's a good guy," says Travis, "but too easygoin' for his own good. She leads him around by his soft parts. Hell of an accountant, though. But I'm not sure he knows how to play hide-the-wienie Bakersfield style."

"Tell him to go to Esalen for a seminar on it."

"That where you learned?" He is grinning.

"Not quite. I did my seminar over on those hills with your girlfriend Cherry."

Travis winces in exaggerated shock, then smirks. "Hey, don't even *think* that name in the same house with Juanita. She's not all that amused by those ol' adolescent deals."

"I ought to tell her about Garcia's heifer."

"You're still a rank sumbitch, you know that?"

"That's what I hear," I grin.

"I'm sure glad you got a Ph.D. It's given you lots of class."

"Thanks."

"Listen," Travis says, "I didn't get a chance to ask you before the party, but how're your momma and daddy?"

"About the same. Seems like there isn't a whole lot of Pop left."

"Damn." He shakes his head. "That's rough. Whenever we were kids, ol' Earl was a *force*—the one father I could imagine beatin' the smart-ass outta people, includin' me."

I can only nod. "Not many ever gave him trouble twice, that's for damn sure, but he's not a force now, poor guy."

"And your momma? She still livin' alone?"

"We've got Mitch and Jared—mostly Mitch—taking turns staying with her. She *says* she wants to live alone, but . . . " I shrug. "It's like she's another person, rough to deal with—complain, complain, complain. No one can stand to be around her for very long, which leads to more complaints."

I stop, because pain is tugging at my heart. After a moment, I say, "I'll tell you something else, pard', I really miss her. I didn't realize until all this came down how close I'd been to her when I was a kid. She was like the air, always there, so I just took her for granted. Now I just can't seem to get close to her. It's like . . . " I search for words. "Like a wedge's been driven between us."

"Life's a fuckin' piece a work, ain't it?" he says. "Are you goin' broke payin' for their care?"

"Naw. Pop had a great retirement package, plus they made money when they sold their house and bought that mobile home. We're okay for a while yet. Then, I guess, we can bill Medicare. Anyway, right now Mom's mad at us for coming down here this weekend. We offered to bring her too, but no, she wanted us to stay up there. We left Mitch with her."

Travis takes a long pull from his beer, then says, "She didn't look too good when Juanita and I were up there the last time. Did I tell you that when you guys weren't around she claimed Yvonne forced you to sell the old family house?"

I start to protest, but he waves me off. Travis is an attorney, and he helped arrange the actual sale. "I just reminded her about the meetin' where she said she already had a place picked out up there, and that she had to sell the old place to pay for it, that she'd told me she wanted you to handle the deal. She said, 'I *did*?' in a way that translated to 'You're full of shit.'"

"I'm familiar with that tone."

"I'll bet you are."

A large brown man lurches through the sliding glass door and calls, "Hey, *putos,* what're you up to?" He pauses there across the deck from us, extracts a cigarette from a pack, lights it, then inhales deeply.

While he's doing that, Travis grins and says, "Would you look at the white sideburns on that *viejo* . . . looks like he's old enough to be our daddy, don't he, Roy?"

"I got your daddy danglin'," snaps Jess Soto, then he takes another pull from his smoke. He walks across the deck to where we stand and asks, "Ol' Travis showin' you where he used to beg Cherry for a little sniff of pussy down there by the river?" He winks at me.

"*He* used to!" I grin. "*You're* the one who turned us on to her."

"Me and Cherry were just friends, man."

"You know," Travis says, "I used to have a hard spot in my pants for Cherry, but now I've got a soft spot in my heart for her. She was just a mix-up gal."

"You got a soft spot in your *pants,* too," grins Soto.

"Eat shit," says Travis, and we all laugh.

A striking red-haired woman sticks her head out the glass door and announces, "We're going to pop the champagne in a minute, Travis." Then she adds, "Aren't you guys *hot* out here?"

"Hey, Marge," I smile, my spirit considerably lightened by this joshing with old buddies, "we're always hot."

"That's *close*," she smiles.

"Damn, Soto," observes Travis, "can't you control that smart-assed wife of yours?"

"Too much Okie, man. I shoulda married a nice Mexican gal like you did."

"Yeah, a subservient little number like Juanita," Travis grins. His marriage to a Mexican girl, and Jess's to a white one, had caused some fuss back in those supposed good old days. "It's a good thing for her she got hitched to a high-class Okie kid like me," Travis adds, "or she might've ended up with a chili bean like you, Soto."

"Get fucked," says Soto, then he veers the subject. "You miss coachin', Roy?"

"Not really." Three years before, after twenty years on the sidelines as coach of defensive backs and linebackers at the junior college where I teach—and nearly twenty years of nickel-and-diming graduate courses at the University of California—I'd quit to write my doctoral dissertation in kinesiology. "I was burning out on it . . . not on the kids, but on all the travel, all the late nights. As it turned out, I was going to have to help Yvonne with my folks, anyway," I shrug.

Soto shrugs in return. "I figured you didn't coach any better than you played, so they canned your Okie ass."

Travis and I are laughing when Jess says, "That reminds me, you guys hear ol' Buddy Duncan died?"

"Buddy?" I gasp. "No shit?" He'd played ball with us in high school.

Travis nods. "I hear he had that Lou Gehrig's disease. And Booker Phillips died too—prostate cancer."

"Prostate cancer? I thought that was an old man's disease."

"It wasn't for Booker. I saw Diane Pellegrini's name in the obits, too," adds Travis. "Breast cancer."

I am shaking my head. Diane had been a cheerleader when we'd played at Bakersfield High. "I guess we've reached that dying age, boys," I say. "We'll see more and more obituaries, then our generation'll be gone like all the others that ever lived."

"Gee, that's *heavy,* Upton," grunts Jess. "Real philosophical." Even back in high school he made fun of what he considered academic bullshit, and I guess what I said sounded highfalutin to him. He once more changes the subject: "How're your kids doin'?"

"They're okay. Right now the boys're just trying to keep up with Grandma. Suzie's still at UC–Santa Cruz. Where're Jason and Caity today?" I ask him.

"They had stuff to do, tennis or some damn thing."

"Just like we used to," I grin.

"I remember you and me took some beer to the tennis courts at East High one night and got smashed," says Travis. Then he nods at Soto, "But this *pendejo* wasn't there. He was out doin' *homework* with Cherry."

We all laugh.

"I haven't seen your kids for a while either, Travis," Jess says. "They take after your redneck side of the family and get locked up?"

"Liz's a junior at Occidental, and she worked down there this summer. Kit's still studyin' overseas on that Stanford exchange deal—at least I *think* she's studying."

"Just like you used to," I suggest. "Good thing she's got a rich father." Travis's success remains as amazing as it is satisfying to all of us.

"You fuckin' A," says Plumley, slipping even more deeply into his Okie drawl. "I hope you two fart-knockers know the clock's a-runnin' right now. I'll bill your ragged asses for consultin' me like this."

"Bill *this, puto,*" Soto responds, grasping his fly.

I can't suppress a grin. "That's what I like about you Soto, you always elevate a conversation."

"I got your elevator danglin'," the large brown man grunts, and he grasps his fly again.

4

For years, I didn't dream much . . . wasn't aware of dreams, anyway. But lately my mind seems to churn with memories every idle moment, waking or sleeping; that long-ago stuff I can't change or escape—my mom and dad as they used to be, Floyd and other guys with Yvonne. It's as though something in me's trying to accept a past that fled too soon. Even happy memories now haunt because they are lost. I can't seem to understand or accept that my life has reached this point, and my belly is frequently eerie.

My wife and I'd stayed up late drinking wine and talking to Travis and Juanita after the party, so when I awaken unrested in their guest room at 5:30 A.M., my mouth tastes like I've been licking cats' rear ends—red wine, whew! I swallow two ibuprofen tablets with a glass of milk followed by several glasses of water, then loosen up in a warm shower. After drying off, I gaze for a moment at the lined face in the mirror—it bears scant resemblance to the boy who'd started school all those years ago—then I swallow more glasses of water, climb into running gear, and stretch my legs.

Travis and Juanita are nowhere to be seen, and my wife doesn't stir, so I kiss her cheek, then force myself away—she's deep in sleep—and walk outside into the coolest time of night or day, the cusp of both—the air still and, in this lush section of town, slightly out of focus, tropical.

Each time we're back, although we usually stay with the Plumleys, I make it a point to drive to the less opulent section where I was raised so I can jog there. I wheel across the dry riverbed, and over canals that channel water diverted for irrigation far upriver, until I pull up at a park behind the grade school I once attended. The back fence of that school had in those years bordered a region of aging wooden derricks, of oil sumps, of a steaming refinery with gleaming storage tanks, and even of company "camps" where workers and their families had lived.

The banks of the nearby Kern River had in my youth been our jungle, but when its flow was diverted at dams and weirs upstream, the forest died of thirst. Desiccated snags, their pleading profiles like bodies buried upright, are all that remain. Water now reaches here only in the wettest of years, and those snags remain grotesque reminders of what passes for progress.

At the park I briefly stretch again, then jog an easy lap on grass before moving onto the street, heading to the main thoroughfare. I run north, then veer west. Pickups and cars bounce past me toward diners or to the oilfields—no sidewalks here near the Catholic church, but disorderly Bermuda grass or puncture vines reach across sandy soil toward the road. In many yards are parked vehicles in various stages of grandeur or disrepair. Unlike the Plumleys' neighborhood, there is little shade here: most people with trees in their yards seem to have cut them back so brutally that scar tissue knots truncated branches like tumors. I once asked my father why he, like everyone else on our block, did that. He looked at me as though I had just confirmed his fears about the mushiness of too much book learnin': "You want them damn *leaves* all over ever'thing come fall?"

"Wouldn't it be cooler if you let the leaves grow?"

Pop merely shook his head and sucked at the snuff he had tamped into his lower lip. "Hell, ever'one keeps their trees thisaway. What're you talkin' about?" End of discussion.

Doves are calling from lawns and gutters as I run by—a haunting, unchanging reality that takes me back . . . back. There are sidewalks now on many of the streets, and I almost trip on a curb, snapping me out of my brief reverie. These houses—none of them large—look more prosperous today than when I was a boy. Many are now surrounded by chain-link fences and small manicured lawns; already this morning a few dark-skinned men, who don't reside in this enclave of working-class whites, can be seen pushing power mowers over grassy patches. American-built sedans and pickups grace narrow driveways, and one yard displays a hand-painted sign: U.S. OUT OF U.N. A corner of it is decorated by a fading sticker: PRO-LIFE, PRO-AMERICA!

That sticker alerts me to others, so I begin examining those I see on vehicles parked in driveways. GOD SAID IT! I BELIEVE IT! THAT SETTLES IT! reads one. HOW'S MY DRIVING? asks another. CALL 1-800-FUC-KYOU. WHEN GUNS ARE OUTLAWED ONLY OUTLAWS WILL HAVE GUNS! asserts a third, and GOD, GUNS, AND GUTS MADE AMERICA GREAT! is plastered over a fading one I can't read. On a rear window I see, THIS TRUCK INSURED BY SMITH AND WESSON.

I see yet another peeling sign stuck to the back of an antique pickup: AMERICA, LOVE IT OR LEAVE IT; a much newer one on the same bumper declares in unfaded colors, FISHING—IT'S A TOUGH JOB BUT SOMEBODY'S GOT TO DO IT. An old man, like a muscular wire in jeans and T-shirt, is washing the pickup. On his head a baseball cap perches at a kiss-my-ass angle. He glances up at me jogging by, puffs at the tiny stub of a cigarette hanging from his lower lip, and nods.

These are the people my father worked with, most of them retired now, having reaped some of the real California promise they once sought—not gold nuggets or movie careers, but *work*. "Give a man a job of work, see," I long ago heard a friend of my father's say, "and by God you've give him respect." He'd had it about right.

Once, back when I was in the army, a soldier from the East sneered something about life in California being soft. I snapped, "You ever chop cotton in hundred-and-twenty-degree heat, asshole? You ever put in seventy-two straight hours on a drilling rig, so tired you couldn't pull your gloves off? You ever bust your butt trying to keep up with a conveyor belt in a packing shed so hot you could bake bread in it? If that's soft, you show me tough."

"Jeez, Upton," he said, blinking, "I never meant *you*."

I only shook my head, embarrassed that I'd flared on him. "I know," I said, "you meant movie stars. But there's a couple of us out there who work for a living."

I hesitate for a moment in front of the Coffee Mill, where Pop had for years eaten breakfast with other oil workers, where he had often taken me when I was a kid. My memories of this place are full of male joshing, laughter, and hot, watery coffee—no cappuccino or latte served here, buster, but many a thermos has been filled. On the window is scrawled BISCUITS AND GRAVY—COUNTRY STYLE, and inside I see unfamiliar men—many the age of my sons—joshing now.

I jog by honky-tonks, beer bars, and card parlors, by Southern Baptist, Nazarene, Pentecostal Holiness, Assembly of God, True Bible, Four-Square Gospel, and God of Prophecy churches, by pump companies, bit companies, chemical companies, pipe companies, fishing-tool companies, well-service companies. The flat country just a mile or so northwest and southwest is spoked by agricultural rows, enormous wealth, but eyes in this community gaze toward those brown hills to the northeast where crude oil is pumped from the ground.

"Whenever we first come out here," my father once explained, "we worked them crops, me and your uncle Clyde, but lemme tell you, boy, that there's nigger work—you gotta do whatever the boss wants you to and take whatever shit he gives you. Here in the oil fields, you can get you a white man's job and earn a white man's pay."

Down Beardsley Avenue near the river levee, a cluster of cottonwood trees miraculously remains from the riparian forest I had so loved when I was a kid; they are untrimmed, so they cast great shady mantles. Beneath them spread trailer parks, some of which now appear prosperous with expensive mobile homes, while others retain the antique travel trailers I remember.

A red light stops me, so I jog in place at the intersection while more pickups and cars buzz past. A woman in tight jeans, high heels, and a frilly cowgirl's blouse joins me. "Gonna be a hot one," she immediately volunteers, and I smile in agreement. Her face is veined and lined like a topographic map, and a long cigarette slopes from her crimson lips; pink hair is elaborately piled and swirled on her head. She is as old as my mother. "This *dern* smog," she adds, exhaling a blue cloud, and I wonder where she's headed so early in the morning.

"See you," I call as I jog away, and she waves.

The bedraggled court where Yvonne's parents lived is still here and little changed; her family's old trailer sits on the same space, its tires rotted. Her father escaped migrant day labor to become a failed door-to-door salesman, always trying to peddle salve or garden seeds or something else that no one wanted to buy; her mother had never escaped work at beer bars. Even together, they could not manage to earn enough to move beyond the small trailer. Yvonne's cousin resides in it now, I know, but my wife never visits. Her memories of this place are not happy.

My own parents bought one of the ubiquitous small houses, next to a canal, and eventually had a sidewalk and a chain-link fence installed to complement their disabled tree. On my way back to the park, I jog past our old family home. The new owner has painted it and removed that lone tree from the front yard since I last visited. I pause to examine it, but an older woman walks out the front door and stares directly at me, hands on hips.

These people have known hardship, and have been toughened by it. They expect life to be difficult and are not easily intimidated. I merely nod at the woman, then turn and jog back to my car, recognizing no one along the way.

5

MEMORY: BAKERSFIELD, 1942

Mommy held my hand all the way that first day. She had dressed me in new red pants, white shoes, a white shirt with a small bow tie, also red, and she led me like a prize up Chester Avenue. Other young mothers were leading their children in the same direction, then into a pedestrian underpass next to the library. That tunnel was full of older kids whooping and echoing, and an especially bold one sang at me, "Kindergarten baby, born in the gravy . . ."

"Get away from him!" snapped my mother, and the boy bounced back toward his pals, giggling, "You guys hear what I told that little kid?"

"*Common*," my mother snorted.

I looked up at her. "This place smells like wee-wee," I said.

"Bad boys do that," she explained, "but don't talk about it. It's nasty."

Out of the tunnel, we walked to a busy room where my mother and many other women filled out forms. There were no men present. "What branch of the service is your husband in?" asked a lady behind a desk.

"Well, he's been deferred because he has an essential job," Momma explained.

"Oh?"

"He's employed in the oil fields."

"Oh," said the lady. "My husband's overseas."

Many kids my age clung close to the women, hugging their legs. A few little girls wore starched skirts, but most were dressed in fading, droopy dresses. No other boys were clothed like me; most wore faded, patched jeans. Several were barefooted.

Momma handed the forms to another lady sitting at one of the tables set up in the room. While my mother talked to her, a thin, shoe-less boy who wore bib overalls pushed me, saying, "You're a yella Jap."

I pushed him back. "You're a Hitler," I grinned.

He pushed me again, laughing.

I pushed him harder.

Then another boy in ragged jeans bumped me—"You're a big ol' Hitler," he giggled—so I bumped him hard and shoved the first one too, giggling all the while.

"You're a Muscolini!" grinned the first boy.

The lady behind the desk glanced up and hissed, "Boys!"—her voice sharp as a rifle's report—"No roughhousing!"

Momma jerked my arm. "Stay away from them," she ordered.

A large, tired-looking woman in a shapeless dress jerked the pusher by the arm, crackling, "Quit that, Floyd!"

"J.D., come 'ere, son," a skinny white-haired lady called to the bumper.

A few minutes later, Momma walked me toward a large room that opened onto an enclosed playground. We were greeted at the doorway by a pretty lady with a flower pinned to her blouse. My mother handed her the paper she carried, and the pretty lady said, "Oh, so this young man is Leroy. I'm Miss Kennedy, Leroy, your teacher." She smiled. "Wel-come to kindergarten."

"His middle name is Clark—after my father," my mother said quickly. "You can call him that if you'd like."

"Whatever you prefer, Mrs. Upton."

"Well, Clark is such a *nice* name . . ." My mother's voice hung there, forcing the woman to decide.

Miss Kennedy turned toward me. "So, what is your name?"

"Leroy Upton," I said.

"Come on in, Leroy."

Momma started to enter the room with me, and the lady stopped her. "We like the mothers to leave the children with us now, Mrs. Upton."

"But . . ." Momma stammered and she gazed at me for what seemed a long time. "Leroy Clark?" she said.

It was too late. I had spied the boys named Floyd and J.D. and was charging across the room to push them.

Two weeks later in the underpass, a big kid tripped me, pulled my necktie, sat on me, and took the quarter Momma had knotted into my hanky. That night I told her at the dinner table that I wanted to wear blue jeans like the other boys. "You most certainly will not," she replied.

"Why's that?" my father asked.

"He will not dress *common.*"

Daddy pushed his plate away and stood up, saying, "You mean you don't want him to dress like a Okie, you want him to dress like a prune picker, right? Marie, how'd you get so all-fired highfalutin? Look at this boy—you dress this kid like a damn sissy. I wear *common* jeans and a *common* shirt to do the work to buy the food we eat. All them kids that wear jeans, most of their daddies work with me in the oil patch and they wear jeans and shirts too, and they're all good, hardworkin', *common* guys." Then he turned toward me. "If you want jeans and shirts like your daddy wears, I'll damn sure get you some."

"Earl, my father wore a white shirt and necktie to work every day of his life." Momma's voice quivered. "My brother Joe is an *officer.*"

She walked stiffly to the sink and, not facing Daddy, she demanded, "*Why* do you fight every decent thing I try to do for our son?" She turned, and tears began streaming down her cheeks. "Don't you want him to have advantages you never had? A person's appearance *does* make a difference."

"You go out and play, Leroy. Me and your momma got somethin' to talk about."

6

We say our good-byes to the Plumleys—Travis looking like he might've cleaned those same cats I did—and I ask his wife, "Does that old poop always sack out this late in the morning?"

"You've heard the term 'sleeping it off'?" Juanita replies.

Travis grins sleepily. "Hell," he says, "I'm just a bedroom cowboy—ride, ride, ride."

"Lie, lie, lie," his wife, sotto voce.

Yvonne laughs, then says, "I'm sorry Jess got so angry last night when Marge wouldn't stay after the party."

"She had homework for the classes she's taking," Juanita explains. "She *told* him he could stay, but he wouldn't."

Travis is shaking his head. "Pussy-whipped, poor guy, just like Roy and me."

"Damn right," I respond gravely, then we both laugh.

Juanita shakes her own head and says to Yvonne, "I swear, it seems like the more these two characters accomplish, the more they try to act like oil-field trash just to prove they haven't changed. Believe it or not, Travis doesn't talk like that if Roy or Jess isn't around. Before they start lighting farts or something, you better get your husband to start the car."

"Hey, Juanita," I explain, "that's what historians call 'class-and-cultural allegiance.'"

"'Class-and-cultural allegiance'?" Travis repeats. "No shit? Is that the term for actin' like an Okie?"

"For acting like an asshole," I say, and he laughs.

Juanita nods toward my wife. "See what I mean?"

Travis suddenly looks grave. "You know, I'm afraid there *is* somethin' goin' haywire between Jess and Marge, though. I don't think he likes her takin' classes a-tall. And he's been actin' downright squirrelly, if you ask me."

My wife shrugs. "She didn't say anything like that to me. Did she say anything to you, Juanita?"

"No, but I think Travis's right. It just *feels* different when we're around them. They're tense."

"Always some-damn-thing," I say, dropping into a heavy drawl. "We gotta get a-goin' if we're gonna get home before dark."

"Yeah," says Travis, "get the hell outta here so Juanita and me can open another bottle of that red wine."

I make a face, then start our car's engine.

"Oh, yeah," Travis says, "there's a country music concert at the civic auditorium next month . . . all local talent. How 'bout you guys comin' back down and we can go? With all the so-called high culture leakin' over the mountains from L.A., some folks around here are embarrassed by country, but it might be fun to see what's happenin' in *real* music nowadays."

"Sounds good," I nod.

"Sure," my wife smiles, "but I'll have to see how much work I've got, and if we can find someone to cover the folks."

"Okay, y'all check and I'll send the details. See you two then, hopefully."

"Thanks again for everything," I call as we pull away.

Driving to and from our old hometown, Yvonne and I avoid the interstate; back roads intrigue us. Today we travel north beyond Wasco on a two-lane, passing only occasional trucks—bumper stickers advertising radio station K-U-Z-Z and asserting AIN'T BUT TWO KINDS OF

MUSIC: *COUNTRY AND WESTERN*. We pass row after green row of crops being irrigated with water that once harbored salmon in the Sacramento River three hundred miles to the north, and whiz by sudden orchards of fruit trees and even vineyards, planted where jackrabbits frolicked only a year or two ago.

Many of the vehicles we see here are driven by Latinos, and as one station wagon wheezes by, I notice a large blue bumper sticker: CRISTO VIENE PRONTO. For a second I think, Cristo? Cristo's *Fence*? Cristo's *Umbrellas*? Then I chuckle at myself and realize I have lived in the swishy Bay Area too long; that sticker is a believer's testament to Christ, not to a chichi European artist.

We are traveling up the core of California, a vast valley nearly five hundred miles long and up to seventy-five miles wide. Land here is flat—flatter than ever before now, since it has lately been laser-leveled to make it easier to irrigate—and the horizon disappears in haze. Parades of shaggy palm trees stand like aging sentries along farm roads. Few houses can be seen despite all the cultivated land: this is a realm of huge agribusinesses, controlled in corporate boardrooms elsewhere while local workers dwell in small, scattered, often impoverished communities. There are few holdings here that can be called farms, and nearly all field laborers seem to be Latinos now.

Near Corcoran we notice alongside the road three small crosses elaborately decorated with plastic flowers. Who was killed there? I wonder. Mexicans, probably. People who worked with their hands in all likelihood. People who were loved.

Just to the north we cross the bed of what was once the largest body of fresh water west of the Mississippi, Tulare Lake. I've become an avocational historian of this region, so I know its sources of water were long ago diverted for irrigation, and its sinuous shoreline is gone. It has been replaced by the geometric grids of agribusiness—plowed, planted, dosed with chemicals, and irrigated with water from elsewhere. Cotton and safflowers and almonds are now grown where once commercial fishermen dragged their nets. We pass a small pond, and on one side I spy a towering stand of rushes. "Look at the tules," I say, pulling the car to the road's shoulder.

"Oh!" Yvonne gasps. "Don't kill us just to see them!" Then she smiles. "I always forget how *big* they are." The tules, for which the extinct lake was named, are nearly twenty feet tall. They were this region's most characteristic and prolific plant, but now they survive only in scattered locations. While we are stopped, a carousel of red-winged blackbirds buzzes our car, warning us away from their nests.

Farther up the road, we pass a few ranch homes in the midst of cultivated fields—large, landscaped yards surrounding custom swimming pools, trimmed palm trees elegantly shading them, vast shining sedans sharing circular driveways with pickups; most houses boast prominent signs announcing security services. In the communities through which we pass houses tend to be small, clapboard, sometimes festooned with fancy cars but more commonly surrounded by brown children playing among the bodies of older autos in the midst of repair or autopsy. Desperate-looking chinaberry trees and occasional vegetable gardens constitute the landscaping. Between those small towns we see farm-labor camps, barracks that were once painted and are today surrounded by patches of flood-irrigated Bermuda grass. Clotheslines are full of faded, waving garments, and various signs in Spanish can be seen from the road.

To our left as we continue north are hills, treeless and burnished with a golden-brown stubble. Those golden stalks are, like so many who live here, imports; they long ago squeezed out native grasses. Precious little that is natural remains in this vast trough. At two more places along the road we pass small crosses decorated with plastic flowers.

It is midafternoon when we finally veer west and slide through mountains toward the Bay Area, where we now live. Already the homeward-bound bumper-to-bumper traffic is creeping east into the valley we are leaving—people who work in bay cities but commute many miles inland. They endure that drive to find less expensive homes or a small-town atmosphere, while reaping the higher salaries and more prestigious positions available in coastal communities.

"Look at all those cars!" Yvonne says, shaking her head. "I can't get over how many people are commuting. We didn't used to see any traffic at all, but now the Bay Area's spreading out, right over the lip of these hills, like fog."

"Maybe the ol' Valley's movin' thataway," I suggest in my drawl.

"Not likely. They'll pave farmland in the Valley to build houses, but they won't plow up parking lots in Oakland to plant potatoes or asparagus."

"Touché," I concede.

We turn off a crowded freeway just before it crosses another range of hills and reaches San Francisco Bay. Instead we drive north on yet another expressway, parallel to the eastern slope of that range and past affluent suburbs—Dublin, Alamo, Walnut Creek, Pleasant Hill, Concord. Fewer of the drivers I notice in this area are dark-skinned, and if they are dark, they're mostly Asian or Black, not Hispanic. There are far fewer pickups and large American sedans on the road up here, too, and many more expensive foreign automobiles: BMWs in particular seem to be breeding before our eyes.

A whole new crop of bumper stickers appears: U.S. OUT OF COLOMBIA! MUMIA WON'T BE SILENCED! A WOMAN'S PLACE IS ON TOP! SUPPORT THE RIGHT TO ARM BEARS! FREE GERONIMO PRATT! CHOICE IS YOUR RIGHT! A top-of-the-line Acura glides past us, and on its plush bumper is a colorful sticker reading FREE TIBET! Only a moment later we pass an aging VW Beetle decorated with FREE LUNCH!

We cross the bay on the Richmond–San Rafael Bridge after driving past seedy liquor stores and bars outside of which crowds of tired-looking black men and women seem to mill at all hours. In Marin County we swing south and soon enter the large, wooded canyon in Mount Tamalpais where Mill Valley spreads up the slopes through the trees—cool and green. It is always difficult for me to imagine that, just a few hours before, I was jogging past coyote brush and tumbleweeds near Bakersfield, only 325 miles south, but in some ways a world away. Now we are motoring among live oaks, bay laurels, redwoods, and ferns, and along a brook that creases our shadowed canyon.

Yvonne and I managed to buy our comfortable but by no means lavish home—then a "Hey-Mister-Handyman!" fixer-upper—when she became a real estate agent, well before a continuing boom projected its value from the $35,000 we paid to the half million that one of Yvonne's colleagues recently suggested it would fetch "easily." We could buy a block of small houses in our hometown for that but probably not find a comparable replacement house here in Mill Valley. When I once flippantly suggested to my wife that we do just that—invest in a block of rentals and return home to manage them—she had simply said, "No" in a tone so unambiguous that I never repeated the proposition. She has shed that place and her life there like a snake ridding itself of an old skin.

As I pull into our driveway, the sun no longer shows over the canyon's lip, and the light in our family room is on. Emerging from the car, I see my dad sitting at the card table we keep set up for him. His hair is still dark, his toothless mouth is working, and his eyes appear to be fixed on the wall ahead of him while Trish, the retired nurse we've hired to watch him, busies herself at the kitchen sink.

"Is something wrong, hon'?" Yvonne asks.

"Just looking at Pop," I reply, but, of course, something *is* wrong: my father is being destroyed before he is allowed to die.

As a result, I am learning what it means to be a son.

7

A small noise jars me from dream or memory or whatever it was, and after an instant I glance toward the clock radio's glowing numbers: 4:07 A.M. Great, I think, then roll over, but that irregular sound, faint yet distinct, burrows into me. I reach for Yvonne, feel her warmth next to me, then lie still, eyes open. Finally, with a sigh, I tilt out of bed and stumble into the hall, my football knees and lower back stiff. I stop and listen.

The sound is coming from my father's room. I limp to it and flip on the overhead light as I enter. Pop stands against the near wall, one hand locked on a grab bar we've installed, the other tugging at a belt. He has somehow managed in the dark to strip off his pj's, then pull trousers on backwards. His belt passes through only one loop, so it rises several inches above the slacks, girdling his pale, flat belly, pants drooping in back to expose a slice of his bare bottom.

I stand for a moment observing the powerful man I had so often seen cut a wide swath, and I blink hard, my stomach swooping in the grip of this reality. Immediately I recall the night, perhaps forty-five years ago, when I'd wandered weeping at some nightmare into my parents' bedroom, and Pop snapped, "Quit blubberin'! Don't never let nobody see you bawl." I returned to bed, tears swallowed, never to weep publicly again.

Now, apparently unaware of my presence, my father continues doggedly working at that belt, his arms decorated by fading tattoos, his chest still deep, his waist still lean. He still looks formidable, especially for a man his age. But his eyes are dull as nickels and he grunts with effort.

I have to arise at six, so I tap his shoulder and ask, "Do you need a fresh diaper, Pop?"

His head turns slowly toward me and he growls, "My belt tightened."

For a change, he doesn't lock his hands on the grab bar, so I am able to easily maneuver him back toward his bed, where I remove the trousers, replace the disposable diaper he has long since shed, then pull a clean T-shirt on him.

As soon as I finish, I return him—still grasping that belt—to the grab bar. I strip his wet lower sheet, finding the soiled diaper he had removed bundled at the bed's foot. I pick it up gingerly, lifting with two fingers, carry it to the bathroom and drop it into a plastic bag there, then wash my hands.

Once when I was a kid, I acted squeamish about scraping dog turds off the lawn, and my dad laughed at me, saying, "Hell, boy, pick them damn things up. It ain't nothin' soap 'n' water cain't wash off." He was correct, of course; most things physical can be cleansed.

Returning to Pop's bedroom, I find him once more grunting with frustration as he tries to buckle that belt over his diaper. "Time to go back to bed, Pop," I tell him, and he allows me to lead him back, tuck him in—belt once more secure around his middle. Finally I turn off his light. I stagger back to my own bed and read those glowing numbers: 4:27.

Two hours later I'm sipping coffee and revising a lesson plan for my recreation course at my desk in the den, while my wife is studying the multiple-listings book at the dining room table. Pepper, our aging mongrel, curls at my feet. I notice the hall light snap on and off several times, then hear Yvonne call, "Good morning, Dad."

My father is shuffling past the doorway toward her, a grin slicing his face. Pepper's tail begins thumping the floor, and my wife asks, "Where're your pants?"

I walk into the dining room and see that he wears several shirts and that belt, but nothing below the waist except socks; the nub that produced me hangs flaccid from a burst of reddish pubic hair. I can't help grinning, and Yvonne winks at me over his shoulder. "Come on," she tells him, "let me help you finish dressing."

Soon they pass my doorway again and I hear my wife ask, "Ready for a hot breakfast?"

"No," Pop responds, nodding yes. He is grinning.

"Did you sleep well?"

"No."

Jared, our sixteen-year-old, enters the family room on his way to the kitchen. "Hi, Grandpa," he sleepily calls.

"How you?" Pop grins toothlessly once more. He abandoned his dentures a couple of years ago.

At 8:00 A.M., my father is sitting at his card table in the family room when the doorbell rings. It is Trish, who will care for him while my wife and I work; she will let herself in, but always rings first. Yvonne has departed for her office, taking Jared with her, and I am ready to leave for the community college. Trish, a retired R.N., dressed as always in her crisp uniform, bounces smiling into the house, singing, "Good morning."

After depositing her purse and sweater in the hall closet, she sweeps into the family room calling in a falsetto voice, "Hello, Earl! Time for our bath!"

"How you?"

I say good-bye, walk outside, and attach panniers loaded with books and notes onto my bicycle's rack. I am laughing to myself at the picture of Trish and Pop sloshing naked and breathless in "our bath," something that might well have happened even a few years ago when my father was still on the prowl. Then I am swept by sadness: Trish and others who have met him in his dotage know only the disabled, demented man he is now, but I see the sum of his life when I view him. If only they knew. . . .

I reenter the house one last time to be certain I've not forgotten anything, and the telephone rings. I answer and hear my daughter's voice: "Hi, Pops. Guess what? I've been nominated to be graduation speaker."

"That's terrific, pumpkin!"

She is bubbling. "That's how I feel. It's an honor just to be nominated. And I got 98 on my morphology test, but it was only second-highest in the class."

"How many students in that course?"

"Two," Suzie giggles, a magical sound that takes me back to the days when I carried her in a papoose pack to and from my own college classes. "About a hundred and twenty," she admits. "I made one dumb mistake—really sloppy—but did okay. Is Mom still home?"

"Long gone for work," I drawl. "If she wants to keep a good-lookin' devil like me, she better bring in that money."

"In your dreams, maybe. Oh, listen, I got a *real* strange phone call from Grandma the other night. She said you weren't my father. Am I adopted?"

This stabs that tender spot. Ever since she's been up here, my mother has been hinting that someone else actually impregnated Yvonne before I married her. I know that's a definite possibility, but by intimidating Floyd and J.D., and by avoiding contact with others who I know had enjoyed her, I've managed to put aside the painful suspicion and all that went with it. I just don't think about it . . . or didn't, anyway. Now Mom has reopened that wound. Nevertheless, I keep my tone light when I respond: "Who'd adopt *you*?"

Again Suzie giggles.

"Grandma's just old and confused," I add.

"Oh, too bad. I thought maybe I was really a princess raised by commoners." Her voice changes and she burlesques, "Yeah, dat's da ticket . . . *a princess.*"

"You are," I say, only half kidding.

"How about Mitch? Is he home? I've got a girlfriend for him."

"Just what he needs, another girlfriend. He stayed with Grandma last night, but he's out in his room. I'll call him. I've gotta go to work—tote that barge and lift that bale—so you take care. I'm real proud of you, pumpkinseed. Stay in touch."

"Okay, Pops. I love you."

I don't say the same thing back to her—those words always catch in my throat—but I am levitated by her saying them to me. Smiling, I walk to my older son's room and tap the door. I hear a sleepy, "Yeah," so I open it a crack and tell him that Suzie's on the phone. "Okay," he croaks and I close the door, then leave for work. Strange that he'd be in bed if he'd slept the night before at his grandmother's mobile home.

Before climbing on my bike, I stand and breathe deeply. We really can't escape our pasts, it seems, no matter how hard we try or how much we change; God may forgive us, but people can't, and even God doesn't forget.

The ride to school remains troubled, because I can't kick the old question of whose baby Yvonne was carrying when I married her—now that Mom has slid it back into my awareness like a rusty dagger. I would never want a child other than Suzie, but . . . Erotic scenes of a young Yvonne with other guys begin to invade me, and I ride harder and harder to burn the familiar pain away.

8

As I wheel onto campus, I cut across the parking lot near the football stadium. Few cars are scattered through this tract, since it is far from classroom buildings. It is littered with trash, so I assume some big event was held here last weekend. I've been so out of touch with school affairs lately that I haven't a clue what it might have been—a concert? a lecture? Then I notice, sprawled under one of the several large oak trees that was left standing when this lot was paved, a young black man sleeping on an unrolled sleeping bag. An old pack rests next to him, along with a clear plastic bag containing a few aluminum cans. His mouth gapes and bits of grass and twigs are caught in his hair.

As usual, I've brought a sandwich and a banana in a paper bag to snack on during the break in my three-hour class. But I suddenly don't need it, so I stop, remove the lunch from my bike's pannier, fish a five-dollar bill from my wallet and put it in the sack too. Then I quietly place the brown bag next to the young man's bag of cans. He does not stir, and up close I can see how dusty and desperate his complexion is. Something in me swoops, but I tighten myself and climb back onto my bicycle. There's nothing more I can do.

A few minutes later, I walk by the Physical Education Department office to pick up my mail, then drop my gear at my own small chamber before strolling to the faculty lounge for coffee.

"How's the new doc?" calls Marty Spielman as I enter. He teaches English.

It's been nearly a year since I finally completed my Ph.D. at the university in nearby Berkeley, and that degree seems to bother, or at least intrigue, some of my colleagues; doctorates are not required or common among faculty at this two-year school. Marty is an occasional weight-lifting partner of mine, one of the faculty's good athletes, and he enjoys male joshing.

"Why aren't you wearing your doctoral hood?" he smirks.

I know he's just hard-assing me, so I raise one fist and drawl, "See this big, bony deal? Well, I'm fixin' to have P-fuckin'-H-fuckin'-D tattooed on it to go with this other attitude adjuster." I raise my other paw, the one with fading L-O-V-E tattooed amateurishly on it.

He laughs, but the smirk doesn't return—attitude adjusted.

I had actually finished the degree for myself and for Yvonne, to complete what we'd started when we left Bakersfield for college a quarter century ago.

"What's up, Marty?" I ask as I fill a cup with coffee from the communal urn.

"I've just been to another of those *interminable* hiring committee meetings. You remember what team meetings were like back in school?" Like me, Marty played college football—he was a safety at Northwestern—and we've many times laughed over the silly pronouncements of our coaches. "Anyway," he continues, "we've finally narrowed the field down to four we can interview."

"Good candidates?" I flop on a couch across from him.

"They're okay, but let me tell you, Dr. Upton, you wouldn't even make the list. SWIMS are out . . . even for coaches, and you *know* how low the standards are for those jobs."

I chuckle and shake my head, then ask, "'Swims'?"

"'Straight white males,' with a vowel added for flavor," he smiles. "Now me, Jewish and gay . . . well, *maybe* I could be hired. Did you ever think *those* two categories could be a help?"

This time I smile. "Only in Hollywood."

"Maybe," he responds, "but only one would help . . . I'm just not sure which." He laughs this time.

"I'm still in favor of Affirmative Action and Title IX—God knows, there's historical justification for both—but I hope we don't overcompensate. The biggest myth making the rounds nowadays is that reverse discrimination is a myth. Smart folks can rationalize anything, and they do. As far as I'm concerned, though, if something's wrong when *I* do it, it's wrong when *others* do it, period."

"Well," he says, "you're lucky you got your job when you did, Roy, as a coach, let alone as a classroom teacher. Really. It's a different world now, and neither one of us would be invited on board."

He sips from his coffee, then adds, "Listen, have I told you that your son is a darn good writer, maybe as good as Suzie was?" Mitch is enrolled in Spielman's advanced composition class, and my daughter had earlier completed two courses with him. "They must take after their mother," he adds.

"Right."

"How'd a big dumb jock like you end up with a classy lady like her . . . ?" he muses. "Oh, well, she's probably doing penance for some past life."

I only smile, "I reckon."

The door opens and in hurries Vijay Patel, another English teacher. He is from India, and he also holds a Ph.D. from Berkeley. Suzie took English lit from him and loved the course. He carries a teapot.

"Hi, Vijay!" calls Marty.

I wave at him and smile.

"Vell," he grins, "vhat are you two plotting? Grand conspirators." He pronounces each syllable.

Marty, noted for not attending many departmental or divisional meetings, is a maverick who disdains campus politics. He says, "We want to elect you faculty chair, put you in charge of everything, then manipulate you."

"I vould send you a chit immediately upon my election, and I vould have you cashiered, you rogue!" He trills that *r* deliciously.

We laugh because Vijay is serious.

While filling his teapot with hot water, he asks, "Your classes are huge this semester?"

"Mine are," I reply.

"Mine, too," agrees Marty.

"And my students vant all A's and no vork," Vijay reveals. "It is so sad."

"They aren't all Berkeley students," I point out.

"No, they are not Berkeley students," he agrees.

Marty did his M.A. at Stanford, UC's archrival, so he chuckles, "No, they're not *that* bad, but they are slow."

Patel gazes for a moment at his colleague, then says, "Another chit for you!"

"That was a Stanford joke," I grin.

"Oh, Stanford," Vijay says to me, "that is the place they call 'the farm'?" Then he steps out.

I am laughing, and even Marty chuckles. "See you, Marty," I say, standing up to leave. I've only fifteen minutes before my first class.

In the hall I pass Marge Chilton, a sixtyish English teacher and a long-time favorite of mine. "Hello, Leroy. How's the family?"

"Okay," I smile. "How're things at your place?"

"If you don't count our bodies falling apart, fine," she grins as she enters the faculty lounge. "After sixty, it's patch, patch, patch."

On my way back to my office I'm hailed by Shirley, the administrative assistant. "Leroy! Your mother just called. She says it's an emergency."

"Thanks." I hurry to my own desk and dial Mom's number.

The phone rings only once. "Yeah," my mother grunts.

"This is Leroy, Mom. What's wrong?"

"Where've you been? I haven't seen you for *ages*."

"We were in Bakersfield last weekend, Mom, for Travis and Juanita's anniversary. I called last night when we got home and Mitch said you were asleep. He left a note on the fridge for you."

"He *did*?"

"Yes. What's wrong?"

"I'm out of bananas."

"That's the emergency?"

Her voice deepens with reproach. "*You've* probably got bananas."

She is correct. "I'll pick some up on the way home from work and drop them by."

"What time?"

"After work, Mom. Maybe four, four-thirty."

"That late? I'm *starving* for a banana."

"Listen, did you call Suzie?"

"Poor little shy Suzie? Oh, I should call her."

"*Did* you call her?"

"Poor little shy Suzie? I feel so sorry for her."

I exhale heavily. "I'm asking *if* you called her. She said you called."

"I certainly need to call her. She hasn't talked to her grandma for *ages*. She never calls me."

I let the question go. "I'll bring you some bananas as soon as I can."

Her voice darkens. "At home Earl would always go to the store when I asked him to. This place is the bunk. I'm going to cash a hundred-dollar check and buy my own bananas."

"Fine." I am gazing at my watch. Class is scheduled to begin right away. "I've got to go to class, Mom. In fact, now that I think of it, Mitch is going to pick you up and bring you over for dinner tonight. I'll have him bring you some bananas and buy some milk for you too."

"But I want *you* to . . ."

"Bye, Mom, I've got class." I hang up, my belly now unsettled.

9

"I cain't exactly figger how that bomb deal works," I heard my father say. "Maybe it's like a whole lotta little ones goin' off or somethin'. Anyways, it sure musta blew hell outta the Nips. They give right up."

"Damn straight they did," agreed our neighbor, Mr. Hillis. From all around us in the neighborhood we could hear car horns honking and even firecrackers—or maybe gunshots—in the distance. My momma was in the house talking on the telephone to her sister, Charlotte, whose husband had been due to ship overseas. Meanwhile, Mrs. Hillis was in our kitchen preparing snacks.

The rest of us were sitting in the grassless backyard of our house that afternoon of V-J Day. Mom's brother, Joe, just happened to be visiting when the good news came. He always wore his army uniform, and he sat there in military coat and tie while the other two men wore T-shirts and jeans. "Your Japs," my uncle announced, like he was lecturing instead of talking to friends, "they don't think like we do. They're more like animals. That's a proven fact of military intelligence. So we had to really hurt 'em to make 'em quit. We probably ought to finish 'em all off . . . kill the whole damn bunch of 'em with one or two more of those atom bombs."

Daddy glanced at him, then said, "My brother Clyde, he wrote to me that the Japs was damn good soldiers, damn tough. Clyde he knew somethin' about tough."

"Damn straight," agreed Mr. Hillis. "He 'uz tougher'n tank water, Clyde. I seen him whup the shit outta some big ol' boys."

Uncle Joe looked impatient. He sucked beer from a brown bottle, cleared his throat, then continued his discourse to the other men. "But you've got to look at it from a *military* perspective, boys. Your Japs live on fish heads and rice, and they do anything they're told and they aren't smart enough to wonder why. They even think that Emperor of theirs is a *god*."

"Well, I never knew me a good Jap," Mr. Hillis nodded.

My father's eyes smiled. "Did you ever know one a-tall, Hillis?"

Mr. Hillis grinned. "Well, now that you mention it, Earl, I never did." He chuckled at himself, and my father smiled.

"And you, Joe?"

"Oh, hell, yeah," snapped the soldier. "My boss at the vegetable market, that Sakamoto, was one of your Japs—a little sawed-off runt with glasses, always grinning when he bossed me around." Then Uncle Joe's voice resumed its deeper, official tone: "We need to just send all of 'em back where they came from. They're all spies for that Emperor of theirs. They aren't true Americans like us. They've got no business here. This is white men's country."

My mother and Mrs. Hillis emerged from the house with a tray of snacks and a pitcher of iced tea.

"Me and Clyde we picked strawberries over on the coast for a family named Hata right after we come out here. They was awful nice folks to work for. Their boy he got killed fightin' in Italy I heard, and I heard they lost their farm because some so-called patriots took it away."

Uncle Joe grinned, then said in that deep voice, "Well, if you'd been privy to military intelligence, you'd understand that they're bigger issues at stake than someone's farm. Remember that was land white people couldn't work as long as your Japs had it. You can bet they were sending money back to that Emperor of theirs, anyway."

My father carefully placed his beer on the lawn next to his wooden chair, looked at his brother-in-law, and said evenly, "First of all, they ain't *my* Japs. They're just Japs. Second, you been stationed in California scratchin' your ass the whole war. You ain't seen squat of action since basic trainin', so don't talk down to me or Hillis either one. My brother Leroy fought 'n' died in the war, and so did Billy Hata. *They* had the right to tell me stuff, but you don't." Daddy's voice never changed and his attention never left Momma's brother.

My uncle averted his eyes.

"Earl! That's no way to talk to Joey. He's an officer!" cried my mother, her voice quivering.

"Not now he's not," my father replied without heat. "He's a grocery clerk again now."

"Oh," smiled Mrs. Hillis, embarrassed by the exchange and trying to change the subject, "are you in groceries, Lieutenant Morris? So's my husband."

That prompted laughter from her husband. "Oh, yeah," he agreed. "Me, I'm real big in groceries. What I do is sell fruit and vegetables off the back a my truck. Make a decent livin' at it, too. Now ol' Earl here, he's in iron 'n' steel. The missus irons and he . . ."

Before he could finish, my daddy poked his ribs and said, "Hey!" Both men guffawed, tension broken.

Uncle Joe ignored them and said, "Well, I won't be in groceries much longer. There's lots of new chances opening up for veterans."

Just then a high-pitched voice called, "Leee-roy! Leee-roy!"

My mother's eyebrows arched. "It sounds like that J.D.," she said. "I'll go tell that pest you can't play."

"Hey, Leroy!" called another voice. Floyd was with him.

"How come I can't?" I asked.

"Well . . . we have company."

Daddy eyed her for a moment, then he winked at me. "You can go on out 'n' play with them two rascals, Leroy. This here grown-up talk gets old, don't it?"

"Thanks, Daddy."

"Earl, those two're crude—that *belching* bit . . ."

"They're just bein' boys," my father replied.

Mom wouldn't relent. "My brother Joey *never* did anything like that, did you, Joey?"

"Yeah, I reckon he never," Daddy smiled at Mr. Hillis.

"You stay in the yard!" I heard Momma call as I ran down the driveway toward Floyd and J.D.

In front of the house I saw my two pals standing on the small lawn. They rarely knocked or rang the doorbell when they came over; instead they stood in the yard and howled like coyotes.

"Hey, Leroy, guess what?" Floyd called when he spied me. "We whupped the Nips."

J.D. immediately stuck his upper front teeth over his lower lip, circled his eyes with forefingers and thumbs to imitate glasses, and said, "So solly, prease. So solly, prease."

Not to be outdone, Floyd imitated a machine gun—"Rat-tat-tat-tat!"—grabbed his chest, spun, and fell to the ground.

"Floyd's ol' Hirohito," grinned J.D.

"Nuh-uh," disagreed the corpse. "*You* are yourownself. Anyways, that's how they die. I seen 'em in the picture show. The Japs they always turn around like that whenever they die, huh, Leroy."

"Nuh-uh," J.D. disagreed.

"Go to and stay put!" said Floyd.

I glanced around, saw no adults nearby, and farted as loudly as I could, quickly calling, "No corks!"

"Corks!" yelled both J.D. and Floyd.

"Too late!" I laughed.

J.D. began swallowing air, and I knew what he was going to do. Just as he burped, I cried, "Corks!"

"No fair, Leroy!"

I corked him on the shoulder.

"Ouch! You always hit too hard," he complained.

Floyd interrupted us. "Hey, you guys, there's this parade up on Chester Avenue. A buncha big guys got flags and drums and ever'thang. Wanna go see it?"

A parade? I hesitated momentarily, then sprinted. "Last one there's a nigger baby," I hollered over my shoulder.

10

While a day at the college tires me mentally, I'm always energized by the bicycle ride home, so I arrive frisky. I deposit my gear in the den, then walk into the kitchen and hug my wife. "How about a nap?" I ask.

"Is your mom coming over?"

"Ah, yeah . . . I forgot." There goes our nap.

"Maybe we can get to bed early," Yvonne smiles, kisses me, and her tongue touches my lips.

"Let's hope so." Since our marriage, we have allowed few afternoons together to pass without the intimacy of a nap—the private talk, the cuddling, the sex. In the old days it started (and often ended) with sex, now the talk and cuddling dominate, with sex still a pleasant component. We prefer those daytime encounters because we're still fresh then.

After another kiss and a moment of nuzzling, I ask, "Where's Pop?"

"He's in the family room watching TV with Jared."

"I'll go say hi."

"Wait," she smiles. "Guess what your father said when I got home from work?"

"I give."

"Right after I came in the door, he came out to the dining room and he said, 'Do you know how much time you spent with me today?' I said,

'No,' and he managed to form a circle with his fingers, and he said, 'Zero.'"

"That's an amazing exchange for him." I hug her. "Maybe he *can* get better." I say it, but I don't really believe it. Doctors have told us that his condition is progressive and irreversible.

I enter the family room, and Pepper climbs slowly to his feet—his arthritic hips slow him—and limps toward me, wagging his tail. "How're you doing, big guy?" I croon to the pooch, scratching his back.

Pepper has been lying near where my father sits in an armchair. The card table is in front of Pop, and a music video blares from the television set in an entertainment center against the wall across from him. He is not watching it—he doesn't seem to notice TV much anymore—but is bent forward noisily sucking at a straw that has already drained a large mug of root beer.

Our younger son, who is watching the rock video, grimaces each time the deep, rumbling sound bursts from the straw. As soon as he sees me, Jared asks, "Can't Grandpa, like, have some more? That sound *sucks.*"

I can't help laughing at his choice of words, but I nod, "Sure, get him some."

My father appears not to have noticed me, so I call, "Hi, Pop!"

Slowly his head turns, his cloudy eyes scan, then a broad smile slices his face. "How you?" he says.

I walk over and pat his back, and make busy conversation: "Dinner's about ready, and there's a ball game on the tube tonight." As I'm gabbing, I hear the telephone ring in the next room.

Jared calls from the kitchen, "Dad, it's Grandma!" and my father says, "Tighten my belt." He wears sweat pants.

I pick up the phone. "Hello, Mom."

"Aren't you going to come get me?"

"No, Mom. I told you that Mitch'll pick you up on his way home from practice."

"You *did*? I thought *you'd* pick me up."

"On my bicycle?"

"Don't you have a car? You've got *all* those cars in your driveway. You *could* pick your mother up if you *wanted* to."

I sigh, allow irritation to pass—we have often had this conversation—then say, "I just walked in the house from work, Mom. I'm tired. Don't worry, Mitch should be there any time."

"Is your father wearing his teeth??"

"No."

"He *needs* to."

"He won't wear them, Mom."

"Make him."

"Okay, Mom. I've gotta go help Yvonne with dinner. See you soon."

There is a pause—she dislikes hanging up. Finally she moans, "All right," and clicks off.

Forty minutes later, my mother walks in the door with our older son, Mitch, and she says without a greeting, "I *wish* your father would wear his teeth."

"Hello. He won't."

"You *make* him, then."

She seems to reach right inside me, so I glance up from my newspaper, suppress irritation, then reply, "No, *you* make him." As far as I know, she has never in fifty years succeeded in making him do anything he didn't want to do. My mother sighs dramatically and looks away from me, the back of one hand brushing her forehead in a gesture that was old when Lillian Gish employed it. I have failed her again.

She must know how futile her endless complaints are: he abandoned his dentures even before my parents' failing health forced us to move them north to be near us. "He just does that because he knows I can't stand it," my mother claimed at the time. Now I have no idea where his teeth are and, of course, neither does he.

When we finally got my father transferred to our house, Mom chose to remain independent in their mobile home at a nearby senior citizens' park. But now she demands more and more attention.

Pop's gums seem to have adjusted to the absence of teeth—"My grandpa can, like, chew spikes," Jared tells his friends. Pop has adjusted well to our household too. While it is true that he looks less than enchanting, we're beyond the point where appearance much concerns us.

He is still eating long after the rest of us have finished, smacking his food loudly, dropping bits, which he tries laboriously and futilely to recover before Pepper, who's none too swift anymore either, can claim them. The apron Pop wears is inscribed THE CHEF IS IN, but it can barely be read through the camouflage of gravy and vegetables.

My father has never trusted doctors. When, a couple of years back, I noticed how vague he'd become, I urged him to see Mom's physician in Bakersfield. "Hell," he snorted, "I'm not goin' to no sawbones. If somethin's wrong with me, I don't wanta know about it."

Well, something is wrong with him, and he doesn't know about it—or at least I don't think he does—but we sure do. When we finally got them moved here, he didn't resist when I took him to our family doctor, Jim Cox. Jim ordered a CAT scan, and it revealed scars in Pop's brain from a series of small strokes. As a result of that damage, he has developed both multi-infarct dementia and a loss of coordination called locomotor ataxia, so this untidiness is the price we pay for his continuing, if tenuous, independence.

I find myself at times like this gazing at him, noticing that his expression is frequently puzzled, pained. Dr. Cox assures me that Pop has reached the point where he not only doesn't remember, but also doesn't remember that he doesn't remember. I sure hope that's true. Those thoughts cause me to blink hard.

"Roy?" My wife has walked in from the kitchen, and she rests a hand on my neck.

"I'm okay, honey."

She glances at my father, smiles at me and kneads my neck for a moment, then sits on the arm of my chair.

My mother suddenly insists, "Why can't you feed your father?"

"*You* can, Mom," I reply, still troubled by my own thoughts.

"I can't. Mitchell will do it, won't you, honey?"

Mitch rolls his eyes. "No way," he says pleasantly.

"No one can, Mom," I tell her. I'm attempting to listen to an interview on TV while she repeats this litany . . . or maybe I'm using the TV interview to ignore her.

"He makes a *royal* mess."

This time I sigh. "Mom, I'm really trying to watch the news. You know that no one can make Pop do anything. It's important to him to do for himself. He's a hog on ice if ever there was one."

"He's a *what*?"

"Never mind."

"*Make* him let you," she insists.

My wife correctly judges my growing irritation and replies for me: "You know that Dr. Cox wants Pop to do as much as he can for himself."

Mother's voice changes and she responds simply, "He *does*?" but somehow the message is "Mind your own business."

"Yes, he *does*," I snap. I won't have Yvonne treated that way.

Before I say anything more, Mom rises and once more alters her tone, whining, "Where's the bathroom?"

She has been coming to this house as long as we've owned it, so even her question bothers me. "Right where it was yesterday," I reply.

"Way down that *long* hall?"

"The same as yesterday."

"I suppose I have to walk all the way down that long hall."

Somehow her tragic tone breaks my tension, and I chuckle. "I suppose," I finally reply, ". . . or piddle your britches."

11

Mitch and I are sipping coffee on the deck the next morning. Because he's been sleeping at his grandmother's mobile home, I haven't seen much of him recently. This morning, however, he has no early class, and my dad is sleeping in, so the two of us are granted a few minutes to catch up with one another. "It looks like we could spoon that fog into our coffee, doesn't it?" I suggest.

He grins.

The deck behind our house is built around a vast bay laurel. I often sit out here watching banks of fog dense as whipped cream creep over the wooded ridges of Mount Tamalpais, then slide slowly down this side into Mill Valley's canyons. There was certainly nothing like this in parched Bakersfield.

"How's life with Grandma?" I ask.

"Well"—he looks away from me and clears his throat—"I don't want to let you down, Pop, but ... well, I can't stay at Grandma's much longer. I really can't. She's wandering around all night, talking to herself mostly, and she's a real downer. She complains about *everything*. She really doesn't like Mom very much, does she?"

"No." Tough questions impale me: What are we to do about my

mother? Who will stay with her if Mitch and Jared won't . . . or can't? How can she move in with us if she disdains Yvonne?

"Why? Everyone else does."

The question stops me. "That's a long story, but she probably wouldn't have liked anyone I married."

"Well, I told her to knock off the stuff about Mom or she wouldn't see me anymore," my son adds.

I reach over and pat his knee. "Good. Don't ever hold back about those things or she'll worry you like a hound does a gopher snake."

Mitch grins. "*Like a hound does a gopher snake?* You sure can say some country stuff, Pop."

I suppose I can. I'm a small-town boy, Ph.D. or no Ph.D. My kids are the children of professionals living in the urbane Bay Area. With the blue jeans and cowboy boots I still favor, I must seem like a hick to them at times.

Still thinking *country*, I smile and ask, "Did you know that Grandpa used to always take a leak outside every night before he went to bed?"

"Outside? Why?"

"He just thought it was important to stay in touch with the earth. That great big bush in the backyard at their house was his favorite urinal."

"Gross! We used to play all around it."

"I'm sure it was a healthy plant." I chuckle, then pause before adding, "Those rituals are vital, Mitch; they ground you. I don't always remember, but I try to walk Pop out here before bed, and he has his business out and spraying almost before we reach the trees."

"Ah, *that*'s what you two're doing." His expression changes and he clears his throat. "Pop," he asks, "what's wrong with Grandma, anyway?"

No simple answer occurs to me. "She's just old and sick and away from her home. She lived thereabouts all her life—she's a Californian, born and raised in Kern County—so she misses the town and her friends there. Grandpa's with us now, and she misses him too. None of us've been through what she has, having our lives disrupted like that, so it's hard to judge her. Unfortunately, it's also damned tough dealing with her."

Mitch chuckles without humor. "Tell me about it. She claims you and Mom forced her to move when she could've stayed in Bakersfield. She says Mom put you up to it. She says she wants to move back."

"I sure wish she could," I murmur. West of the deck, the mountain seems to swell, its gullies and canyons filling with that fog.

Yvonne slides open the door from our bedroom and emerges, fresh and pretty, saying, "Okay, boys, I'm off for work. Where's Jared?"

"He's, *like,* primping," says his older brother.

"*Like,* don't you, *like,* start that," advises Yvonne.

"How about, *like,* a kiss," I say, and she lightly punches my shoulder, then gives me a real kiss, the kind that reminds me to return home early that afternoon.

Yvonne enters the house and calls, "Jared! Time to go."

A moment later, we hear, faintly, "Ah, Mom, I'm, like, not ready."

Mitch and I shake our heads and chuckle. "He'll, *like,* outgrow it, Dad. I sure wish Grandma would."

"Don't we all. Listen, you've been damned good about this. Everyone has. We're going to have to hire more help so we can relieve you guys— and us."

"Great. You know, Grandma told me the other day that you're spending all her money on help for Grandpa."

"Yeah, I know," I shake my head. "She's probably right . . . and some of ours, too. We'd rather it be used now for help now so we can all live and not be tied down all the time, but she doesn't understand. We don't want them to leave us anything. Everything just seems *wrong* to her. And it is, but that's the hand we've been dealt."

This subject seems to dominate our lives, so I bid to change it. "Jared says you've got a new girlfriend."

"I'm going out with Etta Sandrini." Then he smiles. "She's a dish."

"There's worse reasons to date someone."

"Is that why you went out with Mom, because she was a dish?"

I pause, then reply, "Well, she was mighty pretty . . . still is."

"That's what my buddies all say."

"That sure attracted me, but I married her because she was a good person, maybe a special one. It's like a Christmas present. You might see one with great wrapping that turns out to be full of rocks, but in your mom's case, the package was prime and its contents were even better."

"You really love her, don't you?" He says this with something like pride.

"Yes sir, I do." For a second, my throat softens and I blink, because I'm telling the God's truth. To lighten the conversation, I immediately ask, "How about you and the Sandrini girl?"

He gives me that grin that so resembles Yvonne's, then says, "Well, I'm real keen on her *package*."

After I stop laughing, another thought occurs to me. "Is she kin to the Sandrini kid that was in your class? The one who won a scholarship to Stanford?"

"Myron? No, not as far as I know, anyway. He's doing real well down there. I talked to him last month," Mitch says. "He still looks like the Pillsbury Doughboy—and you know what else? He's losing his hair, like a halo: the middle's falling out, but the sides are the same."

I nod. "He never had much of a package, but he's a smart kid, and a damned decent one, too. When his folks tried to make an athlete out of him in youth soccer and Little League, he was a disaster."

"I remember. In high school he was so big and so soft, the football players gave him every kind of crap." Mitch shakes his head. "You know, my strongest memory of Myron is going to be of him standing in his underwear in front of the school, his pasty legs exposed to the elements, trying to get his trousers down from the flagpole after some guys pantsed him." My son can't suppress a grin. "The poor guy."

"Is that when you fought the Garzelli kid?"

"Yeah," he nods. "I went out there and gave Myron my jacket to cover his moon, then got his pants down from the pole, so Bud Garzelli and couple of other football players started in on me, called me a faggot and said Myron was my boyfriend. I popped Bud."

"I seem to remember that he hit you back."

Mitch grins, "Oh, yeah. It was about a standoff, but everyone thought Garzelli was the toughest guy in school, maybe in town, and that fight kind of ended his reign of terror. I think those teeth he lost were kind of a permanent reminder that he could be hurt too. He never gave me or my friends any trouble after that—including Myron. It was worth being suspended for a week."

"You did the right thing. I was real proud of you."

"Uncle Travis says you used to be bad news." All of our kids refer to the Plumleys as aunt and uncle.

"I defended myself a few times."

"I'll bet. He also says Grandpa was rough."

"He damn sure was. I saw him knock the pluperfect dog shit out of a few great big guys. He was about as rough as they came in his day. He probably could've been a damned good heavyweight boxer."

"The *pluperfect dog shit?*" Mitch laughs.

I pour myself more coffee. "You know, there were a lot of fistfights in Bakersfield back then. Being tough was really admired."

"Why, I wonder?"

"I've thought about it some," I acknowledge, careful not to sound like a professor, "and I suspect that part of it was that things were churning after the Depression and the Okie migration, then all the changes that happened in World War II. Southwesterners like Grandpa came from a fighting culture, too, and they wouldn't take any crap. When people out here tried to give them grief, they'd fight." I pause and remember a few toughs from my youth, then add, "For a few guys, fighting became an end in itself, maybe the way they defined themselves."

We both fall silent. Mitch drains his cup, and he plays a little tune on it with a spoon. "Grandma keeps asking about Suzie," he says. "When's she coming home? How's she wearing her hair? Who's she dating? Stuff like that. Suzie's sure Grandma's favorite. 'Poor little shy Suzie,' she always says."

"I know." Although I'm not happy to be talking about Grandma again, I have to grin: our daughter is many things, but shy isn't one of them. Girls, in my mom's view, seem always to be timid and beset.

"It used to really bother me when we were little, the way she preferred Suzie," he adds, "but now I feel sorry for Suz'. You know, Grandma still *baby-talks* when she calls."

"I know. That's a real pain for Suzie."

"She might be coming back next weekend for Nicole's party," he tells me. "She's finishing midterms this week," he adds. "She wouldn't want to miss that party. It'll be *excellent.*" He pours himself more coffee.

Since Mitch puts the shot and throws the discus on the track team at College of Marin—is conference champion, in fact—I prod him a little. "Does the coach encourage caffeine?"

"Want to have a weight-lifting competition?"

"I'll take you on in the bench press," I challenge.

He laughs. "For a hundred bucks?"

Now I have to laugh. I can still pump reps at 265 pounds, but Mitch, shorter and thicker, easily tops me. "Okay, you spot me one pound for each year older I am than you—twenty-nine pounds."

"No way, Pop."

We will get together later in the day in the garage, where we keep a bench and weights. Working out together is one of our enduring pleasures, and these challenges add spice to our sessions. I'm just sorry that my younger son has never shown any interest in training with us, or in athletics at all, for that matter. He's missing good times, and I'm missing him.

The telephone begins ringing. I stride into the kitchen and pick up the receiver. My mother's voice, angry, rasps, "Yeah. What time is my appointment today?"

I sigh, then say, "*Hello,* Mom. Your appointment's at ten-thirty."

"Why so early? That's an *awful* time."

As often happens, I am forced to smile, although my belly burns. "You're up, aren't you, so what's the problem? Besides, most other people are functional by ten-thirty."

"What's this doctor's name?" She has been visiting Jim Cox for more than a year and seems to know his name well enough when complaining about him.

"Dr. Cox."

"Well, that Dr. Cox doesn't give me enough nerve medicine. My old doctor at home was *wonderful.* He gave me all I needed. Now I wake up with that nervous feeling in my stomach. I'm going to *tell* that doctor."

"Tell *him,* then, not me, okay?" She won't, of course. When she arrived up here, Jim Cox quickly determined that my mother was overmedicated, drowsy from tranquilizers. While she was recovering from the bypass surgery she'd had then, he backed her away from the mega-doses she had been taking and was now allowing her only recommended amounts.

"I might have to go *home* and see my old doctor if that Dr. Cox doesn't help me."

"Right, Mom."

"This new medicine isn't strong—Katharine told me about it. She gave me some."

"That's great." Katharine had been one of Mom's neighbors in Bakersfield, a world-class hypochondriac who unofficially practiced medicine in the neighborhood, even dispensed drugs from her own bursting medicine chest. "It's good you heard that from an expert."

She ignores my jibe and asks, "Where's Mitchell? He was supposed to spend the night with me."

"He's here and, no, he wasn't supposed to stay anywhere in particular, you know that. He had a date last night."

"What time did he come in?"

"I don't know."

"You and that Yvonne certainly don't pay much attention to your children, do you?"

Mitch is nearly twenty-one, hardly a child, but there's no point trying to discuss this, so I say simply, "I'll be by at ten or ten-fifteen to pick you up."

"*I* wasn't raised that way." She doesn't want to let go.

"*I* was," I snap, then hang up. Maybe I need to call her old doctor in Bakersfield—or Katharine—and order myself a bucket of tranquilizers.

It's almost time for Trish to arrive, so I walk down the hall and look in on Pop. To my surprise, because I've heard no sound from his room, I find him naked on his knees between his bed and the wall where we have installed the grab bar. His breath is rapid, almost panicked, and his skin is clammy. This has happened before, but for a moment I almost panic myself. I steady myself and say as casually as I can, "Took a spill, eh, Pop?"

His hands are desperately locked on the grab bar, and I know from past experience that I can't lift him until I work them free, so I have to pull each finger, force him to release. It is no easy task, for despite my continued weight training, he is nearly as strong as I am, and he is frantic. I tug, explaining that he must let go, but he merely continues puffing, facing the wall, and holds on as though life itself is at stake. "Took my license," he says.

I stop. Memories like these surface from him like flotsam from an ancient shipwreck: his driver's license was indeed revoked a couple of years previously after he drove the wrong way up a freeway off-ramp. With the lost license, his independence and some of his manhood have been forfeited. But something else grasps my attention: I don't hear complete sentences from him very often.

The doorbell rings as we stand there, and I call to Mitch, "Can you get that, pardner?"

"Sure."

A moment later Trish peeks into the room. "Hello, Earl," she calls in her high, singsong voice. "Are we bathing?"

"Your girlfriend's here," I whisper to my father.

A chuckle rumbles up his throat.

12

Yvonne has taken the sedan to work, so I drive our small pickup to Thistlewood, the mobile home park where my mother lives. I glide past a grassy entryway lined with red and yellow flowers, past two small ponds connected by a cement-lined stream. Late-model autos, most of them large and American, are parked beside the manicured lawns and gardens, and well-dressed seniors wave and nod as I pass. Finally I pull into my mother's carport, park, then enter my folks' mobile home via a side door.

"You ready, Mom?" I call.

She walks down the hall, stops at the edge of carpet and linoleum, and stares at me with red, swollen eyes.

"What's wrong?"

"You *weren't* raised that way." Her chin is quivering.

I slump against the sink, hesitate, then say, "When I was Mitch's age, I went where I pleased and stayed out as late as I liked, you know that."

"That was only after you broke up with Lahoma and started with that Yvonne."

"Her name wasn't and isn't *that* Yvonne. It's Yvonne."

"*She* kept you out. She stayed out *all* night with boys. Not like Lahoma. Lahoma was a *nice* girl."

"Let's go," I say. Mom has lately decided I should have married my high school girlfriend, although she hadn't been enthusiastic about her at the time. I have to step away from this, so I swallow quick anger and plunge out the door toward the pickup. She follows.

We drive to Jim Cox's office, mute and uncomfortable—or at least I am. On the way, Mom tries to initiate a debate: "I don't know where all my *things* have gone. I can't figure it out. I can't find anything. I think *somebody's* taking them."

No answer from me, so a few minutes later she tries again. "We can't afford to be paying for that Trish. *You* should be taking care of your father."

I merely nod. Finally, I pull into the parking lot and announce, "We're here."

We sit silently in the waiting room for a time, then my mother turns to me and says, "You tell that doctor I need more nerve medicine. You tell him I'll just go back to my *old* doctor at home if he doesn't give me more." I simply nod, so she adds, "You tell him."

"No," I finally respond, "*you* tell him."

"Well, I just *will.*" Her voice is resolute.

We sit in uncomfortable silence, me staring without interest or comprehension at a magazine open in my lap, then she adds, "You tell him I need a *strong* laxative. *Katharine* got a prescription from *her* doctor." I do not respond.

A moment later, a smiling nurse opens an inner door and says, "Mrs. Upton, we've got a room for you now."

My mother smiles back wanly and rises.

"How are you today?" the nurse asks cordially, and Mom responds, her voice high and faint, "Ohhhhh, not bad."

"Do you want me to go in with you?" I ask.

"Ohhhhh," she says in that same weak voice, "you don't have to."

I begin reading an article on compact cars in a back issue of *Consumer Reports,* then move on to an evaluation of electric razors—I'm in the market for neither. Finally, as I'm scanning an assessment of trench coats, the nurse calls, "Mr. Upton, do you want to come in for a moment?"

"Sure," I reply, suddenly concerned.

"Hi, Roy." Jim Cox shakes my hand as I enter the room.

"Well, your mother's doing well. Her weight's fine, and that rash on her back has cleared up . . ."

"It was nerves," my mother meekly interjects.

"She says she wants a laxative because she's having some problems with constipation, but I think before we start giving her medicine, we need to monitor her diet, make certain she's eating roughage and getting some exercise too. Are you taking that daily walk I advised, Mrs. Upton?"

The answer is no, but my mother says only, "Well . . ."

Jim exchanges a heavy look with me, then says to her, "You really need to start the day with juice and some kind of bran cereal and to eat fresh fruit and vegetables. Roy tells me that you have toast and tea for breakfast, toast with melted cheese on it for lunch, and TV dinners most nights. No wonder you're bound up—that stuff's like eating corks." I laugh, and even my mother chuckles weakly. "Instead of the drugstore, Roy needs to take you to the grocery store.

"Your tattletale son"—he winks at me—"also tells me that you haven't begun taking even short walks yet. You know the cardiologist and I both want you to exercise. It's difficult to start, but you don't need medicine as much as you need to revise your habits a little. Stay active and eat wisely, Mrs. Upton. That's better than anything I can prescribe."

His tone tells me the medical discussion is over, so I ask, "How's Steve doing?"

"Well," Jim grins, "he's riding the bench at Stanford, but at least he's on the team. Must be genetic—warming the bench, I mean. That's all I ever did."

Steve, Jim's oldest boy, has dated our Suzie off and on since high school. He was a local football hero, highly recruited, but turned out to be a step too slow to be a player at a major college. Fortunately, he was also an excellent student, a pre-med major.

"As we both know," I smile, "it'll all have been fun in about twenty years, even the pine time."

Jim nods, then says, "Oh, yeah, he sends his best to Suzie. I think he's still stuck on her."

My mother brightens immediately, and she says, "Suzie's on the honor roll at Santa Cruz."

"No surprise," says Jim, "since she takes after her mother." He opens the door and we walk out.

For a moment, Mom seems not to have understood Jim's gentle joke, then she says, "No she doesn't. That Yvonne wasn't a good student. Leroy was." In fact, that Yvonne was an excellent student.

I lead Mom to a counter, and she takes out her checkbook and says, "You fill it in for me. I can sign it." Then she adds, "Suzie takes after *you*."

I'm thinking, Right, that's why you called to tell her I wasn't her real father. But I say nothing while I write Mom's check. As she signs it, Jim asks quietly, "How's she been acting?"

"Low."

"Is she taking those antidepressants each night?"

"As far as I know."

He nods. "Well, they'll cause constipation if she isn't eating properly and getting a little exercise. When you bring her in next month, we'll take a closer look at that. I don't want to overwhelm her."

"Okay."

"Has she begun to go out at all, visit her neighbors?"

"No, not as far as I know."

"Let me see if I can get her involved in a senior group-counseling program, then. It's an outreach of the hospital, and it can really help."

My mother finishes and says, "Suzie looks just like Leroy."

"Poor girl," smiles Jim. Then he asks me, "You and Yvonne going to the Rotary Oktoberfest?"

"We're going to try."

"Sarah and I'll see you there, then. Save some beer for me."

He smiles, takes my mother's hand, and almost bows, saying, "Take care of yourself, Mrs. Upton. I'll see you next month."

As he turns to enter another treatment room, Mother says weakly, "Leroy is a good-looking man. That Yvonne . . ."

"He was kidding, Mom," I tell her.

"Well . . ."

On our way back to the car, she turns toward me and announces, "I'm gonna take all the laxatives I want. I'll just write a check for a hundred bucks and get all I want." Her voice is firm again. "And if that doctor won't give me more nerve medicine, I'm going to call my *old* doctor. Katharine says . . ."

"Okay, Mom."

After buying her pizza—a favorite treat—then dropping her off at her mobile home, I return to my house. I've a little time before I must leave for school, so I pick up the latest issue of *Track Technique*. Shortly after I begin reading, I hear the front door open and assume that Yvonne is home.

"That you, babe?" I call.

"It's me and Tracy, Dad," Jared replies.

I glance at my watch and realize that it's too early for him to be out of school, so I stand and walk into the kitchen where my son and another long, lean boy are raiding the refrigerator. The latter's hair is purple and spiked like a Prussian helmet. "Uh, hi, Mr. Upton," he says, nervously, it seems to me.

"You guys're home early today," I say. "What's up?"

Tracy looks at the floor, but Jared grins and extends a sheet of yellow paper toward me. "Me and Tracy, we, like, got suspended till Wednesday. But don't get mad," he quickly adds.

I do get mad, of course, immediately but quietly. Life of late has eroded any slack I might otherwise have had. "Why?" I ask tightly, and Tracy flinches.

To my surprise, Jared continues grinning and opens a large pink sheet with PSYCHIC FAIRE written across the top in bold letters. "They, like, posted these all over campus, and me and Tracy we, like, figured that if it was a *real* Psychic Faire, then they, like, didn't need to list the time and the place because all the psychics could, like, *divine* it. We were just tearin' all that stuff off the signs, and Mr. Farrell, the vice principal, he caught us. He's, like, *into* that stuff, so he got mad and suspended us."

"That's all?"

"Swear to God," he says. Tracy, standing behind him, nods vigorously.

My breath eases, and I have to smile. I know Mr. Farrell, and he's a space cadet. "Okay, but right now Mom and I really don't need any trouble. Grandma and Grandpa keep us pretty tense."

"Can you, like, sign that sheet for me to take back?" he asks.

"No problem, but you get to visit Grandma tomorrow when you're out of school."

"Like, *wow*. How come?"

"And take Tracy with you."

"Yeah, *Tracy*," says Jared, suddenly smiling.

"Hey, dude, I, like, *would*"—Tracy bobs his purple spikes—"but I'll, like, be grounded."

No doubt. I know his folks, and their sense of humor has been strained by his continuing antics. "Well, I've got schoolwork to do. You guys stick around here this afternoon. If you can't go to school, you can give us a hand. No going out. I want you to finish moving that firewood up to the deck for a starter."

The purple spikes quickly say, "I gotta go."

"Like, *thanks*, Tracy," hisses Jared.

"Heck of a helper, ol' Tracy," I comment, then add, "Pepper'll help you." I once more pick up that quarterly.

Jared poses in the doorway for a minute, and I am about to suggest that he quit stalling and go move that wood when he asks thoughtfully, "Dad, like, what *are* we?"

I look up, take off my reading glasses, and ponder his query. "That's a hell of a question, Jared. What's it mean?"

"I mean, are we, like, Other Hispanics or Pacific Islanders or *what*? We got this form to fill out at school and Mrs. Hooper, she got mad because I said we were, like, Americans. She said that isn't a category and that I had to be, like, 'White' or 'African American' or 'Chicano,' somethin' like that."

My son is nothing if not original. When he stalls he makes it interesting. I've explained all this several times before, but I once more tell him, "My family is English, Scots-Irish, Irish, and Cherokee. Mom's is Spanish, Portuguese, French, and German, with maybe a little Mexican Indian—Yaquis and Mayos, I think . . ."

"Wow! You mean we're, like, *Chicanos*?" Jared is a fair-skinned, dishwater blond, just as I am.

"I think you were right the first time: Americans."

He turns from the door, grinning and repeating, "Wow! Like, Chicanos . . ." Pepper limps after him.

I shake my head and call, "Hey, Pancho, don't forget to move that wood!"

By the time I've finished reading an article on interval training for middle-distance runners, the Chicano wood mover has disappeared into his room, and only a few sticks have changed locations. It's time for me to leave, and I haven't the energy to hound him.

13

Trader Tom Gilmore threw a shindig when he opened his used-car lot on a large blacktopped corner near our house. There was free barbecue, free watermelon, free beer, and free soda pop, plus a live band and dancing on that Saturday afternoon, with entire families grinning and chatting and eating under a huge neon sign of a buckaroo. To me, it seemed like the whole town was there.

Late spring and already sizzling, the day demanded iced watermelon and cold beer, so the lot filled quickly with women in pressed print dresses and men in clean jeans, their faces brown, their foreheads white—if they weren't sporting cowboy hats. A few, fresh from work, wearing hard hats and overalls spotted with oil, were kidded when they approached the beer keg—"Hell, Slick, you never had to get *all dolled up.*"

In the dead center of the expanse of autos was a small house with a large sign—OFFICE—decorating it. Three anemic trees—reminders that this had lately been a horse pasture—grew around it, but they offered little shade. Kousin Ken's Kern Kowboys—two guitars, a bass, and a fiddle, with four high-pitched voices—entertained on the porch of the house, winking at girls and sipping brew between songs. Most of us kids—already vaguely ashamed of the Okie image—made fun of Kousin Ken and his music, but our parents listened avidly to the twanging Hawaiian steel guitar and nasal crooning.

Used cars had been cleared from a semicircle in front of the office, replaced by picnic tables, with an area left clear for dancing that attracted an increasingly large crowd as darkness edged closer. In seventh grade now, I wandered around with my two pals, teasing girls and watching high school guys dance cheek to cheek with their sweethearts. Several older folks were watching too, and we heard one old woman wearing a sunbonnet complain, "Clutch-'n'-hug dancin'! That's what's wrong with these younguns!" She walked off in a huff, carrying a plate of barbecue.

We controlled our giggles until she'd departed, then we burst into laughter, imitating her—"Clutch-'n'-hug dancin'!"—and wrestling one another as we laughed once more. To us she sounded as funny as a foreigner.

I spied my mother on the far side of the dancers sitting with Mrs. Hillis and Mrs. Pruett, another neighbor. Pop wasn't with her.

With J.D. and Floyd, I wandered among the polished cars and touched them. My dream, mostly unspoken, was to own a big yellow sedan.

"I'm gonna get my license next year," Floyd boasted.

"You can't," I pointed out. "You're too young."

"You can get one when you're fourteen if your folks'll sign, and my momma says she'll sign for me."

"No lie?" gasped J.D.

I eyed Floyd. A driver's license was the dividing line between boyhood and manhood, and it didn't seem possible that a dumb fartknocker like him could have one. Something about that possibility deeply disturbed me.

Before I said anything, J.D. announced, "He's just shittin' us."

"I'll bet ya five bucks," snapped Floyd.

"Put up your five."

"Put up yours," he countered.

"Put up yours first."

I knew neither one of them had any money—and I didn't either—so I laughed and said, "You two sound like ol' Abbott and Costello."

J.D. immediately laughed, but Floyd continued to look aggrieved. "I really will get it. You guys just wait."

"Okay, we'll wait," I said. "Come on."

The three of us wandered behind the office, where a beer keg was doing brisk business. My father stood in a group of men holding cups of brew and laughing. Just above us, the back door of the house was open, and a large, coatless man in suspenders, a white shirt, and tie suddenly stood there swaying slightly, his eyes on those near the beer keg. He was drinking from a small bottle, whiskey, I guess, and he looked like a gangster in the movies. Just seeing him scared me.

A moment later Tom Gilmore himself came to the door and urged the big man back inside, "Come on, Duke. Cool off." Mr. Gilmore noticed me standing there and winked. "Howdy, Leroy." Duke scowled a moment longer, then disappeared back inside.

My father, his pal Hubby Hobbs, and other guys he worked with seemed not to have noticed the dangerous man. They continued telling stories and laughing. A familiar, skinny guy in oil-stained overalls was saying, ". . . so that farmer he said to the travelin' salesman, 'I don't care 'bout you dickin' my daughter, but if you pull one more hair outta my ass I'll whip you from here to Tulsa!'" The crowd burst into laughter, and so did we three—it was a joke we already knew. My father slapped the thin man's back and said, "That's a goodun, Loy. A dandy!"

Then that big guy lurched into the doorway again, stared at the men drinking beer again, his jaw working, his breath heavy. "Hey, you!" he called gruffly.

Loy, the thin man who had told the joke, turned. "You talkin' to me, friend?"

"Yeah. Come 'ere," he growled.

Loy looked around at the others, who quieted, then he slowly walked to the steps. He hesitated before climbing: "What can I do for you?"

"Just come on up here. I got somethin' for you."

It looked to me like the big man, with his suspenders and slacks and tie, might pull a gat. He backed into the house so we couldn't see him, but I could feel him there just inside the door.

Slowly, Loy climbed the three steps. After a moment he disappeared through the doorway, a few gruff words were heard, then a liquid smack, and Loy staggered back to the landing, one hand on his cheek, shouting, "You son of a bitch! You ain't got no call to sock me!"

The big man lunged out the door with another punch that struck the smaller man on the chest and knocked him down the steps. "You ain't man enough to come in here," he slurred. "You ain't got what it takes! Damn Okie!"

My father and several others helped Loy up just as Tom Gilmore appeared at the doorway. "Duke! Duke!" he pleaded. "Take 'er easy, Duke."

"Goddamned Okies!" sneered the big man, as he disappeared back into the house.

My father was already headed up the steps. "You son of a bitch!" he called just as Kousin Ken's Kern Kowboys burst into a fast number. It was like the movies—music in the background—because we heard a rumbling, some fast clicks and snaps, some *ooofs* and *ooohs*, then Duke stumbled out the back door, his face a bloody smear, and my father was still on him, hitting the big belly three, four times, then splattering blood on everyone as he popped the reeling man's face. "Apologize, you son of a bitch!" my father puffed, then he caught the man in the ribs with two short punches and knocked him into a heap at the foot of the stairs with a long right to the side of the head.

Another tough-looking guy in a suit and tie came sprinting out of that door, down the steps heading for my father, but Mr. Hobbs—as large as Pop—drove a shoulder into his chest, then pinned him against the small house, and snarled, "You want a little a this, fancy pants?"

The man hissed something, and Mr. Hobbs quickly wrestled him to the ground, one thick hand on his throat, the other large fist poised over his face. "Yer a-fuckin' with yer pulse, see. One more word and I'm a-gonna have to disconnect you."

People were running from the dance area and a woman shrieked.

Tom Gilmore, his face stricken, once more appeared at the door, pleading "Earl! Hubby! Jesus, Earl! Take 'er easy! Take 'er easy!"

My father ignored him. His face was stone, and he stared directly at the hulk, who had managed to sit up. I'd never seen Pop look like that before, and it tempered my elation at his victory: he looked crazy. "Apologize to Loy, you son of a bitch!" He slapped the crumpled man's face, and blood showered over the nearest spectators. "Apologize!" He slapped him again, hard, the sound of it popping like a gunshot, and blood again spattered spectators. The man beneath Hubby Hobbs stopped struggling.

Finally the guy my father was slapping mumbled something, and Pop relaxed, then stepped away from him.

Tom Gilmore rushed past my father, casting a wary glance at him, then helped the bleeding man to his feet. "Come on, Duke." He turned toward my father and the other men and puffed, "Duke just made a mistake."

Mr. Hobbs released the other tough guy, who quickly scrambled back into the building.

"Yeah, and *you* made one too, Tom," my father snarled, his face hard again. "You made a mistake whenever you took to thinkin' you was a big shot and runnin' around with tough guys from L.A. You better send that joker back where he come from because I'll whip him every time I see him around here. I'll whip him in church or on the street if he even looks crossways at me or anybody else. I never thought you'd high-hat your own folks, Tom."

"Listen, Earl, you got it all wrong."

"I sure as hell hope I do, Tom. You was always a good ol' boy, but now it looks like you wanta be a big shot. Come on, boys, let's go buy us a beer somewheres. Tom wants to be with his big-shot pals." My father's eyes were fevered.

"Jesus, Earl, wait . . ." called Tom Gilmore, his voice desperate.

I stood shaking near the stairs, almost breathless. It had all happened so fast.

14

The following morning, I'm loading my bicycle panniers with quizzes I've just finished grading, sipping the last of my cold coffee, when Yvonne calls me from up the hall: "Hon', can you give me a hand?"

It's one of my early days, and I'm on the edge of being late and must resist the urge to say no. "Be right there," I call, then hurry toward my dad's room. I find him sprawled on the floor, puffing.

Yvonne kneels next to him, stroking his brow. "He's too heavy for me," she says.

For a moment, I simply register this: Yvonne with the father she wishes she'd had; he with the daughter for whom he'd yearned. Then I smile at both of them. "Took a dive, huh, Pop?" I finally say, sounding as bright as possible.

His breathing is rapid, and his face is contorted with what could be fear or rage or both: his body has become a traitor. I move behind him and roll him into a sitting position. His muscles are rigid. "Take his hands," I direct Yvonne, then I squat, reach under his armpits, and lift with my legs. My father is still a large man, and he is unpliable. With a groan, I raise him until he stands awkwardly. "You can let him go now," I grunt.

Yvonne releases Pop, then I muscle him to the side of his bed. "I'll change him," I volunteer, then begin to remove my father's diaper and replace it with a fresh one. He will likely sleep, I know, as he frequently does after one of his spills, too traumatized to do anything else. I cover him. Trish will soon arrive. That formidable woman must know some nurse's trick, for she claims to have hoisted Pop up from the floor on occasion.

Mitch once suggested that she tickled Grandpa, or maybe goosed him, propelling him to his feet. Dirty-minded young Jared, on the other hand, had simply leered, "I'll bet she knows how to, like, *get him up.*" I merely shook my head when I heard that.

My wife and I pause arm in arm in the doorway of my father's room and gaze at him. In my dreams I still see Pop as I remember him: tall, tan and muscular, winking and grinning from beneath a cowboy hat. I see the heads of pretty women at the county fair turn to gaze as he passes. I see him, at fifty, charge without hesitation into three large, boozy young men at a service station after one had snarled, "Fuck off, you old Okie." By the time he was done, they had been the ones who fucked off.

Now I see him broken in this bed beneath me.

"Are you okay, hon'?" Yvonne asks.

"What?" I take a deep breath, then smile. "Sure."

"I feel so sorry for Earl," she says, gazing at him. "Sometimes I wonder if he even wants to live like this."

"I do too, but at least he knows that we're with him for the long haul."

"Yes," she agrees and squeezes me, "he can be sure of that. Do you think we ought to see about a wheelchair? Or at least a walker? He's falling more and more."

In truth, I really don't want to think about those things, but I nod and say, "I'll talk to Jim." Then I change the subject: "Listen, I'm sorry about last night."

Yvonne smiles and squeezes my arm. "I'm surprised you even manage a *temporary* erection, with all this stress. Don't feel bad."

But I do feel bad. That inadequacy has been occurring more and more often. Our intimate life—previously robust—has lost its edge. "Maybe if I give *you* the back rub tonight we can make it work better."

"Let's try." She squeezes my biceps again. As we wander back down the hall, my wife asks, "Oh, did you see Jared's arm? He burned it. He's in our bathroom putting on a bandage." She must gather her papers and leave for work, so she adds, "Look at it, will you?"

Her tone tells me that she's concerned. Great, I think, worried that I really will be late for my first class. I say, "I'll check it out."

When I enter the bathroom, Jared jumps, then quickly turns his back on me. "Uh, hi, Dad," he grunts. "Need to, like, use this bathroom?"

"How's your arm?"

His eyes widen, then he replies, "Oh, it's okay. Just a burn."

"Really? How'd it happen?"

He is wearing his usual school outfit—carefully torn jeans, black boots, black shirt, black cape. A patch of his blond hair has been dyed black, and he today seems to have applied black eye shadow. "Oh, me and Tracy were, like, just messin' around. Swear to God."

That clears things right up, I muse to myself, then I say, "Lemme see it, pard'."

He flinches and pulls his sleeve over the fresh bandage, saying, "It's okay, Dad. Swear to God. I gotta go or Mom'll, like, leave without me. Swear to God."

Anytime he starts swearing to God I suspect that he's lying, and now I sense that he's concerned as well. I can't stay home right now for a long explanation. I'll save that for after work, give myself something to look forward to. "I'll look at it later. You may need to see a doctor."

"No, it's okay. Swear to God."

"Right."

I return to the den and finish packing my bike bags, grab my helmet and cycling gloves just as the doorbell rings. It's Trish. I tell her that Pop's fallen again, that he has a rug burn on one knee. Although this has happened many times before, she says, "Oh," appearing shocked, and asks, "How is he?"

"He's fine, but he'll need some antibiotic ointment on that knee after you clean him."

"Don't you think he needs a hospital bed? You could rent one. He might break his hip if he keeps falling."

"He didn't fall out of bed, Trish."

This is an old suggestion. She has long urged that we obtain a bed in which my father can be secured, but Jim Cox says it's not necessary. "Let Earl have as normal a life as possible," the doctor told me. "A feisty guy like your dad might kill himself trying to climb over the rails on one of those things. Besides, that old nurse probably isn't comfortable with the kind of independence you give him."

To Trish I say merely, "I'll talk to the doctor."

"All right," she says, then she turns and, to my surprise, we both see my father wobbling down the hall toward his bathroom. Her voice rises two octaves: "Where are we going, Earl?"

"We're going to take a leak," I mumble; fortunately, she doesn't hear me.

After a day of teaching and meetings at the college, I return that afternoon and find a note telling me that Yvonne has been home but has returned to meet some clients at a house in San Rafael. No surprise. I open the refrigerator, then pour myself a glass of milk to consume with graham crackers and seat myself at the dining room table. Jared bounds in the door. "Hey, Dad," he calls, and he, too, raids the fridge, then veers toward the family room, but I hail him and a moment later he returns.

"Yeah?"

"Before you get engrossed in your homework," I say without a grin—he's already turned on the television set—"let me ask you something. What really happened to your arm?"

He sways there for a moment, his expression suspended between a sneer and a smile, then he eases and transforms from the pharaoh of punk rock to the boy I knew just a year or so ago. "Oh, me and Tracy thought we'd, like, tattoo our girlfriends' names on our arms, but mine, like, sucked so I, like, tried to scrape it off."

"What sucked?"

Jared grins. "My tattoo."

"Want to show me?"

"No. It, like, looks awful."

"How'd you scrape it off?"

He is moving slowly back toward the family room as he says, "With a razor blade."

"Well, we'd better get Doctor Cox to look at it, just in case of infection. It'll give him a chance to give you a shot."

"Okay. Can we, like, rent a movie tonight?"

"Sure." This has gone too easily. He's also worried.

The telephone distracts me, so I pick up the receiver and hear my daughter chirp, "Hi, Pops. What're you doing home. Get fired?"

Just hearing Suzie's voice makes me smile. "Naw, I quit. I'm gonna let my kids support me—and about time too."

"Fine. Go right on out and order a Cadillac and I'll send you a check." She pauses for a quick giggle.

I hear a car door slam and glance out the window. Trish is returning my father from his meal at the senior center, and I notice him struggling to emerge from her auto. All the while my daughter's bright voice is regaling me.

"How's Grandpa?" she asks.

"About the same," is all I can honestly say. "He'll be here in a minute and you can say hi."

"I feel real sorry for him."

"Yeah, well, he probably wouldn't want that, folks feeling sorry for him. But you can bet he'd love the fact that you think about him. You were his girl when you were little. He used to love taking you down to the bar and showing you off."

"I know. I remember." Her voice catches. After a pause, she asks, "Is Mitch home?"

"Not yet."

"Jared?"

"Yep."

"May I talk to him?"

I like that, her interest in her brothers, so I say, "I reckon."

She deepens her voice to imitate mine and growls, "I reckon." Then she giggles.

The door opens and Trish leads my father into the house. "Here's Grandpa," I say.

"Hey, Pop." I wave him over. "Suzie's on the phone."

He hesitates, his eyes blank, then they switch on, and he smiles as he shuffles forward. "How you?" he says into the telephone.

15

The next day I pick Jared up at high school and drive him to Jim Cox's office. The waiting room is full, and my son is obviously pleased at the shocked expressions on the faces of two older women when they spy his outfit. "They, like, can't believe how rank I am," he whispers triumphantly.

I only shake my head. He is by far the least aggressive, least venturesome of our kids. His no-effort stance in school is, I'm sure, a way of avoiding competition with his successful siblings. I pick up a magazine but can't develop any interest in it. Finally, I turn toward my son, who seems to be practicing intimidation in this safe setting—scowling, curling his lip in studied adolescent disdain—and ask, "How about going canoeing this weekend? We can go up to the Russian River, or we could just tour Richardson Bay."

He grins immediately, then catches himself and once more curls his lip. "Well, can I, like, bring Tracy? Me and him . . ."

"One canoe, two people," I reply. "Unless Tracy wants to swim, no." A swim might cost Tracy his spiked coiffure.

"I guess not, then." His lip remains curled.

"Think about it. Just let me know by Friday."

We fall silent again until a nurse finally calls, "Jared."

He stands, takes a step, then turns, "Uh . . . aren't you, like, comin' in, too, Dad?" His lip has uncurled and his eyes have grown uncertain.

"Sure." I've been waiting to be asked.

"What seems to be the trouble, Jared?" the nurse asks as he seats himself on a treatment table in the small room.

"Oh, I, like, got this scrape on my arm and my dad's, like, worried about it." He is a boy indulging an unnecessarily concerned parent.

She does not look at it, but says, "Fine. Doctor will be with you in a few minutes."

A moment later the door opens and Jim Cox strolls in, white coat open, glasses pushed up onto his forehead, a chart in his hands. "What trouble've you been up to now, Jared?" he demands with mock anger.

My son grins.

Jim turns toward me and asks gravely, "This kid still sucking his thumb?"

Before I can answer, my son snaps, "No, but Dad, like, is."

"Your thumb or his?"

That cracks Jared up, and he can't answer, so Jim adds, "Just because you're tougher than the old man doesn't mean you ought to pick on him. Let me see that arm."

The doctor removes the bandage from Jared's wound, whistles through his teeth, then says, "Thank God for your family, Jared. I'd be broke if you guys didn't keep figuring out new ways to pay me for visits. Your old man was in here for an inflamed bursa last month when he thought he could still play basketball."

"Hey," I interject, grinning, "my faculty team won intramurals at the college. It was worth it."

"And with those football knees of yours," Jim adds, rolling his eyes.

"How does Jared's self-surgery look?" I ask.

"It's a mess. What exactly did you do, Squirt?" He has called Jared that since my youngest son, an infant, sprayed him with urine during an examination.

"Me and Tracy Whitmore we, like, borrowed this dude's stuff and gave ourselves these tattoos, but after I, like, did it—this heart with Mary Bordessa's name over it—it, like, sucked."

"Whose needles, exactly?" Jim's tone has changed.

"Just some dude at the park."

"Do you know him, his name?"

"No, just some righteous dude. I don't think he even, like, lives around here. Tracy, like, knew his brother."

"Okay." the doctor's tone again lightens and he asks, "Do you love her?"

"Who?"

"Mary."

"No way," Jared grins again. "I, like, scraped it off with a razor blade."

"A surgeon you're not, Squirt."

"Pop says you're not either." Jared is learning the rough camaraderie of men, so Jim and I both laugh.

"Well, at some point we're going to have some skin grafted over this mess, unless you want to tattoo over the scar."

"No thanks," Jared says. "Once is, like, enough. I'll let my dad be the tattoo champ."

Thank God this kid *is* learning something, I reflect, but do not say. I've determined not to be too direct in my responses to him.

"Okay," Jim tells him, "I'm going to take you across the hall to Millie's station, and she'll clean this up and dress it. She'll also give you an antibiotic shot just in case, a tetanus booster, and take a blood sample. I'll tell her to use the old blunt needles. If I could figure out a reason to give you more shots, I would."

"Thanks," grins my son. He sounds relieved.

"You're welcome. Follow me. Your old man can begin loosening up that fat checkbook of his. I've got dues at the country club to pay." Jim gives me a high sign, so I remain seated in the treatment room.

A moment later he returns and sits on the table where my son had perched a moment before. "Damn kids," he says. "They're all immortal."

"How bad?"

"Probably not bad at all, but disfiguring as hell. He'll want that graft after he sees the kind of scar he ends up with." Jim takes off his glasses and rubs his eyes.

"What else?"

"We've got to monitor his blood for HIV and hepatitis, among other stuff. There's no way of knowing what was on the needles he used. Chances are slim, but it's a test we've got to make." He is shaking his head. "We'll have to keep testing at intervals for a while."

"That means he could develop AIDS?" I ask, shocked at that unconsidered possibility.

"Extremely unlikely. Hepatitis B is a larger worry, but neither is worth staying up nights over. We've got to test, though. It's sure gotten to be a more dangerous world, hasn't it?"

I glance at the homemade L-O-V-E tattoo on my own left hand, and an icicle invades my gizzard. "That's for damn sure," I grunt. Then I ask, "Jim, if it was Steve with this mess, would you worry?"

"I'd make the tests and be a little concerned, I guess, but not worried. At this point, I wouldn't even mention it to anyone else, least of all Jared. It's that long a shot."

"Let's hope it stays that way."

A few minutes later, my son and I are driving toward the high school so he can attend his last class, and I am examining him out the corner of my eye, still seeing the jolly little kid, now hidden in black clothes and eye shadow, when he turns toward me and says, "Let's, like, go canoein' Saturday, okay, Dad?"

"Right," I reply. "Sounds good to me." My voice is crisp, but my heart has wilted a bit: I love this rebellious boy and don't want to lose him.

Later, as I wheel into our driveway, Mitch emerges from the house, hair freshly combed, wearing pressed jeans, white running shoes, and a patterned dress shirt.

"Hey, what's the occasion?" I call.

"Hi, Dad. Just an early date. I'm taking Etta to eat and then to a play at school."

"The cheerleader?"

"Yeah."

"Your little brother says she's got a great personality."

"My little brother says she's got great boobs. That's as far as his insight goes."

I'm laughing because he's got Jared pegged.

In the house I see my wife in profile before the kitchen sink—her breasts, her legs, the swelling of her hips—then she turns and her smile dazzles me. "Hi, hon'," she says.

We hug, and I explain what transpired at the doctor's office with Jared, not mentioning HIV but telling her everything else. Yvonne just shakes her head and says, "That *boy.*"

Then we hear a thump and, for a second, our eyes meet.

"Your dad," she says. "He's taking a nap."

He's fallen out of bed, I assume. I say, "I'll take care of him."

He's on the floor between bed and wall, wearing only his disposable diaper. The room reeks of feces. I take a deep breath in the hall, then say, "You diving today, Pop?"

He grins, but still breathes heavily. "How you?" he grunts.

I move behind him and hoist him to his feet. When he grips the grab bar, I again grab a breath in the hall, but when I return I can't break his grip from that bar. Rats. The stench is so dense that I again plunge into the hall for air, then quickly remove his diaper, and gingerly rush it to the bathroom, where I seal it in the plastic pail.

"Do you need some help?" my wife calls.

I need someone else to *do* this, I'm thinking, but I reply, "We're okay" and launch the always difficult task of forcing him to loose his grip—a father-son contest of strength between us, but this one is unfair and I am swept by guilt even as I pull his fingers. When at last I succeed, I move behind him and hoist him to his feet. A shower will warm him and clean his hindquarters, so I say, "Let's clean your pasture, Pop."

He's still unsteady, but I walk him down the hall into the bathroom, where we've had a unit installed that is designed for handicapped bathers: it's flush to the floor, with seats, a grab bar, and a hand-held shower nozzle. Pop stands, tight but insecure, holding the bar, and I direct steaming water at his neck. After several moments, he visibly relaxes and seems to gain strength. When he is thoroughly warmed, I remove the nozzle from its holder and direct the stream at his dirty bottom, soaking, soaping, then rinsing. I hand him a washcloth and drawl, "Clean the family jewels, Pop. I'm not touchin' them nasty devils."

He chuckles. Good. He's feeling better.

Slowly, ever so slowly, he scrubs his pubic area, then finally lets go of all but one corner of the cloth, allowing the rest to drop between his legs. I grasp the other end of the cloth and raise it until it fits snugly into the crack of his rear, then he pulls. I pull. He pulls. I pull. He pulls and we both let go, and the dark-stained cloth drops to the shower floor— I'll take care of it after I dry him. This is a functional method of his own invention to clean the nooks and crannies of his butt. I rinse that region with the hand-held nozzle.

"Ready to get out?"

"Yeah," he grunts. I had expected him to say no, but there is no consistency in his responses.

Finally, I lead Pop, dressed and relaxed, into the family room and plop him into his favorite chair with a card table in front of him, then bring him a can of beer. Pepper curls beneath the table, tail thumping the floor.

I open a can of beer for myself and sit down with the newspaper. On the TV, local news features a segment on an aging country musician, decorated with a vast Stetson, who sits grinning in a wheelchair. I don't catch the name. "You remember that old boy, Pop?" I ask.

My dad stirs. His cloudy eyes turn toward the set—we're not certain how clear his vision is anymore. After a long moment, something rumbles out of him. It sounds like a word.

I don't understand, so I say, "Come again?"

Once more, he rumbles, but I can't understand. Then he says distinctly, "Delano."

"He's from Delano?" I ask, naming a small town just north of where I was raised.

Pop rumbles again, then turns his attention to his beer, and I'm left wondering exactly what we've been talking about, but aware that there's still plenty trapped within him.

As I gaze at my dad after that near-conversation, part of me could weep, but *Stop blubberin'* echoes inside me.

The phone rings and is picked up in another room. A minute later Jared calls out, "Dad! It's, like, Grandma."

"Hello, Mom."

"Leroy? Is that you?"

"Yes, Mom."

"Is that you, Leroy?"

"Sure is."

"Where've you *been*? I haven't seen you for *days*." Her voice is high and jagged. "Why aren't you *here*? I've been waiting and waiting for you. I'm all dressed. I'm out of milk."

"Out of milk? I just brought you a gallon."

"Besides, I think those girls are stealing from me."

"Girls? What girls?"

"Where's Mitchell? He's *supposed* to stay with me." She is on the edge of tears.

I sigh, then say, "I'll be over with some milk, Mom."

16

The next afternoon I meet my Physiology of Exercise class, surprise them with a pop quiz, then spend the next hour and a half in my office correcting their efforts. Students usually visit during this period, but none stop by today. My colleague Marge Chilton does stick her head in the doorway to remind me that we've got a faculty ethics committee meeting next Wednesday. "*Great,*" I groan.

She laughs, then adds, "Ah, the delights of educating America's youth," and departs.

Marty Spielman knocks and stands in the doorway. "Hey, can I talk you into speaking to my sports-and-lit course next week? There's still a few kids around here who associate you with football."

I perform this service every semester, so I drawl, "I reckon."

"You *reckon,* do you?" he grins, then drops into an inexpert Gary Cooper imitation. "Well, thanky, Tex."

Later, tests graded, I change clothes, climb onto my bicycle and pedal over the hump of coastal hills into Mill Valley and home. I will take my father to his meal at the senior center; Trish leaves early on Fridays and I drive him there. When I enter the house, she calls, "We're all ready, aren't we, Earl?" in that high, singsong voice, then immediately departs. Pop is nowhere to be seen.

I walk down the hall to my father's room, where I find him sitting on the side of his bed struggling to pull a second pair of trousers over the ones he already wears. His face is knotted with effort. For a moment I stand in the doorway, my heart swooping, then I have to grin. He notices me and mumbles, "Tighten my belt."

"Come on, Pop," I urge, "let me help you. You don't need those extra britches." I pull them off his legs, then help him to his feet and walk him toward the nearby bathroom. He lodges there, fingers desperately gripping the doorjamb, while I brush his hair. I loosen his grip and lead him slowly down the hall.

The ataxia has so blasted his coordination that this route is becoming slower and slower, one handhold to another, his body struggling along a bookcase on one wall where his fingers can wedge themselves. Frequently his awkward feet and hands become so planted that he cannot move, and he must stand locked in one place like a pillar of salt until someone rescues him. Although his once-thick arms increasingly resemble tattooed wires, he remains strong, and it takes all I can muster to break his desperate grips.

At the senior center, we park in one of the spaces for the handicapped, and I climb out and walk to his door, then open it. I reach in and tug his legs. He is staring straight ahead, and that confused, pained expression I've seen before suddenly covers his face; "took . . . my . . . license . . . ," he mumbles.

I spin him in his seat and one of his feet reaches pavement and he slowly extends his hands toward me. I pull him out of the car, saying, "Come on, Pop, you don't want to be late for your meal." We begin the short, slow walk to the door, me cradling one of his elbows to guide him.

At the doorway, we are passed by a hustling oldster, who calls, "Come on in and eat, John." I look up into the leathery face of Ben, one of Pop's table companions, who has for some reason renamed him.

"He'll be there in a second," I say.

Six long tables, vases of plastic flowers on their white plastic tablecloths, are set on each side of the room. A wide row is open down the center, its far end blocked by an old upright piano where a woman sings and plays, while two others stand and sing with her: "I'm forever blow-ing bubbles . . ."—old songs, always old songs, old ways of expressing life's triumphs and tragedies. Many people are already seated, most at the same places they daily occupy, while others, women mainly, stand and chat. All the men sit on the hall's right side, while tables on the left are being occupied by women. Since there are so many more ladies, they are also sprinkled among the men on the right. The aroma of cooked chicken fills the room.

My father moves directly to his customary seat. Across from him sits a sour-looking man, his bald head gleaming, who grunts, "'Lo, Earl."

"How you," Pop responds. That is apt to be the extent of their conversation.

"I'll bet them old heifers blew bubbles," winks Ben, his large, yellow teeth grinning, "and half the guys in town too. Get it, John?" He removes a soiled baseball cap, plops onto the chair next to my father, and props a cane against it.

"How you," Pop says, smiling slightly.

"You guys read in the newspaper about that kid that tied up the old lady and took all her money? I dunno about these damn kids nowadays. I dunno." Ben shakes his head.

"Who ever told that goddamn woman she could play the pianer?" grunts the bald-headed man.

"Not me," barks Ben. "I might play somethin' with 'er, but it damn sure wouldn't be no piano!" He laughs and those horse teeth dominate his face. "But *she* might sing when I's done with 'er. Get it, John?" He laughs again.

My father grins.

From the next table, a woman demands, "Is Ben cussing again? Is he talking dirty?"

Ben ignores her. "Yessir, I ain't too old. I can damn sure get it up." He wears a dirty double-breasted coat over a stained flannel shirt and patched jeans. Cheap nylon running shoes, worn and soiled, cover his feet. "Never got married," he adds. "Never found one worth it."

Pop mumbles something.

"Like I told my boss one time, sheep don't talk back," Ben nods, and his yellow teeth once more dominate his face.

At the next table sit two men in business suits. They are talking quietly. Ben notices them, gestures in their direction, and hisses, "See them two high rollers? Their kids put 'em out to pasture. Now they're in the same boat as me and you." Ben, who as nearly as I can determine worked as a laborer in this area all his adult life, seems pleased. "Big shots, hah!" he spits.

There is a definite class layering in this microcosm, with one table dominated by well-dressed, alert men and women who seem to disdain social contact with all the others. My father's table is populated by male laborers and one crumpled lady who is fed each day—or each Friday, at least—by her middle-aged daughter.

"Time for our prayer," calls a young woman in a cook's cap who stands in the central row between tables. Her name is Cindy, and she manages this operation. Everyone quiets except Ben—"One time I seen this thing that it was supposed to be half-seal and half-guy in the sideshow. Hah! Whadaya thinka that?"—and Cindy calls his name. He grins and quiets.

"Thank you, Lord, for these gifts we are about to receive," she intones, "and thank you for the blessing of these friends. Amen."

Amens sprinkle from the audience.

"We have some birthdays," Cindy announces with a smile. "Hazel, Joseph, and Hope all have birthdays this week. I have cards for you, but first let's all sing 'Happy Birthday.'" She waves her hand and the piano begins playing, too fast for the singers, who never quite catch up.

Ben grunts, "That woman can't play shit."

As soon as the song ends, trays of steaming food are wheeled from the kitchen, and the few seniors still standing scramble for seats. I move to the back of the room to read and observe while my father eats. I am looking at myself twenty-five years hence and am not pleased. The golden years do not lure me.

"He took my bread," I hear a woman protest.

"Bring Myrtle some more bread," calls another woman's voice.

"He *took* mine."

Cindy walks to a table with bread in her hand, pats a woman's back, then returns to her customary position near the kitchen door.

I can hear Ben: "Nuts, some of 'em. Right, John?"

The piano still plays—rapidly and slightly off-key—though only the pianist now sings—also rapidly and slightly off-key—"You were six-teeeeen, my village queeeeen, down by the ollllld . . . millllll . . . streeeeeam." The tune ends with a flourish. Before the next song can be started, Cindy calls, "Thank you, Helen. Let's all give Helen a hand." A few diners put down knives and forks to clap.

Helen grins and immediately launches into "Mademoiselle from Armentières."

"Thank you, Helen," Cindy calls, louder this time. "That'll be enough, dear. Your food is getting cold."

"Mademoiselle from Armentières, parlez-vous," quavers Helen's contralto. "Mademoiselle from Armentières, parlez-vous . . ."

Cindy shakes her head, then strides over to the piano. After a few moments the tune trails off, and Helen reluctantly gathers her handbag before walking to a nearby table.

17

Most fall Saturdays, us guys gathered at McCray Park for a game of football—tackle not touch. Ages ranged from ten or eleven, maybe, up to fifteen or sixteen—little kids and big ones, Okies and prune pickers. That day J.D., Floyd, and I, along with a new kid in our eighth-grade class, Travis Plumley, assembled with other guys. Because I was fast, I was always selected early, this time by a high school soph' named Willie Williamson, who also took Plumley. Mickey Harrison, another high school guy, chose both Floyd and J.D. for his side, and eventually thirty-plus boys were divided into two disorganized teams, everyone on the field at once.

A few of the rich prune pickers wore helmets and shoulder pads, and two of the worst players sported complete uniforms—Christmas gifts from hopeful fathers—but most of us wore jeans and T-shirts, and abandoned our shoes in order to run faster on the grass. We played a roughhouse version of the game, but all followed unwritten rules: The largest boys did not devastate the smallest. In return, we smaller guys didn't cheap-shot the big guys . . . not that we'd be dumb enough to do that.

That day, our team was well ahead, something like 50 to 20, and I'd caught three touchdown passes, when Harrison decked me. I was going through the motions of a block, sort of tapping at Floyd while Willie ran around end, and big Mickey blindsided me. I literally saw stars and, for a second, almost let myself cry. Harrison was a thick, fair-skinned kid with a thatch of black hair and fiery blue eyes. He played JV football at the high school, and was slow as a slug but tough. No one wanted to tangle with him.

That included me, but I had also learned that you didn't let guys, even big guys, push you around unless you wanted to be pushed around forever. His blind-side block did no great damage, so I stayed in the game, swallowing tears that turned to anger, biding my time and watching Harrison. Finally, on one of the many kickoffs, I caught him standing next to a clutch of players wrestling a runner to the ground, and I accelerated, lowered my shoulder, and hit him at the knees with all my weight. The force of my block carried me through him and he flipped high, landing on a shoulder with his feet above his head. It was the greatest block of my life. "Ooooof!" he grunted, and everyone went silent. The tacklers stopped tugging, the runner ceased resisting.

Several guys burst into laughter, but Williamson, one of Harrison's teammates on the junior varsity football team, barked, "Shut up!" then turned to me: "You better get outta here, Upton."

Mickey moaned, held his shoulder, and I stood in the surrounding silence and faced him, worried that I'd really hurt him. Then his eyes began to glow and his jaw jutted. "You fuckin' little Okie," he snarled, climbing to his feet and moving in my direction.

He was a head taller and maybe fifty pounds heavier, but I snapped, "Fuck yourself, prune picker!" as I grabbed my shirt and shoes and took off.

Harrison's dad and mother were teachers. They didn't associate with my parents, but Mickey had never been stuck-up. If he didn't invite me or any of my friends to his house, he always chose me for his teams when he could, and he always said hi. By junior high school, I was well aware that even in our small section of town, there were differences of status. Lots of kids at school dressed better than my friends did, and some of them took skiing lessons every winter and swimming lessons every summer. They went to uptown churches. Most of their fathers worked the same oil fields as ours did, but they were bosses and they drove company cars that made them look like cops to me; they also lived in larger houses in nearby tree-lined neighborhoods that had sidewalks.

Some of the bold rich kids might call us Okies, grinning when they did, and we'd call them prune pickers, also grinning: an exchange between friends. J.D. used to tease me, "Hey, Roy, you're a Okie-prune: half them, half us." I'd slug him on the shoulder. To most of the rich kids, I was a plain old Okie, while some of the Okie kids considered me a prune picker.

I had even heard a few grown-ups hiss that word, "Okie," and veer away from us in stores or even on the sidewalk. "Them pissants," my dad said when I told him, "real desperate to believe they're better'n *somebody*, but they ain't better'n nobody. Don't take no shit from 'em."

Well, that Saturday, sprinting home from McCray Park, I wasn't concerned with being an Okie or a prune picker. Survival was my goal. Harrison couldn't close the gap as I dashed over railroad tracks and down California Avenue, on a beeline for my house, the enraged high school guy puffing behind me and the rest of the players jogging and laughing behind him. Our parade continued—me glancing back, Mickey puffing, the gang laughing and shouting behind us—while ladies working in their yards glanced up with shock as we passed: "Would you *look* at that!"

At Decatur Street, I jogged up a block to the bridge so I could cross the canal, then saw the tiny bungalow on the grassless patch where we lived. My father was in the front, his body hidden in the maw of our aging automobile, on which he seemed to be constantly working. Harrison was falling farther and farther behind, so I slowed to a puffing walk and casually strolled to the car, calling, "Hi, Pop."

"Howdy, boy. What're you up to?"

"Oh, nothin'."

"Who're them?"

"Just some guys I was playin' football with."

"Who's that bigun with the red face?"

"That's Harrison," I said. "He's mad because I knocked him on his ass."

Pop grinned at me. "Ya did? Well, he looks crazier'n a three-peckered 'possum."

"He is."

The next Saturday when I returned to McCray Park, Harrison wrestled me to the grass, gave me a Dutch rub, then chose me for his team.

18

My father eats slowly, so most others finish and depart while I wait for him. A large, white-haired man wearing a tailored blazer and dress shirt with an ascot, approaches me and smiles, "How're you today, Coach?"

"Fine, Mr. Dwyer, and you?"

"Not bad for an old goat. How's the dad doing?" He never sits with my father—is, in fact, a prominent presence at the high rollers' table—but unfailingly stops to inquire about Pop's health.

"As well as can be expected," I smile.

"Yes," he nods, "that's true of all of us, I suppose." His eyes are sad, but he smiles. "Enjoy yourself, Coach. Life gets pretty ragged toward the end . . . pretty grim." I know from past conversations that his own children live far away, but they have had the power to strip his involvement in business and his driving privileges. I know, too, that his wife is dead, that last year he was injured by a mugger, and that he has recently had heart bypass surgery. Still, he looks like a movie star, pink face decorated by a trim white mustache.

"I'm trying to."

"Your father's a lucky man, Coach, to have a son like you, but I think he knows that."

"I hope so." I decide to change the subject. "What're you working on now, Mr. Dwyer?"

"Oh, just a little poetry—nothing special. Still trying, though. It keeps me going." He had been a screenwriter and minor producer of films for years, so this subject pleases him.

"I'd like to read some, if you think to bring it in next week when I'm here with Pop."

"Why, I'd be delighted. Yes, I'll bring some next week."

I smile, then say, "Looks like Pop's stirring over there. I've got to go help him. I'll see you next week, and I look forward to seeing your poetry."

"Yes, I'll see you then." He walks toward the door smiling, the telltale bulge of a plastic diaper distorting his trousers.

I'm smiling too. I have made his day.

Driving Pop home I swing by Bud's Barber Shop—almost the only one left in town that hasn't become a "shoppe" or a "hair care center." This cubbyhole, next to Mill Valley's only remaining blue-collar bar, the Buckhorn, shares clientele with it, and I've more than once seen thick men holding glasses of draft beer while Bud trimmed their locks. When my father used to visit us in the years before he was stricken, he always spent spare time in these two establishments, so he's no stranger. Bud has two chairs, and one of them has never, in my experience, been used. The head of a startled-looking elk dominates one wall.

My father and I shuffle into the shop, and Bud, who slouches in the spare chair reading a newspaper, looks up and grins. "Come on in, boys. Who's my first victim? How 'bout it, Earl?"

My father is grinning. "How you?"

I help him into the chair, asking, "What'll it be this time, Pop? A pompadour?"

This masculine enclave, these male rituals, are nearly all that remain from the long-held patterns of my father's life, and he slides into them without a hitch.

"I could give Earl one of them permanents the young guys wear, make him look like a fairy," the barber winks.

"You ready for a flattop, Pop?"

"No." Still grinning.

"Give him one of your boot-camp specials."

"Sure thing. Say, when're you gonna get back on the field again, Leroy? The team hasn't been worth a shit since you quit coachin'."

I smile. "Not anytime soon, Bud. I've got my hands full at home."

The barber winks and nods. I settle down to scan photographs and cartoons in *Playboy*, while Bud trims and levels my father's hair. When I glance up, I notice that Pop sits, eyes closed like a contented cat, while the barber shaves his neck and trims his sideburns. There are pleasures left for him, and although I am impatient to return home, so impatient that I nearly didn't stop here, I'm now glad that I did.

Haircut finished, Bud places a vibrator on one hand and buzzes Pop's neck and scalp—my father appearing to be on the edge of happy sleep. "If somebody'd give me one of these machines when I was a kid," comments the barber, "I wouldn't ever've got married."

I laugh more than necessary.

As we leave the shop, I suggest, "How 'bout a snort, Pop?"

He says nothing, but veers toward the Buckhorn's door. Inside, the knotty pine room is dim. Two small pool tables and an old-fashioned bar fill it, while several racks of deer horns decorate the walls. I help my father onto a stool, then seat myself. The bartender, as old as Pop, recognizes us. "Where you been keeping yourself, Earl? In jail again? How are ya, Leroy?"

He seems to know every name in town, but I can't remember his. I order brandy and water for my dad, a draft beer for me. I have placed a twenty-dollar bill in Pop's wallet, so I take it out and put it in his hand. He pays and when change is returned, he carefully, though awkwardly, piles it on the bar in front of him and places a small glass ashtray atop one edge of the bills: he remembers the ritual.

My father needs a straw in order to drink now, but he manages to empty his glass while, on the jukebox, Johnny Paycheck is telling his boss to take this job and shove it. In that dim light I can see my father five years ago or twenty-five or even fifty, sitting in a neighborhood saloon, his money on the bar, country music in the background, talk of sports or women or nitwitted bosses buzzing through the room.

I'm about to suggest that we leave when Pop, having emptied his drink, replaces it on the bar, taps the glass, and the bartender immediately refills it, then slips a bill from the stack beneath the ashtray.

It happens quickly, smoothly, and I realize that I have not seen that characteristic move in a long, long time and that I may never see it again. For that moment, though, he is Earl Upton, in Earl Upton's milieu, and I'm grateful for one more glimpse of him. I reach over and pat his back while, deep in my heart, something softens.

19

At home, I situate Pop at his card table, open a Coke for him, then wander outside with a cup of coffee in my hand and hear "Hey, Leroy!" from the wooded hill behind me.

We don't have next-door neighbors in the sense that my folks did in their compact neighborhood. Houses here are built up and down the slopes of this wooded canyon, each private from others. Sixty or seventy yards above our place a natural redwood residence cantilevers into space, all angles and glass. Bill and Twila Brody live up there and we see them occasionally—a young, successful, and friendly couple. Twila waves at me and strides down the earthen path that connects our property.

"Hi, Leroy," she grins. "Is Yvonne home?"

"Hi, Twila," I smile and nod. "She's at the office."

For a moment, her face droops, then she smiles once more.

"What've you been up to? We haven't seen much of you two lately. I thought once you stopped coaching, you'd be home all the time."

"Wrong. I've still got to teach. Lately, though, we've been pretty busy taking care of my folks."

Her handsome face, which as usual looks as though it has been professionally made up, grows suddenly grave. "Your dad?" she says.

"He's okay, but there's just been *stuff* going on, keeping us busy. What're you two up to?"

"Well, Bill got another promotion at the bank, and I closed that deal to develop a hillside up in Petaluma, so we're on a roll right now."

Both M.B.A.'s, they've always been on a roll as far as I can determine. She's a real estate developer and he's an investment banker. A little over thirty, they live in that million-dollar house above us, drive two new Mercedes-Benzes, and own an airplane. "Good for you, Twila," I say.

"Listen, can I ask you something?" Still smiling, she glances furtively around us.

"Sure."

"Have you run up against this New Age stuff?"

I can't suppress a grin. "You selling crystals now?"

She smiles briefly, but quickly grows grave. "Don't laugh, but Bill got in with some other people at work, and he says he thinks one's a *channel,* that some dead Indian medicine man is speaking through her. They've been meeting every Thursday night and giving this woman money to hear the Indian. It seems crazy to me, but he acts like he really believes it." She is shaking her head.

"Come on . . . ," I grin, thinking that maybe he's hiding an affair behind that story. "How can an educated man like him fall for that crap?"

"That's what I can't figure out. But he's always been a believer. When he was a Marxist back in college, he was *the* Marxist. And before that, he was *the* Catholic. Anyway, now some guy's gotten into the act. He's supposedly a mediator between whales and people. I'm afraid Bill's buying that too."

"*Really?*" I am genuinely amazed.

"He told me that there's all kinds of stuff in the world we don't understand . . ."

I nod, "No argument there."

". . . so just like a lizard can't imagine what a bird knows, we can't imagine the other invisible life-forms around us that live on separate planes. He says *angels* and *demons* are superior life-forms that we can't understand . . ."

I guess my face changes, because she hesitates, then continues, "Honestly, he *said* that. He also says my objections to it just prove how limited I am. He says a New Age is coming when all life-forms will be able to communicate."

"What's he been smoking?"

Twila doesn't smile. "I'm afraid our marriage is going to go ka-boom if I don't shut up and go along with him on this. There's a Psychic Faire in town here at the arts center this weekend, and he's insisting that I go. I can just see myself walking around with a pyramid on my head or something." She rolls her eyes.

"He's gotta be puttin' you on."

"He says that we've all lived lots of times before, and that he's not really going to have to die."

"To die?" I sip again from my coffee and lean on the car's trunk. "Ahhh . . . and so by paying some phony he can buy the illusion of immortality. He could do the same thing at any of the churches in town. I used to hear preachers talk about eternal life and demons at the Assembly of God down in Bakersfield when I was a little kid. But I'm afraid death ain't optional."

Twila suddenly looks embarrassed. "I just thought maybe . . . at school or someplace . . . you might've run up against this stuff. I really don't know what to do." Her voice catches, her eyes glisten, her face goes slack.

I pat her back. "I sure as hell can't tell you what to do, but, yeah, we see a little of it at the college, but most everyone—the students, the faculty, the groundsmen—considers it a joke, a scam, a moneymaking scheme. For all the stereotypes about this, Bill's the first educated person I've ever heard of who takes it seriously."

Still averting her eyes, she says, "Bill says his psychic advisor tells him that he's got real power that needs to be unleashed."

I interject, "I'll bet that advisor's willing to help unleash it and to bill him accordingly."

"Yes, unfortunately, that's about it. I don't *care* about the money, but I *do* care about Bill. I don't want to see him like this."

"Amen," I sigh. Twila has treated Yvonne and me as foster parents ever since she and Bill moved in, but I'm not used to having grown women speak to me so frankly. I can tell that she'd rather have told all this to my wife, so I say gently, "Why not point out to Bill that enlightenment's a personal matter and that real mystics don't accept credit cards. Ask him how much Confucius or Jesus charged."

"That's a good point, Leroy."

"He must've taken logic when he was an undergrad at Stanford. Remind him of the fallacy called reversing the burden of proof. *If you can't disprove it, then it's true*—remember that one?"

She nods.

"Tell him there're gremlins that insert belly-button lint and steal one sock from a pair, unless he can prove there aren't. That's the kind of argument he seems to be falling for. The burden of proof is always on the *asserter,* not the doubter, that's the key."

"Whew! Slow down. You're not quite the hayseed you pretend to be, are you, Coach Upton?" She smiles briefly, then adds, "Anyway, if I tell him all that stuff, I'm afraid he'll leave. Leroy . . ." She hesitates. "Could *you* talk to him, please?"

"Sure. Just tell him I was looking for him. I'll ask him where all the extra souls come from if we've lived past lives. The world's population is growing exponentially. There are far more people alive in this century than ever before in the history of the world. How can all those souls have multiple past lives?"

My neighbor cups her chin with one hand. "You know, that's another good one. I'll ask him that. I've been so emotionally churned up that I haven't been able to think clearly about this at all. Maybe I'll start calling you *Doctor* Upton."

It's my turn to smile. "Hey, I understand. It's easy for me because I'm *not* involved. And, Twila, don't get in trouble over what I said," I quickly add. "Send the old boy down the hill, and I'll talk to him. But remember, you may just have to go along with this till it passes . . . and I'm sure it will. Remember when it seemd like everyone around here was into tie-dyes or macrobiotic diets or acid rock?"

She smiles. "I remember . . . just barely." Touching my hand, she adds, "I always like talking with you, Leroy. Excuse my French, but you cut through the bullshit faster than anyone I know." She takes my right hand in both of hers and shakes it. "Men baffle me, so I have to get some insights every once in a while."

Suddenly a light goes on. "Hey, Twila, isn't Bill's brother pretty sick?"

She says, her voice lowering, "Cancer."

"And they're pretty close, aren't they?"

"Real close."

"That may be your clue. When the world goes haywire, folks tend to become otherworldly, to try to escape into mysticism and that stuff."

After a moment, she says, "*You* seem okay . . . despite the pressures about your folks and all, I mean."

"Don't bet on it," I smile, turning toward my house. "Take care of yourself, Twila. And try to be patient." It's advice I need to follow myself.

"I will. Oh," she calls over her shoulder, "did I tell you we bought a partnership in that little winery? I'll bring some Merlot down to you."

20

Up before Yvonne on Monday, I wander through the hall to the kitchen to heat water for coffee. Pepper, who slept on his rug in the family room as usual, sees me and slowly rises—hips worse each day, it seems—his tail nonetheless wagging, but off to one side now. He tries to walk, but those hindquarters of his won't cooperate. I give him an aspirin in a small ball of margarine, then scratch his head as he smacks it down. "Hey, old-timer. How're you doing this morning?" I croon, and he finally manages to limp back into the family room and flop on the rug. He'll be better in half an hour.

Water is boiling, so I pour two cupfuls through filters, the aroma of fresh coffee crisp in my nostrils. Down the hall, I see the light in my father's room snap on and off and on, so I walk there and find him standing, one hand on the grab bar, the other on the light switch.

"Hey, Pop, going swimming?" I ask because he is naked.

After a long moment of thick confusion, he grins, "How you?"

I run my hand over his fresh burr haircut, then suggest, "How about if I put some clothes on you?" While he's still standing locked in that position, I slip a fresh disposable diaper and a clean T-shirt on him. His bed is a tangle of blankets and sheets, and I begin to straighten them out so I can sit him down to finish dressing him, but I realize that urine soaks not just the center of the sheet, but spreads all the way up onto his two pillows, all the way down to the foot of the bed, and even onto the blankets.

"Damn," I whistle through my teeth, then drawl, "I believe you've went and set a new pissin' record, Pop." I move him back to the grab bar. "Wait a second while I get this cleaned up."

Still grinning, he slowly begins to sit down. Yvonne and I have positioned his bed close to the wall so he can use the grab bar to help himself climb in and out.

"No, wait, Pop." I push his butt to straighten him while I continue stripping sheets. He laughs as I wedge my body between the bed and him, then pull the last of the soaked bedding free and walk it to the nearby laundry hamper. As I return, my father is slowly, slowly lowering himself to the bed—his joints emitting an eerie creaking sound—so I again push his rear and he laughs once more. I'm not certain if he's playing with me, but I choose to believe he is. Finally I finish rapidly and sloppily tucking in his sheets and he seats himself on the bed's side, arms extended so his fingers still grip the bar. "Want me to tuck you in?"

"No," he replies after a pause, slowly nodding yes and smiling.

"Okay, let go of the bar, then."

One hand releases it, then the other. I grasp his feet and pull them onto the bed so that his body spins and ends up with his head on his pillow. He chuckles again, and this time I'm delighted; he likes that spin move we've developed.

"I'll give you more than an airplane spin next time," I say and Pop, long a fan of TV wrestling, grins. "Get ready for an atomic drop, and a Japanese sleep hold, too."

From behind me I hear Yvonne say, "It always tickles me when I see Earl's clothes piled on the floor like that." She stands in the doorway in her robe. "I wonder if he takes them off five minutes after we put him to bed or if he does it in the morning just before we get up." She picks up the rest of my father's soaked bedclothes and I turn off the light. Pop will likely sleep until Trish arrives.

Yvonne and I, trailed by Pepper, carry coffee into the living room, turn on some music, then sit in front of the picture window where we can see the sun come up through branches of the great bay around which our deck is built. "Morning, babe," I say, kissing her.

She kisses me back, then asks, "What's on your agenda for today?"

"I've gotta check on Mom, grade a set of papers, two classes to meet, some reading to do, and that yard work I'd like to finish once I get home. Other than that, I'm free and easy. How about you?"

"Oh," she smiles, "Monday as usual. We caravan to see the new properties on the market, but I'll get home as early as I can. By the way, I think your dad likes his new flattop. He keeps rubbing it."

"Yeah, he does." I find myself grinning.

Yvonne blinks then, as though just remembering something, and her face is suddenly somber. "Roy, Suzie told me your mother's been hinting ugly things about me. That's one thing I won't stand for," she says quietly. "I don't care what she thinks about me, but if she harasses the kids . . ."

"Whoa! Wait a minute. I won't put up with that either, babe," I soothe, my arm around her shoulders. I don't want to think about those bad old days, let alone talk about them. "She just seems to get wacky all of a sudden . . . or depressed."

"I sure hope her antidepressant medication helps her," my wife says. "I don't want her to be sick, but sick or not she'd better leave the kids alone."

"I agree." I'm still rubbing her back and shoulders.

The telephone rings, and I answer it in the kitchen. "Hello."

"I'm surprised an old guy like you's up this early." It's Jim Cox.

"What're you up to?"

"No good. Listen, I've got the results of Jared's blood test and they're negative, as in *no* bad stuff in it at this point. He's clear as far as we can tell."

"Oh." I allow breath to explode from my mouth. "It's too early in the morning. Thanks, Jim." That test's been hovering on the back of my mind.

"So far, so good," he adds.

I return to the living room, and Jared is in the kitchen pouring cereal when the telephone rings once more. After a moment he calls, "Dad! It's Grandma." His voice lowers and he whispers to me, "She, like, sounds wigged out."

Great, I think, just what I need. I answer the phone and she grunts, "*Yeah*. I want my tablecloth back, the good one that your Uncle Joe gave me."

"Hello, Mom. Can't you even say hello?"

Undaunted, she plows forward, her tone as raw as a tent preacher's: "That Yvonne *took* it. She touches all my stuff, and she *smiles*. I don't have much, and she *steals* it."

"We don't need your tablecloth, Mom. What's really wrong?"

"I couldn't sleep last night because I just worried and worried about my tablecloth that my poor brother Joey gave me. I'm worried *sick* about it. Poor Joey *died*." Suddenly she is sobbing.

"Uncle Joe died years ago, Mom." But I sense that she has indeed been lying awake constructing scenarios of her victimization, disparate events and varied suspicions assembled into a mansion of threats. And she is its lone resident.

"That Yvonne sneaks in my house and takes things when I'm having my hair done," she asserts.

"She's working then, Mom."

"Her parents hung around bars. Her mother was cheap, and her father, that Shorty Trumaine with his *nasty* mustache!"

"What's that got to do with anything?"

"She was a trashy girl from a trashy part of town. Her mother served *beer* to men and with that *red* hair!" A pause, then, "She'stakenallmythings!" Her words merge into a cry. "Whywon'tyoulisten?"

"I'll be right over," I say as I hang up.

Then I hear a thump.

Yvonne hurries by in the hall, calling as she passes the doorway, "Your dad."

"Yeah."

We find Pop, his legs somehow thrust into the arms of a red sweat-shirt, neck hole gaping midthigh like a horrible wound. He lies next to the bed in a tangle of blankets, his face screwed with effort as he struggles to rise.

"What're you up to now, Pop?" I ask.

He frowns, then grunts, "Tighten my belt."

21

"Coach! Parker's down," called a player from the field.

"Parker's down? Damn," said the thick man. He hesitated, then asked his assistant, "What's that fast freshman's name?"

"Upton."

"Upson," barked the coach, "in for Parker at linebacker."

I struggled with my helmet and almost tripped over a water bucket as I vaulted off the bench and ran to the right outside linebacker's position. I arrived too late to ask teammates what to watch for, so I simply bent forward with my hands on my knees as Delano's junior varsity snapped the ball and chaos developed in front of me: their yellow uniforms and our blue ones seemed to struggle in all directions, then a small guy in yellow was running directly at me, football tucked under his arm. I dipped my head, felt a jolt, wrapped my arms, and we were down.

"Good tackle, Upton," said a teammate, and he slapped my butt.

The next play went wide, and I drifted tentatively outside until all the yellow jerseys seemed to move away and I was chasing that same small runner toward the sideline. He couldn't outrun me, and I grasped him from behind, then rode him out of bounds in front of our bench.

"That's the way, Upson!" called the coach.

"Watch a pass! A pass!" warned our safety man as the Delano team once more broke their huddle. The ball was snapped and their tailback poised, his eyes searching my area. I simply drifted into an empty space, confused again by the disorderly array of blue and yellow developing in front of me, then I saw the football—floating, floating so slowly, it seemed. I began moving toward where the ball was heading, feeling as though I too was floating, and from the corner of my eyes I noticed a player in yellow also moving there.

We leaped, our bodies bumped, but I managed to slap the ball firmly against myself while he fell, then I was running. Veering right, a boy in yellow moving the wrong way fell as he tried to twist toward me, and a second one bounced lightly off my thigh. At full speed by then, curving toward the sideline, I sprinted toward the end zone, concentrating on lifting my knees, on pumping my arms. Just before I reached the goal line, I felt a jolt and my feet fluttered out of bounds for a step, two steps, then I was jogging in the end zone.

I had been pushed out of bounds on the two-yard line. A play later, Travis Plumley scored on a sneak.

Following our victory that afternoon, parents and students milled around outside the locker room congratulating us, even after the varsity game started. The coach assembled us, said he was proud of us, then grinned and added, "But, Upson, tell me how in the world that boy caught you on your interception?"

I grinned, then said, "He had the angle, Coach."

Soto couldn't resist. "He had the *Anglo,* you mean: you slow white *pendejo.*"

While my buddies laughed, I heard the coach say out the side of his mouth to his assistant, "That Upson kid's gonna be a *player,* Gene. Only a dang ninth-grader, too."

Travis, Jess, and I emerged together from the locker room into the happy crowd and were met by our non-athletic pals Floyd and J.D. Off to one side I saw my dad, not shouting or celebrating, just standing there smiling. Our eyes met for a moment and he winked, then turned and walked away.

While the other three guys walked back to the small stadium, Jess and I headed off campus. "No shit, man," Soto assured me. "It's all fixed up." We walked only a couple of blocks down a side street and stopped outside a small house.

"You're sure her folks aren't gonna come back?" I asked.

"Naw, they go to some church meetin'. Come on."

I followed Jess up the steps and he rang the bell. Immediately, the door was opened by a tall brown girl with full lips and glistening black hair. She wore a blouse unbuttoned so that a flash of white brassiere showed when she moved. Tight white shorts encased her hips and her legs were long. She was prettier than I'd anticipated—much, much prettier. "Hi, Jessie," she said, shyly eyeing me as she talked.

"Hey, Cherry, this is Roy, the guy I been tellin' you about."

"Hi," she smiled, and that snowy bra once more sparked against her coffee-and-cream flesh.

Despite sudden shyness, I felt an immediate tingling in my jeans. "Hi."

"How do you like our tattoos?" Jess thrust his hand in her face and pulled mine up at the same time.

She studied them briefly, then purred, "They're neat."

"Hey, let's listen to some music," he suggested as we entered a darkened living room. "I brought a new King Cole record." He produced a small 45-rpm disc and walked directly toward a phonograph in one shadowy corner.

"What year are you?" the girl asked.

"Same as Jess, freshman. How 'bout you?"

"I'm a freshman at Garces." Ah, so she attended the Catholic school. She stood close to me and her breath smelled like spice.

"Do you play football?"

"I'm on the junior varsity team with Jess. We just beat Delano."

"First string?"

"Yeah. We'll play varsity next year maybe."

"Roy's our big star, except he let a spook catch him today."

I laughed.

"Are you really the star?" she asked.

I didn't know how to reply, but before I had to, Jess called, "Hey, aren't you two gonna dance? I gotta go in the kitchen and use the phone." From the phonograph, Nat King Cole began to croon.

Jess departed and Cherry moved closer, saying, "Let's dance." As I encircled her with one arm, I again glimpsed the flash of her brassiere and my breath quickened.

She kissed my cheek immediately, kissed my neck, then I kissed her smooth cheek—Nat's velvet voice crooning, crooning—and we kissed, her lips soft and warm, her tongue immediately darting into my mouth. Our bodies were tight against one another and I felt something firm begin to slowly push against my thigh.

As we kissed once more, gobbling at one another, I finally slipped my left hand gently onto one of her breasts, and the nob of its nipple nonplussed me.

She immediately popped her mouth free from mine and stepped away.

"I . . . I'm sorry," I gasped, not certain what to say or do.

"Do you have a rubber?" she asked breathlessly.

I had never heard a girl say "rubber" before and could only gasp, "No."

"Come on," she said, her voice deeper, "I know another way." She took my hand and led me through a nearby doorway into a small bedroom, where she shucked her blouse—that white bra outlining her body in the dimness—then removed the brassiere too. "Take your shirt off," she ordered, and I quickly obeyed, then her mouth was on my chest, her warm breasts pressed against my belly until her mouth moved down my chest to my navel, then farther down . . .

Later, a minute or an hour later, I wandered into the kitchen where Jess Soto sat drinking a cola and listening to the radio. "Hey, that took you a long time. How'd you like it?"

In fact, there was nothing I could say, but I repeated what I'd heard others say: "She was pretty good stuff."

"That was your first time, huh?"

It was indeed the first time a girl had done that to me, but I said only, "Are you shittin' me?"

He grinned, then said, "Hey, is Cherry still in there? Listen, you go on, okay? I'm gonna stay here a while."

I didn't sleep well that night. Too much had happened. Tossing on the edge of slumber, I sensed the door to my darkened bedroom opening, then felt my mother's hand touch my head. Then I at last drifted toward sleep.

Later, jolted awake by the front door slamming, I heard my mother's voice: "Where've you been, Earl? Do you know what time it is?"

"I seen the game and he's good, Leroy, damn good. No kiddin'."

"It's after two. And look at you—drinking again."

"No kiddin', he can really play."

"I *hate* that drinking bit."

"Ever'body said so, damn good. No kiddin'."

22

"Jared was right," I tell Yvonne as we heft Pop back onto his bed. "Mom really sounds bad. I'm going to call Jim and see if he can take a look at her right away."

When I reach the physician and explain what's happened, he hesitates, then says, "Roy, it sounds like this has gone beyond me. I think she needs to see a psychiatrist. Do you know Ted Nakamura?"

"No."

"Well, he's a good guy, one of the few shrinks in town who'll actually deal with *sick* people like your mother, not just collect fat fees for listening to yuppies complain. I'll contact him, ask if he can work her in immediately, then call you back. If he can't, you can bring her here. One way or another, we'll do something. You go get her ready."

Relieved, I hang up, and immediately the telephone rings. After a moment of hesitation, a weak female voice says, "Leroy?"

"Yeah."

"This is Velma?" Her voice goes up at the end of each sentence as though she's asking a question. "Velma Martin? Your momma's next door neighbor? I'm afraid she just come to our place and—" the voice hesitates, almost chokes—"she's . . . she's not dressed? I brung her back to her place, but she don't know where she is? I think somethin's wrong with her?"

"Please stay with her, Velma. I'll be right there—and thanks for calling." I grab keys, calling to Yvonne, "I've gotta go get Mom," and jog out to the pickup.

A few minutes later, I park in front of my mother's mobile home, see Velma's concerned face at a front window, then walk hurriedly through the back door. Mom stands in her good coat, her eyes dazed, a lopsided grin on her face.

"I'm sorry I had to call you, Leroy," Velma says, "but when Marie come to my house, she"—her voice lowers to a whisper—"was only wearin' her girdle and she didn't know where she was? I thought I might should call?"

"Thanks, Velma. You did the right thing. I'll take care of her now."

The neighbor is a thin, weathered woman who wears a tightly curled, honey-blond wig. I know that she is one of those quiet heroes I'm increasingly encountering in the nation of the old, minding without complaint a husband who swirls ever more deeply into Alzheimer's disease. "I hope Marie'll be feelin' better?" she smiles.

"Thanks again."

"Thank you," says my mother, her eyes looking away. As soon as the neighbor departs, Mom turns toward me. "Who was that woman? I think she stole my checkbook."

I ignore the remark and hurriedly gather clothing for her, then lead her out the door. "Where're we going? Who're those people?" She smells sour.

No one is visible. "Which people?" I ask as I help her into the front seat, then get in on the driver's side and start the motor.

"Those people that hate me." One of her eyes is wide and unfocused, the other nearly closed.

"I don't see anyone, Mom."

For a few minutes she sits silently on the seat beside me. Then she asks, "What town is this? Your town or my town?"

"Our town, Mom."

"Bakersfield? Oildale? Arvin?"

"Mill Valley."

"Mill Valley? Huh. It's too cold up there."

We are nearly at my house when she speaks again. "Are those people in the backseat taking our picture? I didn't know I was on television."

"There's nobody in the backseat, Mom."

"Then who's taking the pictures?" she demands.

I glance at her, and her jaw is jutting, that eye remains wide and askew. "I don't know," I reply. I also don't know what the hell she's talking about, but I sure don't like it.

"Oh, *no*," she hisses, her voice suddenly crafty. "Of *course* you don't. Who *are* you, anyway?"

That stops me and I face her. "Leroy, Mom. Your son."

"Leroy Clark Upton? . . . Drinking when he named our son. *Leroy.* Could have had a distinguished name. Earl wouldn't listen to reason. *His* father's name . . . that *Leroy* bit.

"They put poor little Leroy Clark in the *slow* group at school with that Floyd and that J.D. and those others . . . Maybelle and Cletus and Sarah Jane and . . . and . . . that other one? . . . that DeeDee. All those *common* names. Leroy was *not* one of them. I marched right down to the school!"

Deep resentments and buried slights are festering here. I listen to this recitation and find myself hoping desperately that Jim is able to connect with the psychiatrist.

He is, and an hour later, my mother and I are in a converted Victorian house nestled in a small redwood grove. The psychiatrist, Dr. Nakamura, is talking to my mother in the next room. Unable to concentrate on the magazine I'm holding, I gaze out the window at the frayed shadows of redwood leaves playing against the curtains. I am thinking "nervous breakdown," the term used by my father when I was a child to describe what was happening when my mother stayed in bed for what seemed like a year. I don't even know for certain what that abstraction, nervous breakdown, actually means. I do know that Mom no longer makes sense. I am beginning to grasp that I have not seen these events for what they are—no, I am far too close, part of the problem, myself, so I haven't put things together.

The door to the inner office opens, and Dr. Nakamura smiles at me. "Dr. Upton," he beckons, "will you come in now, please?" He is a short, husky man who wears a peasant smock over faded jeans and Birkenstocks. His graying hair is modishly long.

I plop myself in a plush seat in the office. My mother, smiling wanly, sits in an identical chair across the small room. The psychiatrist seats himself at a rolltop oak desk. "Well, Marie tells me she had shock treatments in 1943. Were you aware of that?"

"For nerves," Mom interjects.

For a moment I say nothing. *Shock treatments.* This is new and utterly unexpected information, and I infer that such drastic therapy was hardly standard for "nerves." "What were those treatments for?" I ask.

"In those days, severe depression was commonly treated that way." His eyes meet mine and I know he'll explain more fully, probably not in my mother's presence.

"For nerves," Mother repeats.

"And she tells me she's been troubled for a number of years by agoraphobia."

"Yes." Before moving north, she had built a safe world for herself at home where she seldom ventured outside her own yard.

"She also took a lot of meprobamate back in Bakersfield and she thinks Dr. Cox doesn't prescribe enough now," he continues.

"So she tells me."

He turns toward Mom and says, "Dr. Cox is giving you the maximum recommended dosage for a person of your age and size, Marie. If you were given more before, you were being overdosed by your physician in Bakersfield."

I know that she had been prescribed pills virtually carte blanche.

Mom seems not to understand. "He was a *wonderful* doctor," she says.

"And now you feel as though you're losing everything, Marie?"

"That Yvonne took my dish towels. They were *good* ones . . ."

"Now, now," smiles Dr. Nakamura, his voice as soothing as a hypnotist's, "it's not *things* that're important, is it, Marie? No, it's people and love. What you've lost isn't things, it's your health, your safe home, and your old friends. Age and illness, not your daughter-in-law, have taken them from you. That's the loss you've got to deal with, not dish towels, isn't it?" His tone is soothing, and my mother smiles weakly.

She averts her eyes and sighs, "I guess." Then she adds, "They were *good* ones."

"I'm certain they were, but we have to look at all you have—three grandchildren who love you, a son, a husband, a daughter-in-law. A home of your own. Do you realize how fortunate you are?"

"I guess." Her voice remains faint as yesterday's breeze.

Turning to face me, the psychiatrist says, "I'm giving your mother two new prescriptions. One is a nonconstipating antidepressant, so I expect her to take it regularly." He exchanges a glance with my mother, who once more averts her eyes. "The other is specifically to reduce her sense of victimization. She says she can't stand being alone. Will she be able to live with you?"

"Of course," I reply.

"I'm very close to my grandchildren," Mom remarks.

"That's wonderful." The doctor turns his attention to me once more. "It's essential for her to take the medication *as prescribed*. Isn't it, Marie?"

"I guess"—her voice again fading. Then it grows suddenly stronger as she says, "Suzie's real smart and pretty, too. With the *cutest* figure." She sounds more relaxed, but her eyes still wander, and she adds, "*Somebody's* been moving my sewing basket. It's a *good* one."

"I'm certain." The psychiatrist turns to face her. "Remember, Marie, it's not the loss of things that really troubles you, is it? It's the loss of control in your life—your health and your old home—but you've got a resource that many older people don't have: your family. You be sure to take your medication, and I'll talk with you again next week . . . or sooner if necessary."

As we rise to leave, the psychiatrist says quietly, "It's paranoid depression. Keep an eye on her and, if you can, don't let her be alone—have you someone in the house when you're working?" I nod yes. "Move her into your place right away or move someone in with her. *It's crucial,* Dr. Upton. If you can't, she'll have to be hospitalized so we can stabilize her. She may very well have to be anyway, but let's try this first."

"Okay. We'll keep her at home."

"Bring her in next week at this time and call me daily and let me know how things're going. If she regresses, bring her right in. She *should* show improvement almost immediately with these medicines, but it's tough with someone her age. She's had a psychotic episode. I should also tell you that my dad suffers from nearly the same condition . . . he thinks it's still World War II and that he's back in an internment camp. I know more than casually what you're going through. It's bad, bad business."

As we reach the car, my mother stops and asks, "Was he a Chinese doctor?"

"American, Mom," I reply.

She looks vexed for a moment, then says, "I know that, but what is he *really*?"

"I think he's Japanese American."

"Well," she finally says as I open the door for her, "he certainly has pretty hair."

23

We install Mom in Suzie's room, and she sleeps most of the next two nights—perhaps because of the new medicine—and that allows us to get some welcome rest. When she is awake, however, she says little, and she seems to glare at Yvonne. Even in repose my mother's face appears distorted, jaw thrust forward, eyes agog; she seems to be gnashing her teeth.

Sunday evening, I walk into the master bedroom after finally depositing my mother in bed—over her objections, of course—and Yvonne sits in robe and slippers reading a newspaper. "You look beat," she looks up and says.

"I am." I feel damned ragged.

"Well," she smiles, "I've been waiting for you. Sit down here. I want to play a little game with you."

"I'm too pooped," I reply, but I'm really afraid that I once again won't be able to provide much of an erection.

"Try it first," she advises, then she takes a pair of dice out of a pocket and hands one to me. "We'll roll for high number. The winner can take one piece of clothing off the loser." She tosses her die onto the bed: five.

I toss a three.

She turns me and places both arms around my neck, removes my shirt, kissing my ear softly as she does so. My AWOL erection immediately reports for duty.

We toss again and I win, six to two. I remove one slipper, note three small blue veins under the bulge of her arch, and kiss each of them, and her ankle. That erection is at attention.

She wins the next roll, and removes my undershirt—touching one of my nipples with her tongue as she works. She wins again, kneels before me, and pulls my trousers down—fondling first one of my knees, then the other.

The game is a total success, and, as I drift toward sleep, I refuse to wonder where and when she learned it.

Arising rested for a change the next morning, I check on Mom, then on my snoring father. Yvonne has preceded me and has coffee ready. As I walk past her to the kitchen for my cup, I notice that her face is drawn and she keeps her eyes on the mortgage update she's been studying. Steaming mug in hand, I return to the dinette and walk behind her, scratch her back. It's taut as oak, so I kiss her neck. "Are you okay, babe?" I ask.

She sighs. "When I got up this morning, your mother was awake. She said some . . . *things* . . . to me."

I know what's coming, so I say, "Let's wait a few more days, babe. Maybe this medicine'll snap her out of it."

"All right, but if she's still the same . . ." My wife leaves the rest unsaid. Her chin is up and she gazes toward the deck door at the shimmering leaves of the oak as she speaks.

"I know, I know. Let's just play it by ear, okay? Please."

"Okay."

I hug her and we kiss. "Thanks for last night." I smile.

"Thank *you*." She smiles back. "We need more nights like that, Roy."

"Amen."

After Yvonne and Jared leave, Trish calls in sick. Just what I need. I have no choice but to telephone Alberta, the substitute recommended by the Senior Services Office; she can't come early. As a result, I then have to telephone the college and explain that I'll miss my morning class. At ten-thirty, Mom still isn't up, so I gently shake her shoulder, crooning, "Good morning."

"*Don't!*" she spits, her eyes tightly shut.

"It's ten-thirty. Don't you want breakfast?"

"No. Leave me *alone.*"

Half an hour later, I try once more. This time my mother beseeches me: "Why are you *doing* this to me? I'm so, *so* tired. *Pleeease* leave me alone." She does not open her eyes.

It isn't worth the stress to force her up, so I do indeed leave her alone. Nothing is simple when dealing with my folks, and I begin to wonder if I'm really just asserting myself—a child who can at last dominate a parent—if I persist in trying to awaken her despite her entreaties. But I also wonder if I'm taking the easy way out when I cease trying. Guilt plagues me.

Shortly before lunch, Alberta arrives. She is a large middle-aged woman with olive skin and black hair streaked with white. I'm relieved to see that she doesn't wear a nurse's uniform as Trish does. I explain to her that the regular caregiver is ill and, after telling her that Mom seems unwilling to wake up, ask her to please look after my father for me. "That's fine, Mr. Upton. Has your father eaten?"

"I gave him breakfast."

"Well, I'll bathe him, then give him lunch. I'll do these dishes too. I like to stay busy."

That startles me a bit. Trish does what she considers nurse's work but no more; she is a professional, not a domestic. Already Alberta, in her pink dress and bright bandana, is bouncing around the kitchen putting things away, humming as she works. She may be a pleasant variation around here, especially if she can get along with Mom . . . and pick Pop up.

As much as I hate it, I skip my bicycle ride and drive our pickup to school in order to meet my next class on time. I later return home dissatisfied and with the hope that I can at least jog a bit before dinner.

"Your mother's been up to go to the bathroom, but that's all, Mr. Upton," Alberta tells me.

Crap! I'll have a sleepless night with her tonight; her long naps are warnings to me. Oh, well, nothing I can do about it now.

"Please call me Leroy, Alberta. I'll be taking my dad to the senior center for his weekly meal today. If you can feed Mom, please do, but don't push it," I advise.

"I tried to wake her up," the large woman explains with a smile, "but she was *so* angry that I gave up."

"Just keep an eye on her. If she does get up, please help her bathe. She doesn't smell very good."

"Doesn't she like to bathe?"

"She doesn't like doing anything other people want her to do."

"Well," Alberta says, "if she wakes up, I'll urge her to take a shower."

"Thanks."

I walk Pop to the pickup, and the two of us drive silently to the meal site. After parking, I hold one of his hands and walk him into the hall—he is slower than usual today, but finally we reach his seat. Ben and the bald-headed man are already there. "Hell, John, I figured you was skippin' 'er today. I figured me and Henry here'd just have to split your dessert," Ben guffaws. "Right, Henry?"

The bald-headed man says simply, "'Lo, Earl."

Pop settles into his chair, then says, "How you?"

Before I can depart for my customary seat at the back of the room, Ben grabs my arm. "Say, you hear about them three gals that they died and went to heaven?"

"No," I say.

"Wellsir, them three they got there and ol' Saint Pete, he says, 'This place ain't like what you think. Nosir, this place lets you do whatever you want. Why, right now you can sleep with any guy in the world if you want.'" He grins, and those large yellow teeth dominate his face.

"This first gal, she says, 'Any guy, whether he's alive or dead?' and Saint Pete he says, 'Yeah.' 'I'll take ol' Valentino,' she says and poof!—there he is and off they go. The next gal she sees that, so she says, 'I'll take ol' Frank Sinatra.' Poof!—there he is and off they go."

Ben pauses and a mischievous grin crosses his face. "Wellsir, that third gal, she frets and frets, then she finally says, 'I'll take ol' John Upton.'"

Ben sneaks a peek at my father. "'John Upton!' Saint Pete says, 'Why in the world would you take him when you could choose ol' Casanova or Don Juan or famous guys like that?' 'But he *is* a famous lover-boy,' she tells Pete. 'Why, all over Mill Valley I seen wrote on walls, *Fuck John Upton!*' Ha! Ha-ha-ha! Get it?"

The bald-headed man doesn't seem to, but I do, and I can't help chuckling, and my father's face is slit by a broad grin: he too gets it. Ben slaps his back.

Before I can say anything I hear a woman's voice call from the next table, "Cindy! Ben's cussing again!"

"Fulla bullshit," grins my father.

"Cindy!"

I depart for my customary seat at the back of the room. Later Mr. Dwyer, the ex-screenwriter, stops by my table. "How are you today, Coach Upton?"

"Fine, and you, Mr. Dwyer?"

"About as well as an old poop can be. There was a man I knew back in the business, a comic, and he used to say that old age was like being nibbled to death by ducks. It seemed funny at the time." His grin is sad. "Now I have to pause and wonder occasionally at how quickly my good years fled and left me . . . like this."

He is a man of accomplishment, but his eyes become pained and baffled. After a moment, he smiles. "Oh, excuse me for waxing philosophical." He shrugs, then we shake hands, and he slumps away, with what seems infinite sadness, that plastic diaper bunched under his tailored trousers. He has said nothing about my offer to read his poems.

Near the doorway, Ben, in his soiled baseball cap and overalls, steps lively, and I hear his braying voice—"You guys read about them dope fiends?"

24

That next weekend, Mitch has volunteered to watch Grandma and Grandpa so Yvonne and I can take Amtrak to Bakersfield and attend that country music concert with the Plumleys. We were on the verge of canceling, but Mom quite unexpectedly improved. Besides, I realize that my wife and I really need to get away, if only for a day or so. The concert is an afternoon affair, so we can return home in the evening—just an overnight trip. We're departing on the Friday evening train, and Yvonne orders Chinese food delivered.

We've just seated ourselves when Jared bops in the front door and calls, "Hey, Mom! Guess what! I, like, got my band started."

Yvonne, Mitch, and I exchange grins because Jared plays no instrument and has never been able to sing. "That's fine, honey," my wife replies. "There's Chinese food on the counter."

"Great. Like, how many shrimps do I get?"

"Four."

He joins us in the family room a few minutes later, and Pepper, who as usual hovers beneath Pop's TV tray awaiting dropped morsels, immediately moves to Jared's location, knowing that food will be passed to him there. "Hi, Grandpa," calls our younger son. Pop continues toothlessly smacking his food, although his eyes slide toward the boy.

Jared is bubbling. "Yeah, it's, like, far out," he tells us. "Me and Tracy we, like, met this dude that just transferred into the school, and he, like, wants to form a group too. We dig the same kind of music and we came up with this *rude* name for our group: 'Post Partum.' Do you like it?"

"How about the Texas Playboys?" I ask. "There's a name for you."

"Huh?"

"It's fine, honey," smiles his mother, giving me the evil eye.

"What instrument you gonna play, dude?" asks Mitch.

"How you?" my father finally says to Jared, then he fills his mouth with food once more.

"I'm gonna, like, sing lead and learn the tambourine . . . and maybe the harmonica."

"And Tracy?" Mitch asks. We all know that Tracy also boasts no musical training.

"He's gonna, like, learn the drums."

"And the new dude, what's he play?"

"He's gonna, like, learn the guitar." Jared turns to Yvonne. "And wait'll you hear about the *rude* outfits we're, like, gonna wear. White leather pants and boots with those real frilly tux shirts and black coats with, like, tails and black top hats. It'll be *real* rude."

I smile. "It sounds rude to me."

"Me too," agrees Mitch.

"And we're, like, gonna get these real good-lookin' chicks to, like, back us up."

"That's good, honey," Yvonne smiles. "Want another shrimp?"

"Maybe, like, *black* chicks. Oh, look at Grandpa's nose. It's *gross*," swoons Jared.

A long, clear dollop sways from my father's nose, and he poses, unable to coordinate his activities well enough to wipe it with a napkin.

"Hey, Pop," I call as I rise, "lemme get that for you."

"Listen, dude," Mitch tells Jared, "if you need someone who, like, *doesn't* know how to play bass and, like, *can't* sing, I might, like, join your group too."

Jared hesitates, then says, "Ha-ha, like, very funny, fart breath."

"Ouwww," winces Mitch, and he grabs his chest like a man absorbing a bullet, "what a put-down!"

"You don't need to cuss, Jared, but I'm sure you'll have a good group," Yvonne says, and she glares at Mitch. "I seem to remember somebody who entered the Boys' Club talent contest as a magician but didn't bother to learn any magic."

Mitch raises his hands in supplication. "Okay. Okay. I give."

"And Suzie signed up for *The Nutcracker* at the grade school without benefit of dance lessons," I add, "so it's a long-standing tradition in this family. And . . ."

"Dad," Jared interrupts, "Grandpa, like, just ate his fortune cookie."

I turn and give him a so-what look, then notice half of the paper fortune protruding from my father's smacking lips. "Hey, Pop," I call, rising again, "you don't want to eat that," and I slip the half-chewed paper out of his mouth.

"Roughage," says Mitch, and Jared laughs. I fight not to smile myself: this is humor my father would have enjoyed.

Through it all, my mother has not stirred from bed, and I am not willing to ruin this meal by rousting her. "Are you sure you can deal with Grandma?" I ask Mitchell.

"Yo, Pop," he grins, "for a day or two I can deal with *anything*. Besides, you two've been uptight. We'll all feel better if you guys have a good time and come home happy. Isn't that right, shit-for-brains?" he pleasantly asks his brother.

"*Stop* the cussing!" snaps Yvonne, and both Mitch and Jared, who's about to reply in kind, look at their plates, grinning.

They're just kidding, but Yvonne's tension is evident, so I add simply, "Cool it, guys."

"Oh," I hear my mother's voice, "did I miss dinner?"

She stands at the end of the hallway, silhouetted—small, slight—by a light behind her, and her voice does not harbor the harsh rasp that has so frequently characterized it of late.

I stand and walk to her, extending a hand. "You're just in time, Mom. Come on, it's Chinese food, your favorite."

I walk her to a chair and my wife prepares a plate for her. Both boys sit warily in the dinette eyeing their grandmother. I hear the microwave beep, then Yvonne gingerly delivers a plate with steaming chow mein, noodles, egg foo yung, sweet-and-sour pork, rice, and shrimp. "Oh," says Mom, "I can't eat *that* much. It smells delicious. Did you make this yourself, Yvonne?"

"No, Mom, we ordered it from a restaurant." My wife glances at me because this pleasant tone is so uncharacteristic of recent experience that it is shocking.

"It's certainly delicious," mushes Mom, her mouth full.

"I'm glad you like it," my wife says.

"It's delicious."

Pop turns his head. "How you?" he grins slowly.

"It's delicious, Earl," Mom says, her face eager, like a child's.

And I think, yeah, it is delicious, seeing them together, almost the way they were, and I am their son. Each moment like this may be the final one, so my heart lurches, and I look down, blinking hard. Yvonne moves to my chair, puts both her arms around my shoulders, rests her chin on my hair, while I continue blinking and remember that long-ago rebuke, "*Quit blubberin'!*"

"Isn't this just *delicious,* Earl?"

"Took . . . my . . . license," he mumbles.

25

"Oh, Earl, you're not going to make him work with that foulmouthed Hubby Hobbs, are you?"

"First of all, I ain't makin' him do nothin'. Leroy told me he'd like to work out there, didn't you?"

I nodded. Now that football season was over, I appreciated the chance to earn some spending money.

"Besides," Pop added, "Hubby's a good ol' boy and funny as a bone. Him and me've worked together in the oil patch for a lotta years, and he can sure show a feller how to pull his weight. Give him a real day's work, and he'll be as good to you as can be. Don't, and there won't be nothin' left a you but blood and chunks."

I chuckled and nodded because I knew from past experience that Mr. Hobbs was funny but plenty tough too.

"But he's so. . . ." Mom seemed to search for just the right word, then said, "so *common.*"

Pop didn't get mad. He only paused, then said, "Ain't that a shame. Come on, boy."

I laughed again because Mr. Hobbs seemed uncommon to me, uncommonly nasty, but her voice told me this didn't amuse her.

Although I wasn't old enough for a driver's license, my father allowed me to pilot the pickup out to Shafter and, once there, he directed me to a dilapidated motel on a treeless stretch of Pond Road, not far from some packing sheds. An old hand-painted sign near the road read, MONTHLY RATES. The units were clapboard shanties connected with small carports. Barren dirt lay between each, but Mr. Hobbs's own residence, otherwise the same as all the rest, featured an aging pepper tree near the door and a small, irregular patch of Bermuda grass.

Before we could knock, the thick man lunged out of the door and raised a vast right hand. "Damn," he called, "you boys must work them banker's hours. Hell, it's near seven o'clock." He spat in mock disgust. "Me, I had to bump up on Momma two 'r three extra times just to kill time a-waitin' on you, see."

My father grinned. "We was just eatin' some of them bonbons and drinkin' some of that champagne, Hubby," he called. "How you doin'?" He extended a hand and Hobbs shook it.

"Doin' good, Earl. Just ask ol' Momma," he winked. Then he turned toward me. "How you doin', hoss?" His paw swallowed mine. "You ready for a little honest labor?"

"Besides, what's this *two or three times* shit?" demanded my dad.

"Why, hell, yeah," grinned the big man.

Daddy grinned back. "You ain't done nothin' no three times in thirty years."

"Shit, I jacked off three times just yesterday, see."

I laughed. That wasn't a topic I was used to hearing adult males discuss.

Daddy was laughing when he said, "You mighta 'jacked' some, but I bet there wasn't much 'off' about it."

Mr. Hobbs didn't back down. "Hell, I'd beat my meat more, but the doctor he told me not to lift nothin' too heavy, see."

"Shit, Hubby," guffawed my father, "I gotta get off to work. Don't you go to talkin' nasty around this boy."

"Who, me? Hell, you know me, Earl. But you know, if I coulda screwed half as good as I jacked off, I'd'a went to Hollywood and got rich keepin' them stars happy, see."

"It's a comfort to know you won't be talkin' nasty in front of my boy," Daddy said, winking at me.

"You damn right," grunted Mr. Hobbs.

Five minutes later, we were on the roof scraping off rotten shingles with shovels. From up there, I could see miles of cultivated fields, different shades of green, the wrinkled configurations of irrigation rows, plus some orchards. Everything disappeared into haze, though, with no distant hills or mountains visible in any direction.

Mr. Hobbs said little once we began working, and I was too occupied trying to keep up with him to initiate a conversation. He was fast and efficient and, as I learned when we were moving bundles of shingles, much stronger than I was, despite all my weight training for football.

"Yessir," Mr. Hobbs said an hour later, as though the earlier conversation had never stopped, "whenever I'uz your age, hoss, I jacked off in that shower so much I'd get me a hard-on ever' time it rained."

I nearly fell off the roof guffawing, then I heard a screen door slam and a voice call, "What's all that laughin' up there? Ain't you two s'posed to be workin'?"

I glanced down and saw a handsome gray-haired woman built like Mr. Hobbs, blocky with no shape showing in the dress she wore. "You talkin' nasty to that boy, Hubby?" she demanded.

"Who, me?"

"Y'all come down here and drink some a this ice tea I brought you."

Mr. Hobbs winked at me. "Alright, darlin'," he called.

"Don't start that *darlin'* stuff."

"Momma don't like me sweet-talkin' her in front a company, see," he said.

"I'll *company* you," she threatened, then she turned in my direction. "Here, sweetheart," she handed me a beaded glass of tea.

"Thank you, ma'am."

"You're welcome. Has this old man been talkin' nasty?"

Behind her, Hubby raised his eyebrows and shook his head.

"Not really," I stammered.

As soon as his wife disappeared back into the small house, and we once more mounted the ladder onto the roof, Mr. Hobbs winked at me. "I'd surely like to take me a little break, see, bump up against Momma a time or two."

I grinned.

"Yessir, I'd like to have me the three best thangs there is in the whole damn world, see. Know what they are?"

Prurient answers filled my mind, but I shook my head and grinned again.

"A shower before and a nap afterwards, see. Ha! Ha-ha!" After a minute, he added, "Say, you gettin' any nooky, hoss, good-lookin' young buck like you?"

I was scraping the last dried shingles, tossing them onto a pile on the ground. "Oh, a little," I said.

"Don't be missin' out on no nooky, see. I'm sixty year old and I ain't *never* found nothin' better. The *worst* fuck I ever had was better'n the *best* strawberry shortcake I ever et, see. Better'n the coldest beer I ever drunk. Better'n the . . ."

"Hubby!" called his wife through the screen door. "Are you a-talkin' nasty to that boy?"

"Who, me?" he called. "How come you to ask me that, darlin'?"

26

When we emerge from the train in our hometown—dark yet warm out-side—Travis and Juanita are leaning on the hood of his Mercedes. After hugs and greetings, Travis says to his wife and me, "You two sit in front. I'm ridin' in back with Yvonne . . . givin' her a good goin' over on the way to the place."

Juanita chuckles. "Maybe we could just go to the 99 Drive-In Theater so Roy and I can play a little doctor in the front seat, too."

"Well," Travis says, "if you two're gonna get nasty . . . ," and he slips behind the steering wheel.

Once we reach their house and are settling in their family room, Travis calls to his wife, "Honey, get Roy a glass of that Thunderbird."

"Mix mine with Dr Pepper," I call.

The mention of that poisonous combination we'd tried in our youth causes Travis to laugh. Then he asks, "How're them cookie-crumblers of yours doin', Roy?"

"I told the boys they could come down here and work for you next summer, make some easy money like you do."

"You tell them two little prune pickers I might just have to knock some religion into 'em if they aren't real careful."

"How's your dad?" asks Juanita.

"About the same."

"And your mom?"

"She was fine when we left, but I wouldn't bet a penny on how she'll be by this time tomorrow. It's like I told you on the phone—she's been rough to deal with."

"She sure has," agrees Yvonne.

"Sorry to hear that." Travis's face turns grim. "Well, I hate to be the one to tell you, but we got some bad news a couple days ago. Marge left Jess."

"She's *left* him. No shit?"

"No shit. I guess she wanted to go off to some law school down in L.A., and he said no way, so she took off. That's what I heard anyway, and he's takin' it real rough. I'm surprised he hasn't called you. He's on the horn with me most every day."

"How're their kids?"

"Not good," Juanita answers. "I think they both blame Marge."

I shrug and say, "Crap." Sometimes it seems that our world is slowly coming apart.

"If anybody ever fought long odds to make it, they did," I say. "Now this."

Yvonne shakes her head. "I can't understand why he doesn't just support her in this. Roy practically forced me to go back and finish college after Jared started school."

"Mexican," explains Juanita. "Jess is like my father was. He's never really trusted school, and he can't let his wife get ahead of him. He's a lot more conservative about that stuff than you guys imagine. Remember, he didn't go away to school like us. He's lived right here all his life, and he *is* a Mexican male."

"Shit, he's just like the rest of us," says Travis. "We all come from blue-collar families."

"No," Yvonne quickly disagrees, "I don't think he's like you two, and if you think about it you know it, too. He's a generation behind you, doing work like your fathers did, and maybe thinking like them, too. You two've been successful, you've had educations, and even when you act like rednecks, you can do that because you've got a choice. Jess doesn't."

She is, of course, correct, this bright woman I married. And I gaze at her for a long moment.

"I saw ol' Tommy the other day," Travis says, then he nods toward me. "You know him and your ol' high school flame Lahoma've split too."

"Who hasn't?" I croak.

"He said she just about cleaned him out financially. She told the judge he'd got the best years of her life. I said, 'Well, hell, no wonder me and Juanita're still together. She had all her best years *before* she married me.'"

"You can say that again," grins his wife.

"Roy, you know what this ol' hide said to me the other day?" He pats his wife's thigh as he speaks. "She was gonna hang a picture up, and she asked me where I'd put the stud-finder. I told her she didn't need one since she'd already found me."

Juanita rolls her eyes and shakes her head.

"Well," he nods, "she says, 'I want a *stud*-finder, not a *stub*-finder.'"

While we chuckle, he shakes his head, then says with mock gravity. "I oughta work her over for knowin' the difference. It'll all come out in the divorce."

I don't know about Juanita, but Yvonne certainly knows the difference, so I don't pursue that topic. But this couple, our best friends for many years, always amaze me: they seem to play with one another, teasing almost like kids, each truly enjoying the other. Yvonne and I do that too, though not as much or as freely as they do, but I never saw Jess and Marge banter.

Merle Haggard's baritone is surging out of the large stereo speakers, and I ask Travis, "Don't I recollect you doing your best *not* to listen to country music back in high school? Your favorites were Billy Eckstein and Jo Stafford and . . . what's his name? . . . ah, Johnny Ray."

"Not me! It was *you* who did that, peckerhead."

"You guys know what Tex Ritter there"—Juanita nods at her husband—"gave me for a Christmas present when we were going together? The very first album Johnny Mathis ever made."

"Ol' Johnny was a-singin' country in them days," snorts Travis. "Besides, I seem to remember ol' Roy here sittin' on the team bus with all the colored boys singin' that song."

" 'Night Owl.' "

"Yeah, 'Night Owl.' " He rolls his eyes and breaks into a scratchy, atonal baritone: "Here comes the niiight owwwl, comin' in the back dooo-ooo-ooor . . ."

"Enough!" I yell, covering my ears.

"But you know what's real funny hereabouts. We've had world-class country music for a long, long time: ol' Ferlin Husky, ol' Jean Shepard, ol' Tommy Collins, and you know, most of the high rollers here, they ignore that and crow about our local symphony, or the operas or ballets or Shakespeare that comes to town . . ."

"We send checks to support all those things, Mr. Plumley," inserts Juanita.

"Yeah, we do," he acknowledges. "And I'm glad. This is a good little city with lots of stimulatin' stuff goin' on, but there's still too damn many 'suedeo'-intellectuals embarrassed by those Okie roots."

"Hey," I say, "they can come up to our place. There's a psychic faire up there next week."

"I knew that," snaps Travis, and I have to laugh. He's a quick study.

"A *what*?" Juanita asks.

"You know, one of those New Age shindigs like your friend . . . what's her name? . . . Dolores . . . she's hot for."

Juanita rolls her eyes. "Earth calling Dolores," she says in a metallic voice. "Earth calling Dolores."

"Hell, I'd go to one of those psychic deals," her husband announces. "Is it like a 4-H fair? I'd like to see the fat-calf judgin' or maybe the pickle contest."

"One a those mystics might pickle your fat calf," I warn.

"And he just might be suckin' buttermilk with his ass by the time I get through with him, too," Travis growls.

"What a vocabulary! These two old coots need a *physic* faire," his wife says to mine.

"Ol' Leroy ain't gonna need one after I knock the shit outta him," snaps the attorney, and even I have to laugh at that quip.

"How much did you pay for this red rotgut?" I ask. I know he's in the process of assembling a formidable wine cellar.

Travis grins. "Ninety-nine cents a jug. Want me to bring the cap out for you to smell?"

"Nope, but I'm curious."

"Well, if you buy this by the case, it's about sixty bucks a bottle. I buy us two cases a year—one to drink, one to lay down. It drinks pretty good right now, doesn't it?" He finishes his glass, then refills it, plus ours.

After we, for perhaps the fifth time, touch glasses in a silent toast, I say, "Did I tell you I heard a lecture up at Sonoma State on the importance of California? All of our families, except maybe yours, Juanita, were foreigners—from Texas or Oklahoma or just points south or east, and from whole different social and economic systems. They got here just before World War II expanded the economy, and now look at us, drinking sixty-dollar Cabernet . . . thanks to an Okie lawyer."

"My family was from Mexico," says Juanita. "My grandparents came north during World War I, but you're right. It wasn't until our generation got to school that changes began."

Travis adds, "Part of that was that we were able to marry whoever we wanted—at least if you were both outsiders, Mexicans and Okies like us. Juanita's family—the older folks—sure didn't want her marryin' a paleface like me, and my folks said, 'Cain't you find no *white* girl to have you?' I said, 'No.'"

"Hey!" His wife pokes his shoulder. She had been our class's great beauty, the school's first ever Latina homecoming queen, and she'd married the Okie quarterback. Then, without help from their impecunious families, they'd put each other through college.

Travis's voice deepens. "But, you know, none of 'em—our folks, I mean—none of 'em knew at first how this California deal works. But they damn sure figured it out, and pushed us in school. Second-generation kids, like my brothers and me, we've done real good because we learned to play the game out here, got those educations, broke out of bein' laborers like the folks, and made ol' California work for us."

"That's the real gold in this state," I agree, "education and more . . . what? . . . a sense of the possible. You can dream of being more than your folks thought was possible back *there* . . . in Oklahoma or Texas or Mexico. Of course, then you have to work your ass off."

"You damn right!" agrees Travis.

Yvonne has been gazing away. Now she says, "My folks—my dad especially—never caught on. He really kept searching for gold nuggets or something. He fell into one get-rich-quick scheme after another, and he died broke. Momma followed him, and she died broke too."

"People complain about the younger generation today," Juanita says, "but one big problem is that we've given them too much. We couldn't help it, but we have. There isn't as much 'up' for them."

"That's the dilemma, Juanita," I agree. "I bet they'll all do okay, but I'd be more certain of that if they'd chopped a little cotton."

Yvonne's chin is up. "I'd rather we give them too much than too little," she says in mild disagreement. "Poverty's only romantic when it's over." She knows what she's talking about, since she endured deeper destitution than the rest of us.

Travis reaches over and squeezes Yvonne's arm. "Yeah, I guess most of us like to sound like we were born in log cabins and walked a hundred miles through snow—or maybe through tule fog—to school. Tell you the truth, I wouldn't wanta be a kid now, what with dope and AIDS and gangs and all the rest."

"Me either," I agree. We all fall silent while Merle continues crooning from the stereo speakers.

Finally, Travis says, "But you know, it's funny how *countrified* outsiders think us Bakersfield-types are. Hell, I use this ol' Okie twang to lull big-city lawyers before I cut their balls off. Nothin' I like better'n some slick L.A. shyster comin' to Bakersfield to show us hicks how the law really works, then sendin' him home singin' soprano. Those smart L.A. guys paid for this house . . . and that wine."

I can't help laughing. Travis does indeed castrate a high percentage of his foes, and that is indeed why we're in this air-conditioned mansion instead of the Quonset hut south of town where he lived when we were in high school. I drawl to the gals, "Nothin' worse'n a rich damn Okie."

"Oh, *yeah?*" Travis counters instantly. "A poor one's a hell of a lot worse, 'specially if you've been him."

27

The next afternoon, as we walk across a vast parking lot, Juanita observes, "There aren't as many cars as I expected for a free concert."

I stop dramatically and snort, "*Free*? Did you say free? Well, hell, your husband told me the tickets cost twenty bucks. I already paid him cash on the barrelhead."

"And you probably want your damn money back," Travis feigns disgust.

I'm still chuckling as we slide through the civic auditorium's main door into a smoky lobby. "Jeez," coughs Juanita, "what's this, a tobacco growers' convention?" In the background, taped country music—Buck Owens and Dwight Yoakam singing "Streets of Bakersfield"—resounds from speakers.

All four of us know well the streets that are Buck and Dwight's subject. We also know twanging guitars—their sound is an intimate echo of our youth. My first impression as I survey the folks milling around the lobby is that I have stepped into my past. The attire, the stances, even all that smoke evoke country dances of long ago. This crowd is long on men in boots and pearl-button shirts open to hairy chests, long on women in skintight jeans and spike heels. And many women add frilly blouses to those tight jeans, with cigarettes bobbing like white exclamation points in their crimson lips. I spy no neckties, and although the lobby bar probably provides fine wines for most concerts, these tipplers suck on cans of brew purchased there, evidence of the concessionaire's pragmatism.

This crowd is certainly different from any Yvonne and I have seen at performances in swishy Marin County. Of course, prosperous Bakersfield now hosts many swanky, prestigious events too, but this sure isn't one of them. These are working people, and it shows in their clothes, in their cosmetics, and especially in their less inhibited behavior. A sociology prof years ago joked that there were rich folks who don't get enough sex or laughter, and poor folks who don't get enough money or respect. This lively crew appears to have enough of some of those things and plenty of others. Hair, for instance, seems big among many men and women both—big in attention paid to it and big in dimension as well. I haven't seen so many self-conscious coiffures since the heyday of the Haight-Ashbury . . . and they were sure different than these.

While we stand near the door, a family dressed in their Sunday best—three, perhaps four generations, very old to very young—passes us, children chattering. One youthful man wearing a billed cap and an inscribed T-shirt holds a baby, while a young woman—his wife?—pushes him in a wheelchair. Behind them a middle-aged woman helps an elderly version of herself, saying earnestly, "I know, Mama, but Earlene Mae really *likes* her hair thataway."

The men who fill the lobby—their skin sun-damaged, their lungs smoke-damaged—expect life to be tough, and it frequently is. Most make decent salaries, but they work hard for them and, like my dad, these guys do not flinch. Most have worked outdoors all week, paid their bills—some barely—and bought their beer, but tonight, with cheap gold chains decorating their leathery throats, tonight they will play. From the speakers, Charley Pride is singing.

These women likely have their jobs as waitresses or clerks or they wrestle with gangs of kids and creditors and perhaps overdue child-support checks, but tonight they are coiffed and foxy. They have camouflaged twenty or thirty or even forty years of hard travel on their faces, and maybe they will prompt these fading stallions to battle over them.

Tonight they will hear their lives celebrated in song—Tammy Wynette now moaning over the lobby speakers.

Travis pokes my ribs and winks. "This must be a conference of Juanita's ol' boyfriends."

"Well, that one over there *might* be if he's willing," his wife says. A vast, bearded man is wearing a stained ten-gallon hat and a T-shirt that doesn't quite cover his belly, the bottom of which is exposed like the hairy slice of a planet. His thick arms are decorated with scrolls of swirling names and scenes, the heels of his boots are worn on their sides so his feet slant away from one another.

"Excuse me," I say. "I've gotta use the men's room."

Travis grins. "Well, I can't guarantee your wife'll still be here when you get back . . . or mine either . . . all these studs cruisin' the lobby."

I glance at Yvonne and smile, but see tension in her eyes. She'll be here, I know.

I swerve into the rest room and, to my surprise, find it almost empty. Then Floyd turns from a urinal shaking his heavy tool, and our eyes meet. For an instant, his take on an expression of surprise . . . almost like one I've seen so often in my daughter's face. My throat constricts and my fists clench.

"Roy," he nods pleasantly as he tucks his business back into his jeans, then extends an unwashed hand. "Good to see ya."

I am immediately ready to punch him, and I hiss, "Stay away from me and my wife, Floyd. If you see either one of us, walk the other way."

His shoulders slump, but he does not turn away. "I'm not crawlin' for nobody, Leroy. You can whip me, we both know that, but I'm not crawlin'." His face is quivering when he adds, "We been buds for *so* long, Roy, and I told you and told you I'm sorry about what happened. You *know* I am. I never ever meant no harm. Never." He pauses again, and seems to search my face, then asks, "Can't you forget that stuff and forgive me?"

"Never."

He slumps even more, then passes me and departs, and I can't help thinking of that expression of his . . . so similar to Suzie's, it begins to seem to me.

Unnoticed by me, a heavyset gent has observed all this from the far urinal. He is grinning when he approaches and asks confidentially, "You fixin' to kick that ol' boy's ass?"

"No," I snap, "but I might kick yours, you nosy bastard."

I'm not kidding.

He flinches. "Jesus," he says, "I didn't mean anything," then he scurries out the door.

After doing my business, almost too upset to be aware, I wash my face in cold water, breathe deeply, then return to my gang. I force a smile.

Beside us, a middle-aged stud about my size grips a can of beer in a large paw. Shoulders husky, face sagging and veined, he entertains three fiftyish women who have been poured into jeans. "You gals hear 'bout the husband that asked his wife why she never told him if she had them orgasm deals?"

They hadn't.

The man's fading red hair has been swirled and sprayed to cover what appears to be increasing parking space above his forehead, and it does not move as his head twists and turns. "Well, sir, she said, 'I would, but you aren't never around when I have one!' Ha-ha-ha!" The gals guffaw with him.

Eyeing those tight britches, Travis says, "Me, I could go for that middle one if it wasn't for that big pimple on her butt."

That breaks the tension I've been feeling since encountering Floyd, and I laugh. "Come on," I say, deciding to move on before Travis gets us into a beef. We find seats near the front of the auditorium.

Lights blink and the rest of the crowd hurries in from the lobby. The master of ceremonies turns out to be the sagging redhead who had entertained the three gals with his joke. "Evenin', ladies and gents," he calls, "I'm Wilbur Dellue that owns Wilbur's Place over in Taft, home of the finest country music west of Nashville—or even Bakersfield"—more laughter—"and I just wanta welcome you to Kern County's own Grand Ol' Opry and Barn Dance Show. Before the music starts, lemme thank our sponsors: radio station KREW, another radio station KKOW-FM, Jack's Pump and Well, the Twin Palms over in Weedpatch, B.J.'s Body

Shop, Old Adobe Records, and, of course, Wilbur's Place, home of the coldest beer and the hottest women."

Travis grunts, "I believe ol' Wilbur might be one of them sexist deals."

"Where's Gloria Steinem when we need her?" smiles Juanita.

"Probably waitin' out in ol' Wilbur's pickup," whispers Travis, and we all laugh.

"We'll talk more about our sponsors after while, but first lemme introduce our openin' act—and this ol' boy's gonna go a long ways in this business. All the way from up in Delano . . . let's give a big welcome to the great *Leroy Remington*!"

"They fly him all the way in?" asks Travis. Delano is thirty miles north on Highway 99.

"Connector flight," I say, "on a crop duster."

"Will you two *hush?*" Juanita requests mildly.

There is a poking and probing at the curtains while the band plays a fanfare, and it appears that after his long, long journey from Delano, Leroy isn't going to find his way onstage. The band repeats its fanfare while the poking and probing of the curtains continues. The master of ceremonies chuckles into the mike, "I believe ol' Leroy's got lost." More laughter.

Finally escaping the drapes, ol' Leroy turns out to be a slight blond youngster in a fringed leather jacket and a straw Stetson with brim dipping front and back, curls falling to his shoulders. His face is bright red.

"One, two, three, four," he quickly calls, and the band swings into a version of Buck Owens's "Act Naturally." The youngster begins singing, and his voice is a deep baritone, obviously well trained. He intones pleasantly, though without any noticeable style or emotion of his own. His stage manner is uncomfortable, as though he has been choreographed by Pinocchio.

"That kid moves like a white guy," Travis can't resist saying, and a large, bouffanted lady in front of us turns and glares at him. "Will you jest *hesh?*" she snaps. Travis rolls his eyes and grins but says nothing.

The singer follows with a ballad, "For the Good Times," and does a better job. Looking at him, though, I can see only a life of frustration, of singing at Wilbur's, and at the Twin Palms in Weedpatch, of expensive hairdos and low-paying jobs, of selling his own tapes locally. But at least he has dreams.

"Let's hear it for the great Leroy Remington, a boy on the way up," calls ol' Wilbur. "Put your hands together and give him a big round a ammunition, folks. He's gonna be back a little later in our show.

"Me and Larry that owns the Twin Palms we just a cut a demo tape of Leroy singin' those same two songs, and we'll release it soon as we raise a little money. If any a you rich millionaires out there wants to sponsor a future star, you look me up at break time," he grins.

"Me and Larry we go way back. Hell, I knew him when he still had hair," Wilbur winks, and the crowd laughs. "I'll tell ya what, though, you'll get the coldest damn draft beer in the Lamont-Arvin-Weedpatch area at his place and find the friendliest waitresses, but don't go to messin' with ol' Larry's wife, Hester, 'cause he keeps a shotgun behind the bar." Laughter. "You bring the war department tonight, Larry, or that purty waitress you're always sportin'?" he calls, and once more the crowd guffaws.

"He runs a great joint. Oh, one time I busted my knuckles out there, didn't I, Larry?" Masculine laughter dominates this time. "You folks just ask ol' Larry 'bout that little deal.

"Anyways, our next act is one of the greatest singers in this part of the country. He's opened for lotsa big-name shows, and he's played at the Twin Palms and at my joint, at Trout's out in Oildale, at the Lucky Spot on Edison Highway, and even at the Blackboard before it closed up— the great *Red Richards*."

Travis sounds serious when he turns to me and observes, "Wilbur's worth comin' to the concert for. I sure hope his knuckles're okay, though."

"He might be using 'em on you if you don't shut up," Juanita advises.

Red, whose hair is gray, strolls stiffly onstage, wearing a large guitar and a western-cut suit that does not hide his ample belly.

Travis can't resist. "I believe ol' Red's been neglectin' his sit-ups," he whispers.

"Thank you, thank you!" calls Red. "We'd like to start with a number made famous by our good friend Ernest Tubb. It goes a little somethin' like this right here: '*I'm walkin' the floor over youuu . . .*'" His voice— high, thin, and nasal—caresses the words. He's a pro, and he plays the audience as well as his guitar.

"Thank you, thank you!" Red calls as the crowd claps enthusiastically for his first number, Wilbur cheerleading on one side of the stage. The singer bows, then announces, "Now we'd like to sing another favorite that our old buddy Bob Wills recorded and that Tommy Duncan sang way back when most of you was just little bitty kids. It's called 'Roly-Poly' and it goes a little somethin' like this right here . . ."

After finishing the number and acknowledging applause with a comfortable wave, Red calls, "How 'bout a hand for the fine band we got tonight. Aren't these boys good?" The crowd responds warmly.

"We'd like to close this set with a number for our shut-in frey-unds that couldn't be with us today. It was recorded a few years back by our good friend Hank Snow and it's called 'I'm Movin' On' and it goes a little somethin' like this right here . . ."

"We're fixin' to cut a fart," Travis whispers to me, careful not to disturb the formidable lady in front of him, "and it goes a little somethin' like this right here."

"That was the great Red Richards. He's somethin', ain't he?" calls Wilbur as the singer waves and strides offstage. "We'll have ol' Red back a little later, but first let's give him one more round a ammunition!"

Red is followed by a pretty young woman who seems to be suffering from sinus congestion, by a carefully coiffed young man with a pleasant voice and no style, by another old-timer with no voice but an appealing style—all of them "great." After the band plays "Dueling Banjos" featuring guitar and mandolin, and an elderly fiddler contributes a spectacular "Orange Blossom Special," ol' Red comes back onstage, sings "There Stands the Glass" ("That was made famous by our good friend Webb Pierce and goes a little somethin' like this right here . . ."), then beckons young Leroy Remington to join him. Together they croon "For All the Girls I've Loved Before." Finally, the entire company squeezes on stage for "Take Me Back to Tulsa."

The crowd is raucous and happy by the time Wilbur announces, "It's time to call this deal quits, folks. You been a great audience and I hope you enjoyed the show and that you'll give our sponsors your business. If you did have a good time, how 'bout one more round a ammunition for all these great performers and sponsors." The response is thundering, with many whistles and shouts livening the applause.

"Before we go, though, it's time for a hymn"—he pronounces it "he-um."

Red Richards moves to the mike and solemnly intones, "We'd like to close with a number that was just recorded in his new sacred album by our good friend Willie Nelson, 'That Old Rugged Cross.' It goes somethin' like this right here . . ."

"Now there's a religious zealot for you, ol' Willie," whispers Travis. I manage to bite laughter.

28

Sleeping soundly after our big day away from home and the train trip back that followed, I am jolted awake when the overhead light in our bedroom snaps on. After a dazzled moment I see my mother standing at the door, her eyes wide and unfocused. "Whose place is this?" she demands.

"Huh? What? Are you okay?" I blink.

Yvonne sits up and I slide out of bed.

"Who's that woman?" Mom asks. "Is this the restaurant? Do you know Leroy Upton? He's my son. I'm trying to find my son."

"I'm Leroy."

"Oh, *you're* Leroy." Her eyes narrow.

"Come on, Mom, let me tuck you in." I take her arm and she is pliant, so I guide her toward the guest room, where she had earlier been put to bed.

"Do they serve hamburgers here? I'm hungry. I haven't had anything to eat for *days*. No one feeds you in this hotel."

"You ate dinner with rest of us earlier, Mom."

"I did? With all those people?" She demands, "Who *were* all those people? I don't like this not introducing me bit."

"That was Jared and Mitch and Yvonne and Pop and me. You talked to them."

"It was? Mitchell and Jared?" She hesitates in front of a color portrait of our daughter in her high school cap and gown. "Poor little shy Suzie," she says. "I feel so sorry for her."

I am sleepy, but her questions and tone alert me. She is not feigning this confusion: are we back to this again? My mother, who built her life around me, who would have done anything for me, would have made any sacrifice, seems to be traveling in and out of a realm where I cannot reach her.

Just then Jared, sleepy and wild-haired, staggers up the hall. "Wow, like, what's happenin'?" he asks.

"Grandma's up, dude," I say.

"Like, righteous," he grunts, then disappears into the nearby bathroom.

"Who *was* that?" Mom sounds frightened; she clasps my arm.

"Jared. Your grandson."

"Oh." She seems to think this over, then says, "I want my hamburger."

"Mom, it's two-thirty in the morning. I'm not making you a hamburger. Come on, I'll get you some milk and crackers."

"Is that all they serve around here?"

Back in bed I lie, owl-eyed, listening to my wife's purring, wondering if my union with her has led finally to the fraying of my union with my mother. I reach over, rub Yvonne's warm neck, kiss her cheek, brush one breast. And I am swept by the need to awaken her, to make love with her. But no, she's had a long day. So I roll away. I'll call the psychiatrist tomorrow and report Mom's bizarre behavior.

I awaken to the smell of coffee, and I hear, "Can you help me, hon'?"

"Huh?"

"Your mother's had an accident. Can you help me give her a shower?"

A shower? I'm still groggy, but I immediately reject this. I can't wash my mother's body. I can't invade her privacy that way—or invade my own, for that matter. I don't even want to *see* my mother's naked body. What's Yvonne thinking? "I can't."

"You can't?" My wife stands in the doorway now, and says, "Roy, she *needs* a shower, and you know I can't do it alone. Do you want me to get the boys to help me?"

Yvonne doesn't understand. We're talking about *my mother*. "No," I croak, "leave the boys out of this. I just don't think I should . . ."

Her expression changes. "Leroy," she says softly, "we both bathe your father. It's not my favorite thing in the world to do either, but it has to be done. And so does this."

"Okay, okay . . . ," I grunt, hating my words.

Mom doesn't protest much. "Isn't this a fine thing," she says at one point, "naked as a jaybird!"

I do my best to avert my eyes while supporting her. Yvonne soaps and rinses and later towels her. It all goes smoothly, but something stronger than fear grips my innards: I can give it no name.

When the bath is finally finished, we return her to bed.

I pour myself a cup of coffee, and hold it in trembling hands.

"Are you okay?" asks Yvonne. "You look pale."

"Yeah," I grunt, "I'm okay." This was something I'd never imagined.

"Maybe Freud was right," she smiles.

I have to smile back. "Maybe," I say. Inside myself, though, I am not smiling; no, my innards simmer. Part of me knows this has been necessary, but another part recognizes that this is simply *wrong,* one more diminution of my mother's dignity—perhaps of her humanity—and of our relationship. Like so many of her losses of late, it has come at my hands.

"I have to get Jared to school. You're on Grandpa-and-Grandma duty until Trish arrives. He's up too, and I've changed him."

After my wife and son depart, I help my father to the family room—he rumbles some conversation at me, but I can't understand what he's saying and am too sleepy to work at it. Afterward, I look in on my mother, sleeping crumpled and gape-mouthed, almost unrecognizable. I am sipping my second cup of coffee when the telephone rings.

"Roy?" I hear the familiar voice say as I lift the receiver.

"Big Jess," I respond.

"She's gonna take the house I built for us, so her and her bitch friends can sit around and talk about me." His words are slurred—it is 7:56 A.M.—and I am concerned that he has been drinking.

"Marge can't just *take* your house, buddy. Talk to Travis. He'll stop her."

"She wants to trade her part of my retirement for my share in the house."

"If you don't want to do it, tell her to kiss off," I snap, not needing these problems since my own life offers trouble enough.

"She fucked guys before she knew me. Now she wants to fuck 'em again. I'll kill that bitch!"

I immediately wish I hadn't sounded so harsh a moment before. "*Cálmese vato*. Don't let her drive you nuts. Talk to your attorney or Travis, they'll know what to do."

"I'll break her fuckin' neck," he snarls.

"All that kind of talk's gonna do is get you in trouble— maybe even *help* Marge get the house . . ." I stop because he's begun sobbing.

"Why?" he cries. "Why's she doin' this? She's the only woman I ever loved."

"Shit, Jess, I don't know," I reply with abject honesty, and I am suddenly thinking: please don't let what's happening to Soto ever happen to me. Please don't ever let me lose Yvonne. Minutes later, after at last managing to urge my old buddy to hang up, I dial the Plumleys.

Juanita answers, and I ask, "Is Travis awake?"

"Barely. You sound upset."

"Jess."

"Oh, I should've guessed. He's been calling Travis nearly every night."

"I didn't imagine he was so bad."

"Here comes my jealous husband. Talk to you later, Roy. That was great fun at the concert."

"We had fun too. You take care, dear."

"Don't you damn Okies ever work?" demands Travis.

Hearing his voice prompts me to grin. "I called to give you one more round of ammunition, and it goes something like this right here . . ."

"What the hell do you want? You shillin' for the Twin Palms or what?"

"Listen, Soto called this morning and he sounded drunk. He was carrying on about Marge, saying he was going to kill her, among other things."

I hear Travis sigh. "Yeah, like I told you, he's takin' it damn rough. You remember ol' Jimmy Silverberg that went to East High? He's Jess's attorney. Jimmy couldn't play football worth a kiss my ass, but he's not too damn bad at divorce lawyerin'. He's tryin' to keep Jess cool, but it's a load right now. Jess's wilder'n a mile of lizards."

"What the hell *happened* between Marge and him? How'd it go so sour?"

"Shit, I don't know. Like I told you guys when you were here, it's been comin' for a while. Both of 'em 've always been real closemouthed about personal stuff. Juanita says it's cultural, a Mexican deal. Her family's the same way; they'll talk your ass off about anything except what's really important.

"As I hear it, though, they'd been havin' some trouble and ol' Marge was goin' to this *counselor*—we got damn *counselors* poppin' up like toadstools hereabouts; how'd we ever get along without 'em? Anyways, Marge went to find herself, and I guess didn't like what she found.

"She's been real steady at takin' night classes and stuff for a long time, and real ambitious too. I guess she felt stuck, and she decided she wanted to go to a barely accredited law school down in L.A. Like I told you, Jess tried to put his foot down and she left, but I think it was just the last straw. Juanita said it's been a long time comin'. The funny part is that he's always been the most pussy-whipped guy I know. If Marge said jump, he asked how high and up he went."

"Amen," I agreed.

"I'll bet Jess can be a load to live with, though," Plumley continued. "He's always been a moody son of a bitch, and he hasn't exactly *liberalized* as the years have gone by. Remember, he was terminally pissed about boys with long hair, about war protesters, about that ecology deal, about . . . hell, I don't know, the *Beatles* . . . well, about damn near everything new.

"Now it seems to me that Marge feels like she needs to be a professional, and that Jess has stood in her way. And, of course, he *has*. He's still tryin' to play by the old rules. He can't understand what's wrong with just bein' a momma like his mother was."

"Change is always tough," I say.

"Anyways, Marge told Juanita that she was just takin' care of herself— that's a quote. You know what my little bride told her? She said that's all a rapist is doin', just takin' care of himself. Ol' Marge she wasn't all that amused."

I let that pass and say, "I remember that Marge was always a damned good student back in high school . . . a whole lot better than Jess ever was."

"Yeah, well, she wants a career is what Juanita says. She wants to be *somebody*—which is natural enough. She seems real desperate, like she doesn't have time to earn a title or a degree, so she's gonna find one or buy one *right now*."

I can only grunt, "It's a tough time to be woman, pard', trying to succeed at two sets of goals, wives *and* career women."

"That's rough, all right. But I get sore sometimes when these young gals in our office act like raisin' a family's no big deal. Hell, they oughta *try* it. You remember when Juanita and I were just startin' out, after she'd already helped put me through college and law school, and she ran the office—and the household—while I hustled business."

"Yeah, I do. Juanita was ahead of her time, and so was Yvonne. They got us through school, too, then earned their own degrees. But I'll tell you what I really think's at the bottom of all this: overpopulation's devalued mothering, so now most of the women I know're trying to find other prestigious roles. Then they find those sexual barriers when they do enter the workforce, so there's another challenge. Anyway, is Jess always drinking heavy?"

"Like a damn fish. He tells me over and over that all he ever wanted was her, and now she's gone. He doesn't know whether to shit or go blind. I called his brother Lou and tried to talk to him about Jess's problems, but he's as closemouthed as Jess is. My ol' uncle used to say, 'Them damn Mex'cans keep it in the family.' Lou wanted me to butt out, so I did."

"Yeah," I add, "but it sounds like Jess keeps butting us both back in."

29

We all piled into Mr. Avila's station wagon, and he drove us north of town into brown hills covered with oil derricks and storage tanks—miles and miles of them. Eventually we began the sharp climb out of lingering ground fog toward Granite Station in the foothills where ragged boulders sprouted among the dried remains of wildflowers and high grasses. We motored past the old ranch station itself, then the climb became more gradual, and oaks and scattered pines appeared—first in creases and arroyos, then scattered over the hillsides near upper Pozo Creek.

Rainless winter so far, with the grasses so dry from fall heat that they appeared charred, but the oaks and pines remained deep green as we swerved along a narrow dirt road in remote ranch country. I had never before visited this area, never really imagined it. Finally, our teacher stopped the vehicle, climbed out, and walked to a wooden gate sealed with a heavy chain. He unlocked it, then swung the gate open.

We were on a field trip to an archaeological site on a private ranch, eight of us from Mr. Avila's general science class for seniors at Bakersfield High School, all sardined into his wagon. Travis and I sat in the rear fold-down seat facing backwards, talking about our absent buddy Floyd, who took no academic courses—"So horny he'd fuck mud," said Travis, "and leave a *real* big dent in it." I cracked up.

He and I were not much interested in archaeology that Saturday either, but this one-day dig would give us extra credit and help us to pass a difficult course.

"Will one of you two scholars in the backseat jump out and lock the gate, please?" called the teacher after driving through. Travis and I were somewhat more dedicated students than the others, but his use of the word elicited general laughter.

"Right," called Plumley. He jumped out, closed the gate, wrapped the chain, and snapped the lock shut, then hustled back to the car, while all the passengers chanted, "Leave him! Leave him!" Mr. Avila allowed the car to roll forward slowly.

"Fuck you guys!" Travis laughed as he scrambled back into the seat—me trying halfheartedly to push him out. This was an all-male outing—only a week after the season's final football game—and we were full of vinegar, but Travis quickly remembered the teacher's presence and called, "Oops! Sorry, Mr. Avila. I didn't mean you."

The driver nodded, suppressing a grin.

Three other ballplayers—Jess, Bob, and Jimbo—sat in the seat just ahead of us, and Soto whispered, "You screwed up, *cabrón*, cussin'."

"Eat shit," Travis hissed back.

We drove another mile or two into sparse, dry woods, with large granite outcroppings all around us, our road just two tire tracks in dry grass. Finally, Mr. Avila stopped the station wagon next to a granite monolith. "Come on," he instructed, "I want to show you boys something."

We piled out and followed him to the far side of the stone, and he pointed at some faded, rust-colored slashes.

While they were clearly human-made, I couldn't tell what they were supposed to be.

"Can you see it?" Avila asked. "That's an antelope. That's a deer. The other one, the big one, we think is Old Man, a kind of half-human, half-god."

I did see them, and I felt eerie.

"Looks like some little kid's paintin'," Soto snorted.

"Hell, yeah," agreed Travis, winking in my direction.

"Someone painted that maybe a thousand years ago, maybe even more. There were people right here just like we are, who lived and died and wanted all the things we want. And they left this . . . this *message* for us."

"I wonder if they fucked mud," Travis murmured into my ear.

"What's that, Plumley?" asked the instructor.

"I wonder how come they got *antelope* on there?" Plumley, always a quick thinker, improvised.

"Because this area, or the Valley down where we live and where these people spent part of the year, was full of them until white people got here and slaughtered them all. I think the last wild pronghorn was killed about thirty or forty years ago."

"Pronghorn?" Bob asked.

"Pronghorn antelope," the teacher explained. "Not a true antelope, but close enough."

"Antelope around here?" Travis said. "No shit?" Then he quickly added, "Oops! Sorry, Mr. Avila."

The teacher chuckled, "I suppose some Yokuts were foulmouthed, too, Plumley. They were just people like us."

Not one to give up, as soon as the teacher turned his attention elsewhere, Travis again whispered into my ear, "Yeah, but did they fuck mud?"

The actual dig was a small site outlined with stakes and strings. Within that oblong block, other strings had been staked to create a grid of small squares. After instructions, several of us were assigned squares, issued trowels, spoons, and brushes, and we began to excavate carefully under the gaze of the teacher. Travis and Jess were unenthusiastically sifting dirt through a wire screen—"We're too dick-fingered to dig," Travis smirked.

Acne-faced Jimbo immediately exposed a shining black arrowhead and handed it to the teacher. Mr. Avila brushed it carefully, then said, "Excellent, James."

"Excellent, James," whispered Jess.

"Eat shit," hissed Jimbo.

"What's that, James?"

"Nothin', Mr. Avila."

A few minutes later, a sharp edge emerged from the soil I was examining, so I delicately probed, then dug around it with my spoon, brushing dirt free, probing and digging a bit more, then brushing once again.

"Oh," gasped Mr. Avila, "that looks special, Upton. Careful. *Careful.*"

Beginning to sweat, I cautiously continued my minor excavation until at last I lifted from the earth a triangular-shaped wedge of pottery about the size of my hand. I handed it to the teacher.

As he examined it, he announced in a loud voice, "I'll tell all you boys something: These people, the Southern Hill Yokuts, were almost the only pottery makers in this entire region of the state, and Upton here's actually found a shard. This is rare."

Plumley and Soto, standing behind Avila, flipped me off. I winked at them so they wouldn't know I, too, was impressed by this discovery.

The instructor continued examining it, then jolted. "My God, look at this!" he said, and he carefully handed it back to me. There, on the inside edge of the brown shard, was the distinct imprint of two extended fingers in something like a narrow V shape. "Someone had to have done that on purpose, probably a woman, judging by the size of the prints, a woman who's been dead maybe a thousand years."

I held the piece and looked at the prints, and something churned within me. Another human being had made that mark, placed her fingers on this clay in just that way, and now she had reached across a thousand years to me. I placed my own large fingers crudely decorated with the letters "L" and "O" over the mark left by hers. Although I dared not let it show, I cared about who this artist was and what she'd been; that moved me the way a special song might.

When Mr. Avila once more took the piece of pottery, I remained there, gazing at the small square of soil that had unveiled its secret to me. As soon as the teacher returned to his car to place the shard in a box filled with cotton, Travis slid up to me.

"You know what they made the pots out of? *Mud.*" He poked me and laughed.

30

Ten days after Mom moved in with us, Ted Nakamura sounds exasper-
ated as we speak on the telephone: "She *still* hasn't stabilized?" He pauses,
sighs, then continues: "Well, let's try giving her five milligrams of Haldol
tonight, plus two chloral hydrates, and stop the Prozac."

"Okay." What else can I say?

"I'm sorry we haven't been able to get a better handle on this, Leroy,
but with someone her age and possible organic brain damage—I'm convinced she's had occult strokes—on top of the mental problems . . . well,
it might be necessary to hospitalize her if we're going to get a handle on
her problems . . . just till we stabilize her. Maybe a skilled nursing facility . . . ," he adds.

The thought chills me. In my family, we have always taken care of our
own. No one has ever been abandoned to a nursing home. "I don't think
we'd ever send her to a *home*."

"Well, I hope you never have to, but remember, paranoid depression
is a real illness, like cancer, and a *terrible* one. I'm not just thinking of
you and your family when I suggest hospitalization—your mother *is*
suffering, Leroy. I'm trying to relieve it, but a hospital or a nursing facility may be the only place we can accomplish that."

I know that Dr. Nakamura has dealt with this problem before and that he's correct, yet my belly still says *no nursing home.* Before I can frame a response, the psychiatrist adds, "And don't think her disease isn't contagious. She might pull all of you into the sump where she's stranded right now. You've still got kids at home, right?"

"Yeah." I'm troubled by the suggestion that I might be allowing guilt to stand in the way of good medicine.

"Keep an open mind. You don't want your family suffering because of some principle or precedent. This condition is real. Those other concerns are abstract."

I know that stress is already taking its toll on both my wife and me, so I impulsively say, "Let me change the subject for a minute. I've got an old buddy down in Bakersfield who's still agonizing over his wife's past. I mean he literally loses sleep over it, and he's been married nearly twenty-five years."

"Is this the pal your mother told me about?"

That surprises me. "My mother?"

"She said you have a friend . . . Soto, did she say? . . . in Bakersfield who's having big problems."

I'm baffled by what Mom does and doesn't know, but I jump on that convenient guise. "Yeah."

"Well, if he'll listen, urge him to find help. That's not just obsessive behavior, it's sick . . . possibly indicative of something deeply wrong in him, not her. He has to confront his problem and get past it because, as one of my old profs used to say, 'that way lies madness.' It really does. No one can retrieve or change the past; they have to let it go. If they can't, they need help. I can recommend a therapist down there."

"Thanks. I'll let him know," I say, uncomfortable at having my suspicions about myself confirmed.

After hanging up, I walk into the family room, where Mom sits before a TV tray. All the pleasantness of just a few nights earlier is gone. Her jaw juts angrily; her eyes are wide and askew. I think about what Ted Nakamura has just told me . . . about my mother, about myself. I know they're linked, because until Mom fell ill and began insisting that Suzie was some other man's daughter, I thought I had put the old, dirty memories behind me. Now I can't get them out of my mind.

"Good morning, Mom," I say.

"Good? Huh!" she grunts. "Nobody took *you* from your home. Nobody steals *your* things. I don't even have my own kitchen."

Refusing to take the bait, I ask, "How's breakfast?" Yvonne has prepared scrambled eggs, toast, jelly, and tea, which Mom has half finished.

"Oh, all right, I guess. Who's the cook at this place?"

"Yvonne."

"Is this a hotel? Whose place is this?"

"Ours—mine and Yvonne's."

She turns to face me. "Sure, everything's 'mine and Yvonne's' now, isn't it? My electric blanket's gone. She'd like to take my rings, too, wouldn't she? Well, I'm canceling all my checks, *mister*. And I'm calling the police. Some people forced me to take a *shower* yesterday. I *hate* that shower bit."

"That was us."

"Naked as a jaybird," she growls.

My bowels are churning. "Okay, Mom. Enjoy your breakfast."

Yvonne and I now have to disconnect the telephones at night as part of our grandma routine because she has indeed tried to call the police. We also have begun leaving a snack on the kitchen counter, blocking all outside doors, removing knobs from the stove, and securing all sharp instruments.

I look up and see my wife leading my shuffling father up the hall from his room. A large grin splits his face. "Hi, Pop," I call.

"I'll take him, babe," I offer, and she kisses my cheek as I grasp my dad's hands, but her face droops.

"You want one, too, Pop?" she asks, and he grins as she gives him a loud smack.

I lead my dad to his chair, place a dish towel on his lap, then pull the card table close and bring him a bowl of cereal, a dull knife, and a banana. He seems to enjoy cutting his fruit each morning—carefully assembling his remaining coordination.

While he works intently at that chore, my mother eyes him. "Who's that?" she demands.

"That's Pop," I answer.

"Earl? What's happened to him?"

"He's had some strokes."

"He *has*?" Her tone tells me I am lying.

My father notices her. "How you?" he says.

"Call the police, Earl," she growls. After a moment, her face suddenly changes, softens, and she moans, "I feel *so* weak. I can't feed myself. *Please* help me, Leroy."

"You're doing fine."

I open the newspaper and begin reading the sports section. On the television's screen, an odd little man in a tight suit and bow tie cavorts with a marionette. The telephone rings, so I pick it up, hoping that I won't hear Jess Soto's voice on the other end. "Good morning, darling. Are you on your second cup of coffee yet?" It's Marge Chilton.

"Still struggling through my first one," I confess. "What's up, Marge?" She's never before called so early.

"I ran into Yvonne at the drugstore yesterday and she told me about your mother. She—Yvonne, that is—is at the ragged edge, my friend. She broke down trying to tell me how tense things are. And since you *so* want my opinion, I think you should realize that you may have to decide soon which woman you're going to keep in that house."

Marge is my favorite colleague precisely because she is forthright and perceptive. This insight, however, doesn't charm me. "You think I don't know that?"

"Yes, I think you don't. I think it really hasn't sunk in that you *could* lose the best gal you'll ever know because of some notion of duty."

Marge is, as usual, correct: I really haven't considered that my marriage might be deeply damaged by this family tension. How would I feel if the situation were reversed? Yvonne shows me only her brave face. "Maybe you're right," I admit.

"Listen, Roy, I'm not trying to be a bossy old cow. I've been through a similar situation too, with my own mother fifteen years ago. She suffered from an intractable depression. I finally faced the fact that nothing we could do could ever make her better, and she was sucking all the happiness out of Bob and the kids and me. It was the most difficult thing I've ever done—I'm an only child, like you—but I placed her in a nursing home. Ironically, it not only helped us, but it helped her. She got constant attention and responded as well as she could.

"So don't close your mind, darling, or you might lose a lot more than you're bargaining for. That's the end of my recorded inspirational message for today. Take care, and give your wife a break—take her to lunch, you tightwad."

"Yes, ma'am."

Just as I hang up, my mother's incensed voice startles me: "Don't you think that's about enough of *that* bit, Leroy?"

"Enough of what?"

"That *ignoring* me bit," she hisses.

"I was on the telephone, Mom, not ignoring you. I'm not an entertainer, I'm an exhausted middle-aged man who needs a little time to himself," I say frankly but to no effect.

A moment later she moans, "*Please* feed me . . . I'm *so* weak."

"Mom, come on, I don't need this."

"You feed Earl sometimes."

"When he can't help himself."

"I used to feed you, he didn't. He was a *terrible* father."

"Not so terrible." This conversation is a whirlpool.

"That drinking bit," she adds. "You feed him, not me."

"Sometimes," I sigh.

"Your kids stay out too late. That Yvonne, I *know* things about her."

"Fine." I walk out onto the deck and take several deep breaths, then sit at the glass-topped table out there. Behind me, I hear my mother's voice, like an alarm, calling my name. I ignore her, although I can't unclench my jaw. I am coming to dread even entering my own house because I'll have to face Mom.

A few minutes later, Yvonne joins me. She has showered and dressed and is, save for her tense face, as pretty as youth.

"Where are the boys?" I ask.

"Hiding in their rooms. They won't come out when your mother's in the family room."

"Great."

"Can you blame them?"

"Why do you think I'm out here?"

"The same reason I was in our room. We've got to do something about this, hon'," she urges.

"We'll keep experimenting with her medication till she's under control. Dr. Nakamura thinks he can find the proper balance . . . he's confident."

Yvonne, however, isn't. "I sure hope he's right. I'm going to pick up our turkey and fixings for Thanksgiving. Be back in a couple of hours." She doesn't sound very thankful.

In fact, the turmoil in our lives has led me to forget the impending holiday, so I briefly contemplate Suzie's return, then other Thanksgivings, with my folks when the kids were small—Pop and me sharing drinks, Mom complaining about that as she busied herself with the turkey, tolerating Yvonne's assistance. Aunts and uncles had often been with us in the early years, even Yvonne's parents once before they died. Those were good, good times.

I reenter the house in a more pleasant mood and, as brightly as possible, call, "Finished? Let me take those dishes." I clear Mom's tray.

"Now what do I do?" she asks.

"Anything you'd like."

"I don't want to do anything."

"Fine," I respond. This is not a new question or answer. I've heard it most mornings.

"There's nothing to do," she complains.

"There's as much as there ever was, Mom. What'd you ever do? Watch TV?"

"You just want to make me do what *you* want, but I want to do what *I* want. Huh! You can't make me do anything, *mister*." Her eyes are again wide and unfocused.

"Do what you'd like."

"I don't *have* to. I'm canceling all my checks, *mister*."

Alberta has agreed to come in on weekends—Trish's days off—so my wife and I have some relief. She should arrive anytime now, none too soon for me. I stand in the kitchen and gaze at my mother and father sitting in the adjoining room. He slops milk and cereal and banana all over himself and seems to relish his meal. She sits stonily, her lips working, her jaw jutting. Suddenly Mom sighs and moans, "What a life," then puts her head in her hands and drops it to the tray in front of her.

We have been told to keep her awake during the day if at all possible, but this scene of abject suffering always blunts my will. Besides, when these sudden swoons of depression strike, they offer blessed respite from her irate non sequiturs.

"What a life," she moans once more.

I walk to her and rub her back, but say nothing. I have nothing to say. The frequent verbal attacks from her are, I know, cries for help. She is miserable and nothing we do seems to help. Maybe Ted Nakamura is right. Maybe a hospital can help her in ways that we cannot.

I see Mitch peeking in the deck door. Finally, he enters, lightly punching his grandfather's shoulder as he passes—"Hi, Grandpa"—but tiptoeing past his moaning grandmother as though she is a sleeping grizzly.

"Hey, slugger," I say.

"Hi, Pop," he smiles and I hear the echo of my own voice thirty years ago speaking to my father.

"Come here, pal," I order.

He glances at me, then obeys, and I hug him.

"What's that for?" he says with a smile.

"For looking like your mother."

"Yeah, I'm lucky," he agrees. He is, in many ways, a slightly shorter, slightly thicker version of me, but with her coloring. He turns and grabs a box of cold cereal from a shelf, then asks idly, "Hey, Pop, what would you say if I told you I was gay?"

My breath catches. What did Emily Dickinson write, ". . . and zero at the bone"? After a couple of seconds, I reply, "If you *are* telling me, I'll say that's the least of my worries."

"Good. It's the least of mine too because I'm not, but Professor Spielman told all of us to tell our folks that we were and see what they say, then write a short paper on it."

To say I'm relieved would be an understatement. Leave it to Marty Spielman. I guess I'm a long way from liberated, but I'm finding life tough enough as a supposedly empowered straight white male, a swim. I don't wish any complications on my kids.

31

Another week into this experiment and Mom is still not sleeping through the night. She does manage to doze during the day, however, no matter how we try to prevent it. Dr. Nakamura and I have many tense conversations, and he continues urging that we keep her awake, especially during the afternoon, but when we try to do so, the confrontations are so angry—"Shove it up your butt!" she shrieked just yesterday when we tried to awaken her for lunch—that we relent and allow her to nap. His juggling of her medication seems to have done little good.

I had never heard my mother curse until this deterioration began, and I remain stunned by her language. Lately Yvonne and I have begun locking our bedroom door at night, but I still lie there on the edge of sleep awaiting her cries—"Leroy! Leroy! Leroy!"—and my own eyes increasingly resemble mud puddles. I honestly used to believe I could find a way to accomplish anything—anything except change the past, anyway—but this situation proves I can't.

In my increasingly uneasy, shallow sleep, I seem to confuse dreams with other experiences. One early morning, I seem to have remembered or dreamed that years ago, shortly after Suzie was born and her parentage was in doubt—in my mind, at least—I had nevertheless admitted to myself how much I needed Yvonne and had been baffled; how could I feel that way? I'm not baffled anymore, just grateful.

I can't seem to accomplish much school work at home anymore—Mom refuses to let Trish or Alberta help her when I'm there, calling me for every need—so I'm spending more and more time at the college, grading papers and reading there, drinking coffee in the faculty lounge instead of on my own deck or in my family room. I'm particularly missing my naps with Yvonne, since she also stays late at her office now, and I sure don't blame her. Those naps have always provided times when we could speak privately, when we could comfort one another, when we could cuddle, and it is no longer clear to me where the talk and the comfort and the sex demarcate—it's all one loving experience. I need those naps now more than ever, and I suspect she does too.

This afternoon in my office, I have groggily been trying to evaluate a set of book reports, but I finally carry them to the faculty lounge where I can gulp some coffee, maybe even wake up. The room is empty when I enter, so I draw a cupful from the urn, then flop onto the couch, eyes burning with fatigue. Only a moment seems to pass when I hear: "Jeez, I heard about a guy that just *winked* at fifty and he couldn't cut it anymore—dozing off in the middle of the day. It must be hell to get old."

I grin, open my eyes, but do not look up because I know it's Marty Spielman.

"I thought coaches were supposed to be tough," he chides.

"I'm all linebacker . . ."

"Oh, *spare* me."

"Are you two foulmouths at it again?" demands Marge Chilton, who entered the lounge after Marty, and who isn't exactly noted for her sanitized vocabulary. "You look like hell, Roy."

"I don't feel nearly that good, Chilton."

"Your mom?"

"You guessed it."

"And Yvonne?"

"I'm thinking about what we discussed."

"You'd best do more than think about it. You've got a gem there, my friend," she observes with arched eyebrows. "I don't know how a big dumb jock like you lucked out."

"Charm," Marty suggests.

"That's must be it," Marge smiles. "Both of you, charming."

When I walk into the house that afternoon, Yvonne looks up from the dinette table where she is doing paperwork. "Your mother slapped Trish today," she says.

"She *what*?" I feel as though I've just been slapped. "Shit!"

Yvonne turns to gaze out the window. "Trish gave us her notice. She can't deal with your mother. And Alberta says she's had enough too. She won't be available either."

"That's *great*."

Yvonne turns and her face is grave. "Roy, honey," she says, "I know you hate to even think about it, but we really *can't* keep your mom here unless she's stable. The few good days don't make up for all the bad ones. We have to find a hospital and see if she can be helped."

Yvonne pauses, and her chin begins quivering as she adds, "She called me a whore in front of Jared and Mitch when I tried to keep her awake this afternoon." Tears spill from her eyes. "I don't know, maybe I deserve that, but the boys don't. Jared told her, and I quote, 'Shut the fuck up.' I think he was ready to hit her, but Mitch stopped him. It was a terrible scene, and I can't take any more like it. I can't stay here if . . ."

I walk behind her, put my arms around her, and nuzzle her neck. "I'm so sorry, babe. I haven't wanted to face this."

Her shoulders begin to lurch. "It's no fun being hated, Roy. I've tried to help her. I really have . . ."

"I know you have, babe. No one could've tried harder. I'm the one who's sorry. I guess I didn't want to know things had gone so far. We'll have her examined at a hospital. There's really nothing else we *can* do. There's no penicillin I know of for this."

Just then, as though on cue, Mom's voice shrieks through the house—"Leroy! Leroy!"—and my throat tightens. I have come to dread that call, but I proceed down the hall, where I encounter my father clutching one of the grab bars. He is engulfed by the heavy aroma of feces. "You okay, Pop?"

"How you?" he rumbles.

"Leroy! Leroy!"

"I'm coming, Mom, but I've got to help Pop first." I unclasp his strong hands and move him toward the bathroom.

"Leeeroy! Leeeroy! *Leeeroy!*" Her voice grows more desperate.

I am about to shout back at her in frustration, when Yvonne touches my arm. "I'll take care of your dad. You see what your mother wants."

She is sitting up in bed, gazing at a blank wall. As I stand in the doorway, she cries once more, a raw, animal sound: "*Leeeroy! Leeeroy! Leeeroy!*"

"Mom, I'm right here."

Her eyes scan wildly and do not stop when they pass me. "I want *Leroy Clark Upton*! I've got to get out of this place. I've got to get to the bank and get some money from those girls so I can cook dinner. I need a hundred bucks."

"It's me, Mom. It's Leroy." I walk to her and rub her back, but she recoils.

"Hah!" she grunts and her eyes narrow.

"I'm going to take you to the doctor tomorrow."

"What place is this? Who owns this hotel? Who's in charge?"

"This is our house—our family's."

"Where's the bathroom? Isn't there a bathroom in this hotel?" she demands.

"At the end of the hall," I reply.

Her tone is suddenly desperate: "Ohhh, I've gotta go. I'm *going* right now! Ohhh, I'm *going.*"

"Come on." I help her to her feet and lead her to the bathroom—she seems amazed at what is happening. Once there, I change the diaper we have begun insisting that she wear. She says only, "Isn't *this* a fine thing. This never happened when I was home, *mister.*" She pokes the top of my head with a forefinger.

The poor, poor woman, I think, as I return her to her bedroom. "I want my checkbook, *mister,*" she growls as I ease her into a rocking chair and turn on her radio. Then I walk directly into the den and telephone Ted Nakamura. His exchange answers.

A few minutes later he returns my call. "What's up, Leroy?"

"I think it's time to see if the hospital can stabilize my mother. We aren't succeeding here. She's much worse."

"Yeah," he replies immediately, "I've expected this call and I think it's the right decision. I'll call Ross Hospital and arrange for you to bring her in tomorrow morning. We can get a handle on things there, I'm sure, and I'll order a brain scan—I really suspect she may be suffering from some organic brain damage. Just pack a small bag for her. We'll look at her for a few days, see if we can move her back toward balanced behavior. If we can't, I'll tell you candidly, and we'll decide where to go from there."

That remark triggers a response in me. "I understand that she needs to go to the hospital, but I really don't like the idea of a nursing home, Ted."

"I know you don't but, first of all, I wouldn't recommend sending her or anyone else to a *home,* in that sense. I might recommend sending someone to a convalescent hospital—a *hospital,* a skilled nursing facility—where she can be cared for properly, but not a *home* where she'd just be hidden away.

"I told you before, Leroy, mental illness *is* an illness like cancer or AIDS and it *is* contagious. I'll bet you'll see that if you just look at your family. I'll bet they're all on edge. Let's get her to Ross and work her up, find out exactly what we're dealing with. *Don't feel guilty.* It could very well be that we can stabilize her and she'll be able to come home. See you tomorrow, anytime in the morning. You know where the hospital is, don't you?"

"Just down the road from the college?"

"Right."

"Okay, we'll be there in the morning."

Yvonne has walked outside, and I sense that she needs to be alone for a while, so I put a Merle Haggard CD on the stereo. With "Working Man's Blues" filling the room, I occupy myself by correcting a set of quizzes, doing *something,* but I can't concentrate. Yvonne's words echo through me, "I can't stay here if . . ."

When night comes, sleep is ragged for me; I lie awake waiting for my mother's inevitable call. At 1:35 it comes: "Leeeroy! Leeeroy! Leeeroy!"

"No one's feeding me around this hotel," she complains. "I haven't eaten for *days*."

I fetch her crackers, cheese, and milk, but when I put them in front of her, she asks, "Do you know Leroy Upton?"

"I am Leroy Upton, Mom."

"What do I do now?"

"Try eating the snack I just brought you."

"Oh, is *that* what you call it? Don't you have any hamburgers? Someone stole my chocolates."

"Fine," I reply, too exhausted to spar. When I was small, my mother occasionally read me a sentimental poem called "Little Boy Blue," and her eyes would always dampen, her voice would always catch; even then I sensed that she gazed at me, her lone child, with wonder and sadness. I now understand what she saw: I would one day grow up and cease to be her little boy blue. Now I am gazing at her with wonder and sadness and my own eyes dampen; poor Mom . . . she has become my little boy blue.

An hour later I'm back in bed, teeth grinding, unable to sleep. The idea of taking my mother to a hospital is upsetting, since in my family's history that is where folks go to die; we've never had much luck bringing people home; hospitalization has always been the final act. The threat of a nursing home, however, is even worse. But the stark possibility of losing my wife is the worst threat of all, so I'll take my mother tomorrow. Thanksgiving is only a few days away, but I don't feel very thankful.

32

"Where're we going, *mister*?" Mom demands as I help her into the car.

I sense that she may bolt momentarily. "To the doctor, Mom," I reply, urging her inside, too cowardly to mention the word "hospital."

Finally she is perched on the seat, and I manage to connect her seat belt and close the door. "The *doctor*," she hisses.

For a moment I hesitate: I am taking my mother to a mental hospital, a nuthouse, and momentarily I am uncertain whether I am doing it for her good or for my convenience. I quickly thrust away my doubt, then fasten my own seat belt.

When at last we're on the road, driving a back road over a shoulder of Mount Tamalpais, I remark on the woods through which we pass, "It's pretty through here, isn't it?" No answer.

A few minutes later, we pass College of Marin, and I say, "That's where I teach, Mom. My office is in that building there." Deep within myself, I am hoping for some sign that this trip is unnecessary.

She does not look up. Instead, she sighs, "What a life," and leans forward, her head in her hands on the dashboard.

Studying her as we wait for a stoplight to turn green, I am once more convinced that this trip is necessary. The light switches and I turn left. A couple of blocks later, I swing the car into a small parking lot shaded by redwoods.

My mother's head jerks up. She says nothing.

"I'll run inside and find out where we go," I tell her, and I do indeed run, my nerves on edge. A young receptionist listens to my uncomfortable question, then smiles: "Just take your mother up that elevator to the third floor. The nurses are expecting her. Once she's settled, please stop by here so I can have you sign a few papers."

"Thanks."

Returning, I see Mom through the car's rear window. Her head's in her hands again. It's my turn to sigh. After a deep breath, I open her door, release her seat belt, and help her out. She does not speak as we enter the building and proceed to the elevator. Waiting for its door to open, my mother finally asks, "Who is this doctor, anyway?"

"Dr. Nakamura, Mom."

"Huh! That *Oriental* doctor."

We enter the elevator.

"They don't give me good medicine up here. My stomach is so nervous because these doctors up here aren't any good. My old doctor was *wonderful*."

I nod, too tense to talk. The door slides open and we're in a sunny central foyer—a skylighted recreation area surrounded by rooms and offices. The far wall is all glass and a deck extends from it out over a wooded creek. I see no hospital gowns or nurses' uniforms, but a number of casually dressed women lounge on couches in the sunlight, talking. To our left I notice an unobtrusive nurses' station and a tall, mustached young man looks up, smiles, and calls, "Hello. Is that Marie?" He wears designer jeans, a plaid sport shirt, and Birkenstocks. A stethoscope is draped around his neck.

Mother says in a weak, high-pitched voice, "Yes."

"Hi. I'm Gino." He takes her hand in both of his and shakes it. "I'll be your nurse."

"You will?" Her voice remains faint. "A man nurse?"

"I'm afraid so," he grins. Then the nurse turns toward me, extending his hand. "Dr. Upton?"

I nod and shake hands with him, saying, "Leroy Upton."

"Ted Nakamura asked me to work with your mother. Does she have a bag?"

"Yes," I reply. "I'll bring it up."

"Do that. I'll show Marie her room, then introduce her to the other guests."

I turn to leave, and my mother's eyes stop me. "Leroy?" she pleads and reaches for me.

My heart swoops.

"Go ahead, Dr. Upton," urges Gino gently. Then he turns toward my mother: "He'll be right back, Marie."

At the car, I open the trunk and extract Mom's small suitcase. Again I sigh. This shouldn't be so difficult, but it is. I feel something like tears welling—I am abandoning my mother, and she would never have abandoned me—but I squint hard, slam the trunk even harder, then carry her suitcase upstairs.

When I return, Mom is sitting at a coffee table with two other older women, and she is saying softly, "I have three grandchildren and my son's a professor." She appears nervous, perhaps frightened, but not agitated.

Gino is back at the nurses' station filling out a form and, before I can approach him, a tall, stylish young woman—strikingly beautiful—passes me, immediately capturing my attention. "You'll remember to have my prescription transferred to the drugstore in San Anselmo?" she asks Gino.

The nurse looks up. "I sure will, Megan. You take care, now."

"You too, Gino," she smiles, then walks to the elevator.

He turns toward me and smiles. "Your mother seems to be settling in already. We'll have some trouble when she decides she needs to sleep today, but we'll deal with it." He stops, seeming to read my expression, then adds, "Don't feel guilty, Dr. Upton. You're doing the right thing, and your mother's one of the lucky ones. Just think of all the poor sick people out on the streets. Here she'll receive the best of care. Most of these patients are with us voluntarily—they want our help."

He pauses and smiles. "We really *will* help your mother. Why don't you just say a quick good-bye—don't drag it out—and we'll stay in touch.

Here"—he hands me a card—"this is the number in the unit. You can call anytime, for whatever reason. There's always a nurse at the station."

I walk into the sunlit lounge where my mother sits and interrupt, "Excuse me. I've got to go now, Mom. I'll be back later."

"Oh"—one hand flees to her mouth—"you're leaving?" She turns to the other ladies and says in a distressed tone, "My son's leaving."

They both nod at me, then one asks my mother, "So then what did the doctor say to you, Marie?"

They are once more conversing as I depart, although Mom's eyes follow me.

My visit to the office downstairs is brief, then I'm out in my car again, certain that I've done the right thing. My palms are so slick with sweat that I must wipe them several times before I can drive away.

That night Ted Nakamura calls and says, "How in the world did you folks deal with her? She's delusional, highly combative, fully incontinent, and her sleep is reversed. You must've had your hands full. She cusses pretty well, too," he chuckles, adding, "I wouldn't've guessed that. Anyway, I've got her scheduled for an MRI tomorrow, and we're doing some other tests. You stay away for a couple of days, Leroy, and let us get this under control, then we'll see where we go from here.

"And *don't* worry about her," he adds. "She'll be fine here, and I'll bet you and your family can use some rest."

"What's the prognosis?" I have been unable to thrust her from my mind all day.

"She won't be worse and she'll probably be better. I'll be able to tell you a lot more after we get test results back. We're already working on her sleep cycle—and she isn't enjoying it much."

"I'll bet."

"But, listen, *don't worry*. At this point *your* feelings are more fragile than hers. She'll be better. How *much* better is what we're going to determine."

But I do worry.

33

"I ever tell you boys 'bout the time I went to buy me my first car right after I got this job in the oil patch?" Hubby Hobbs didn't wait for my dad or me to answer. "Wellsir, I'uz a-lookin' at a Ford in this lot whenever a fancy-pants prune-picker salesman he come up and says, 'You thinkin' 'bout that car?'

"Me, I said, 'Naw, I'm a-thinkin' about pussy. I'm a-gonna buy this here car to help get me some.' Shut him right up."

We were still laughing when he added, "Kept me a old ass-jack piller in the backseat of that car that I used to prop gals up on whenever I give 'em a hot-beef injection."

"Ya don't say," my father winked at me. "Ol' Hobbs here he likes to discuss important subjects at dinnertime, world affairs and that philosophy deal, right, Hubby?"

"It's a nat'ral fact," continued the large gray-haired man, undaunted. "I give that piller so much business that it got real high, see. You know what I done? Wellsir, I cut that sucker up for catfish bait and caught lots of whoppers with it."

My dad was laughing by then. "I believe that story's the biggest whopper, Hubby."

"Nosir! It's a nat'ral fact, see. You believe me, don't ya, hoss?"

"Oh yeah," I chuckled.

Pop shook his head and winked at me again.

"I met this little Mex'can gal right after I bought that car, see. She had the best damn smile I ever seen—teeth glistened like cat shit in the moonlight. Anyways, I nailed her in the parkin' lot after work one evenin', dog-style and ever' other which way. You boys ever heard a anything like that? What the hell *was* her name . . . ?"

"You know," I smiled, "I'll bet if women knew how guys talk about 'em, they'd never put out."

"They'd put out," my father replied unambiguously. Then he grinned and said, "To hear this ol' boy talk, you'd never know he's been married to Momma for over forty years, that he's got nine kids, all of 'em about growed and one a damn doctor . . ."

"Linda Jean," smiled Mr. Hobbs, "that's my doctor's name."

"What if some ol' boy was talkin' about Linda Jean the way you talk about gals?" Pop was still grinning.

"I'd knock a fuckin' lung outta him is what," Hubby chuckled, then he added, "You know, a long time ago whenever I was a-courtin' Momma, this cousin of mine named Willie, he slid up to me one day and he said, 'I heard somethin' about that pretty gal you been a-seein'. Since blood's thicker'n water, I figured I'd pass it on.'

"Wellsir, I just looked at ol' Willie and said, 'And come's thicker'n blood, you sorry fucker. You say anything a-tall bad about her, and I'll *cancel* your useless ass. Cancel it!' He could tell I wasn't shittin'. I never hear no more from him."

"Well, I guess ol' Willie wasn't entirely dumb," chuckled my dad. "He saved his own life."

I had to laugh at that. I'd graduated from high school only the week before, and Pop had snagged a summer vacation replacement job for me in the oil fields. As a result, I was living one of my childhood dreams, joining my dad there in the oil patch. We three were eating lunch that day in the shade of a metal shed. "What they got you doin' today, boy?" my father asked.

"I'm helpin' Ed Johnson load chemicals."

"That's a good deal, stout young buck like you, hoss," grinned Hubby. "Me, it'd kill my back nowadays, see."

Pop gestured toward me and said, "Don't let this old fart fool you. He won lots of strength contests back in the old days. You'd bet him a dollar and he'd pick up one a them full drums in a minute. Remember that time you and ol' Fat Norton raced across the yard carryin' fifty-five-gallon drums? I never seen nothin' like it, Leroy. Ol' Fat he's about half stout hisself, but Hubby give him a good lickin'."

Mr. Hobbs grinned. "Yeah, I won me twenty bucks cash money on that deal, and I had to give it right to the damn chiropractor afterwards. That sumbitch sawbones, he turns out to be the real winner, see."

I was pushing weights several evenings a week then at a gym in Bakersfield, building myself up in the hope I would one day play college football, and I was considered strong by my lifting partners. Still, the idea that anyone could even walk across the yard carrying a full fifty-five-gallon drum astonished me.

My father added, "Hubby he's a mountain man, two hundred fifty pounds a dynamite with a two-inch fuse."

"Yeah, but I got me a pile-drivin' ass, see," Hobbs interjected. "Hey, did I ever tell you about the time I nailed them two sisters after a dance back in Oklahoma, hoss? Wellsir, . . ."

Lunch finished, I wandered toward the pipe rack with my father and he asked me one more time, "You sure you don't wanta go on to school next fall? You always done real good in school. You might could go up to the junior college for a while, play a little more football."

"I will, Pop. I'll go, but not right away. I just don't know what I want to be or where I want to go." I didn't intend to let him down, but I was telling the truth: I had received no offers of football scholarships despite making all-league, but maybe that was best, because I also knew I wasn't ready for college. I had no focus . . . except maybe football. Then I grinned. "Mom asked me again this mornin' when I'm gonna find a nice girl and settle down."

He shook his head. "I know there's still a lotta pressure on you kids to marry young like folks done whenever we'uz kids, but this ol' world's a different place now. You don't have to marry no gal to get a little honey . . . or a lot, for that matter. A fella he needs a education nowadays if he don't wanta sweat all his damn life in this oil patch like me and Hubby."

I nodded, then said, "I'm thinkin' about volunteerin' for the draft, Pop, servin' a couple years in the army, then comin' out and goin' to college. I'd have some GI Bill money to help with expenses."

My father stopped walking. "In the service, huh. Well, that might could be a good deal too, but don't let school get away from you. That's the thang, don't let no chancet get away or you'll be sorry the rest of your damn life. Just take my word on it."

That afternoon, as usual, I arrived home from work earlier than my father. I showered and donned thongs, shorts, and a T-shirt, preparing to drive to the gym to meet Travis and Jess. We'd pump iron before a warm evening of cruising. I heard the front door slam. Relaxed, feeling comfortable, I emerged from my room and called, "Hi, Pop."

No answer, so I wandered into the kitchen and found my parents seated at the table in the small dining nook. My father looked up at me with an expression I'd never before seen on his face. "Hubby died this afternoon," he said.

"He *what?* Mr. Hobbs *died?* What . . . what happened?"

"He just dropped dead out on the job. We was pullin' casin' out at Ten Section, and he dropped like a damn stone. Soon as I seen him, I knew he'd had it."

I sat down, stunned. How could anybody so alive . . . ? I really liked Mr. Hobbs, who had always treated me like a son. "Jesus," I gasped, fighting not to reveal the emotions suddenly surging within me.

"He always said he wanted to go out screwin'," my father observed quietly.

"*Earl!*" snapped my mother.

"Earl *what?*" he snapped back. His face looked ominous.

"The boy."

"He ain't a goddamned boy, he's a man. Take a look at him. And he damn sure knows what screwin' is."

"Well, if he does it's thanks to you!"

34

The next afternoon, Yvonne smiles and urges, "Go ahead and call, hon'. I can see you're aching to."

"Yeah, I am." I have been holding a book but staring at the telephone.

I take the card Gino gave me from my wallet, then dial the number and a woman's voice answers: "Adult Women's Unit. Kimberly speaking."

"This is Leroy Upton. Is Gino available?"

"He's off today—he'll be back tomorrow. How may I help you?"

"I wonder how my mother, Marie Upton, is doing."

Kimberly chuckles softly. "Oh, Marie? She's doing fine, but she's a *character*. Are you her son?"

"Yes."

"She talks about you all the time. We've been keeping her out of bed today, and we kept her in bed last night. That's real hard for her, but generally, she's been pleasant and funny."

"Funny?" It is an unlikely description.

"Yes. She cusses a blue streak when we won't let her do what she wants, then, when we tell her that she cussed, she denies it. 'I don't know those kinds of words,' she says, 'but my husband does.' But we'll get ahead of that sleep cycle problem before long—it usually only takes a few days. We deal with this all the time.

"Oh," she says, "here's Dr. Nakamura."

"Hello, Leroy. Well, we've got some test results. Your mom has organic brain damage, just as we suspected. There are areas of dead cells—infarcts—that've probably led to some dementia; it's not severe, but it is something to consider. I don't think it triggers or has triggered the mental illness, but it does give us more information about what's going on. She's a little anemic and has a slight mineral imbalance. She hasn't tolerated some of the medication we've given her in the past—the Prozac, especially—maybe because of her earlier addiction to tranquilizers. Anyway, we've got a medication, Mellaril, that I think will work. Unfortunately, it normally takes a couple of weeks to become fully effective, but it seems like the right stuff."

He's going too fast for me. "Wait, Ted, did you say 'Mellowril'?"

"It's Mellaril, M-E-L-L-A-R-I-L, a brand name. Actually, it's thioridazine, an anticholinergic . . ."

"I just barely got a C in chemistry, Ted. What's it do?"

"It's for psychotic anxiety—strong stuff—and we have to be very careful using it with older folks, but I'm giving her a tiny dosage. I think we'll see a leveling of her paranoia. I'll adjust her dosage until it's right."

"And her prognosis?" I ask.

"Well, right now she requires skilled nursing care—she has real trouble dressing herself; she's incontinent; she doesn't consistently remember where things and even places are . . . or where she is, for that matter. She can still be delusional and combative. But it's inconsistent: a moment after an outburst she can carry on a complex conversation. She's a *very* intelligent woman, Leroy, as I'm sure you know. Anyway, I suspect she'll have to spend some time in a skilled nursing facility when we release her—for her sake and yours."

My belly tightens, but I say nothing.

"On the other hand," he continues, "I think we're on our way to getting her back to a normal sleep cycle and that we can control that angry paranoia. The depression? Well, just getting her to take her prescribed medication is bound to help. I don't want to overmedicate her, so beyond that, we'll have to play it by ear. I'm looking at a mild compound like Aventyl right now. We may not be able to completely repair her . . ."

"Meaning what?"

"Meaning that there'll probably always be some depression, some paranoia, but we should be able to mitigate acute episodes. You know," he adds almost as an aside, "if she were younger and stronger, she'd be a good candidate for electro-convulsive therapy, especially since she had such good results the last time, but that's just idle speculation. She's much too fragile now."

"Yeah." I have a knee-jerk aversion to that suggestion too: shock treatments. "Listen, Thanksgiving's coming up. Can she come home for dinner?"

"Sure she *can*. Whether she *should* is another question. Let's play that by ear, too, see how she is. Okay?"

"Yeah." But it isn't really okay.

Later I try to explain everything to Yvonne. "The bottom line is that she's getting better, but he thinks she needs to go to a convalescent hospital—for a while, at least."

My father sits near us at his table. He has, for some reason, had difficulty walking today, even with help, and he lists in his chair.

"Well, you know we've got our hands full as it is, hon'," says my wife. "I hate to have to say it, but if you decide to bring her home, you may have to make an exchange—take your father . . . well, *somewhere*. I'd hate that, Roy. I don't think I could deal with losing Pop."

I can only breathe deeply, then say, "I know." She and my dad have grown closer than I ever imagined possible. But I am thinking, why must we make that choice at all?

Half an hour later, Jim Cox returns my earlier call. "Sorry it took me so long to get back to you, Roy, but it's been one of those days."

"No problem." I describe my dad's symptoms as carefully as I can.

"Well, almost anything could cause his problem, as tenuous as his health is, but it sure sounds like another little stroke, doesn't it?"

"I was afraid you'd say that."

Jim says, "I'll swing by on my way to the hospital after I eat. But, listen, Roy, you know we're fighting a losing battle here. Earl's just coming apart. It's a wonder to me that you and Yvonne can care for him at home."

That observation, on top of what I've already heard from Ted Naka-mura, upsets me. "We'll manage," I croak.

Jim arrives an hour later and, after examining my father, he says sim-ply, "I'm not going to subject Earl to a battery of tests unless you want me to. I'll just tell you I'm 99 percent certain he's had another stroke. And I don't think we can do more for him at the hospital than you're doing here. And here he's with family. The golden years . . ." Jim smiles sadly. "A guy at Rotary was telling me the other day how funny old peo-ple are."

"Yeah, they're a hoot," I reply without smiling.

"That's basically what I said: 'It's a matter of perspective. Wait'll you're in the middle of it.'" Then he adds, "Anyway, it sounds schmaltzy, but the only gold in Earl's years now is you guys, his family."

We all fall silent. What can we say?

Finally, Jim changes the subject. "When will Suzie be home?" he asks.

"Tomorrow," Yvonne replies. "Or at least she'd better be. She's sup-posed to help me with Thanksgiving dinner."

This is likely to be the second Thanksgiving I've ever spent without my mother. The other one occurred when I was serving overseas in the army. I've always known that the day would come when neither of my parents would be with us, but that notion was distant, abstract, unthreat-ening. Now it is becoming real.

Jim is smiling. "You'll probably have Steve over here, too. All he can talk about when he calls—other than needing money, I mean—is that temptress daughter of yours. He's really looking forward to seeing her."

"Reckon I oughta polish up my shotgun?" I ask, straining to lighten my own mood, and Jim laughs.

"I'm sure they'd never do anything we wouldn't have," says the physician.

"Polish that shotgun," my wife advises.

35

Our daughter drives in just as Yvonne and I are heading for bed. She is as usual full of stories and enthusiasms—poor shy little Suzie—so she and her mother drink hot chocolate on the rug in front of the fireplace, giggling and tittering like teens—and both look like kids in that light, two beautiful young women. I am swept by pride and sadness because I know that Yvonne as a girl experienced few of the youthful joys Suzie has been able to take for granted. While our daughter regales us with tales and infectious laughter, I nod off on the sofa.

I awaken when I hear Yvonne saying, "I've got to put this old-timer to bed, honey, before he falls off the couch. He's got to be fresh to help us with the turkey tomorrow."

"Who, me?" I blink. "Just resting my eyes."

"Hey, Pops," says Suzie as she pokes my ribs, "let's wrestle."

"I'm going to wrestle your momma," I yawn.

They both laugh and Suzie says, "I don't think Mom's in much danger tonight."

"Pops?" she asks, her voice suddenly deepening. "Will Grandma be able to eat with us tomorrow?"

"I don't know, honey, but probably not."

"Really? It won't be the same. Let's go to the hospital and take dinner to her, then, the whole gang of us, have dinner there."

As unlikely as that suggestion sounds, I know she is serious. I also know that Pop would be unable to accompany us there. I reply, "I'll see what I can do."

The next morning, I wait until eight, then telephone Ross Hospital. Gino answers. "I didn't talk with Dr. Nakamura, but I'm going to come pick my mother up for Thanksgiving dinner."

"No problem. What time can we expect you?" Gino asks.

"Well, about eleven, I guess." I am astounded that this goes so easily. I had prepared arguments.

"See you then."

Ted Nakamura is at the hospital when I arrive, and he calls me aside before I can greet my mother. "Listen, Leroy, I know it'll be hard, but don't get tempted to keep her home tonight. She's *much* better, but she's a long, long way from well. She can slip back in an instant. It'll be tough, but you've got to be firm if you want us to help her. And *please* bring her back before dark—that's when her demons come out."

"Her *demons*?"

"Her behavior regresses pretty badly at night," he explains, and I nod—how well I know. "Do us all a favor and bring her back early, please."

"Sure," I smile, relieved that this hasn't been a hassle.

No sooner do I load Mom into the car—she seems a little dazed—than she asks, "Why was I at that hospital? How'd I get there?"

"I took you, Mom," I reply as we pull onto the road.

"You *did*? When?"

"Nearly two weeks ago."

"Why?" She sounds baffled.

"You were ill."

"I *was*?"

"You had a breakdown." I can think of no other way to explain what occurred.

"I *did*?"

We ride silently for a couple of miles, then my mother pulls a small, almost parched-looking piece of paper from her purse. "Look what I found stuck in a corner of my bag the other day," she says.

I glance over, and see a note my dad must have written years before. It is all bold capitals, and says simply, MEET HUBBY AT TANK FARM.

"Earl has such a strong hand," Mom remarks.

I can only choke, "Yeah."

Mom enters the house, sees my wife in the kitchen, and calls, "Oh, hello, Yvonne. Can I help you with anything?"

For a moment the three of us stand silently, then Yvonne smiles, walks to Mom and hugs her. "You sure can," she says.

Suzie appears from the family room, calls, "Hi, Grams," and bounces up to her.

"Oh, little Suzie Quzie," Mom coos, and both the boys, standing behind their sister, grin. "Little shy Suzie Quzie. Did 'ou miss Gwandma?"

"How you?" Pop mumbles from his card table.

Dinner that afternoon feels as close to normal as it can, with more food than we need, and plenty of laughter. Pop sits next to Yvonne, who helps him, and he eats enthusiastically and noisily. Mom sits just to my left so I can aid her—"Not too much. Not too much! Ohhh, darn, that's *too* much"—and Suzie is seated next to her. My mother seems unable to resist touching her granddaughter, to resist baby-talking to her, but she eats too and is pleasant—"This dressing is *delicious*, Yvonne."

Mom shows no evidence of incontinence, asking where the bathroom is half a dozen times, and commenting half a dozen times too, "Way down that *long* hall?"

Suzie accompanies us back to Ross Hospital late that afternoon, occupying her grandmother so that I don't have to continue answering her painful question: "But why am I going back to that *hospital*? Why aren't I staying home with my family?"

"Hey, Grams, the doctors aren't through fixing you up yet."

"They *aren't*? What's wrong with me? Why, I feel fine. *Earl's* the one who's sick."

In her ward, several women are seated in the communal area drinking coffee and talking. "Oh, it's Marie. How was your dinner?"

"Oh, fine . . ." Mom's voice is pensive. She turns toward me. "Why did you bring me here? Why can't I stay home with my family?"

My heart sinks, but before I can answer, a young woman wearing slacks and a sweater, with a stethoscope draped around her neck, approaches. "Hello, Marie," she smiles warmly. "Did you have a nice outing?" She takes one of Mom's hands in both of hers.

"You're the one who gave me a shower," Mom spits, her jaw suddenly jutting.

The nurse mouths to me, "Say good-bye," but does not actually utter the words.

I hesitate, and my mother turns and growls, "They give you *showers* here."

"I've gotta go, Mom. Suzie's waiting in the car."

"But why . . . ?"

I kiss her cheek, then quickly turn and depart, walking rapidly as her voice follows me, "My family . . ."

On the drive home, Suzie asks, "So when will Grams be able to come home?"

"I don't know, honey. Soon, I hope."

"Me, too. She's odd, though, isn't she?"

"You could say that."

"I am saying that." She pokes my ribs. "And she's funny, but I can see that it's hard for you to laugh at her."

"Yeah, I suppose." I am unable to escape the sense of what my folks have lost.

She pokes me again. "Hey, Pops, who're you supposed to be, Clint Eastwood? *Yep, you could say that. Yep, I suppose. Yep.*" She giggles and I laugh too. "Learn to laugh at her, Pops, or *you'll* be in the funny farm yourself," she advises, and this time her voice is serious.

A mile farther, stereo country music wafting from the car's radio, my daughter asks, "How do you know when you're in love, Pops?"

It is an unexpected question, so I clear my throat. How *do* you know? What can I say? When you don't want to share your girl with other men? When you've been together for twenty-five years and feel your lives braiding? "I don't know, pumpkin."

"You don't *know?*"

"You thinking about Steve?"

"Ohhh, I *might* be."

"What about that musician you were dating last year at school?"

"He turned out to be a dork."

"Oh." That seems to settle that. "Well, you and Steve've been pals for a long time. That's a good start."

"But what about romance?"

"I don't much believe in romance," I say. She's a grown woman and I speak frankly to her. "To me, that's just a fancy word to cloak sexual attraction, what we used to call the hots, and you can have sex with anyone . . . that's the easy part. People say they make love when they really make lust. To me friendship is the place to start, because you can build on it, and maybe weave your lives into the real thing, what I know love is now."

"Mom always said sex is something special for someone special."

My breath catches for a moment, then I say, "It should be."

"Did you and Mom start as friends?"

"Sort of."

"Sort of? Hey, Pops, you and Mom've been together for what, over twenty-five years? You *must've* done something right."

"Yeah, we have. We've built something fine. But I don't really remember how or even when it all started—me feeling so strongly about her, I mean." What I do recall about events leading to our marriage is more prurient than romantic, more desperate and sad. I remember that I immediately took pride in my role as husband and young father—in the role itself—but I also remember that I somehow assumed that it wouldn't last and that I'd be free to go on with a life Yvonne had so unexpectedly interrupted.

But that didn't happen. Away from our hometown, ghosts dissipated—except in a dark corner of my mind, anyway—and I took pride in the beautiful, personable, and bright young woman who was my wife. Most of my male colleagues, men who knew nothing of her past, envied me. Now I can't even think of my life without Yvonne.

"I really don't know, honey," I say to Suzie, and I really don't.

"You're a *big* help." She pokes me again. "In the movies, the picture gets fuzzy, and the father always offers a philosophic soliloquy to his sweet, innocent daughter—yeah, dat's da ticket, sweet and innocent . . . like *me*." She pauses, flutters her eyelids, presses the back of her hand against her forehead, feigns a swoon, then continues, "But what do *I* get?" Her voice deepens to imitate mine: "*Well, pard', I dunno.*"

"Well, pard'," I say, "I dunno."

36

Suzie marches into the family room the following morning and announces to her mother and me, "You guys get the day off. I'm taking care of Grandpa today, so you two can sneak away, have lunch, do whatever you want."

Yvonne and I exchange surprised smiles, then I say, "I hope you don't think we're going to gracefully refuse your offer."

"You'd better get out of here before I change my mind."

My wife stands and extends both hands toward Suzie, who grasps them, grinning, and they kiss; I'm always amazed at how undisguised females' emotions can be. "Thanks, honey," Yvonne says. "We'll take any break that's offered." She hugs our daughter, then turns toward me. "Come on, old-timer," she calls, "time's a-wastin'."

"I think she just wants to get rid of us so she and Steve can have the run of the house."

"Well," Suzie grins, "that thought *had* crossed my mind. Hey, Mom, where do you keep your naughty nighties? I might want to borrow one."

"I'm staying home and cleaning my shotgun."

"Come on before she changes her mind," Yvonne urges, so I come on.

After a brief discussion, we point our car toward the East Bay, driving through San Rafael, then across the Richmond Bridge. Eventually, I wheel us into Albany, suggesting, "Let's walk down Solano Avenue, sniff around the shops, maybe find a new restaurant."

"Sounds good to me."

When I was taking graduate classes at the university in Berkeley, we had often ventured to that pleasant, nearby neighborhood. It's been a while since we've been back, however.

This serendipitous expedition has us both feeling coltish. I almost miss a green light on San Pablo because I am kissing, really kissing, my wife when it changes. A honk from the car behind alerts me.

"Whew," smiles Yvonne, "let's park."

Eventually we do—but in broad daylight on a busy public street, so satisfaction is postponed but by no means forgotten.

We wander past the same Oriental rug store that was offering a going-out-of-business sale twenty years ago; it's still going out of business. Pegasus Books remains open, as do the junk shops and used-book stores we loved. I price frayed copies of Padre Garces's two-volume *Diary*—too rich for my blood—but a couple of old Plastic Man comic books are affordable. My wife shakes her head over that purchase. Then she discovers a small Hispanic rug from New Mexico—she's certain it was woven by one of the Trujillos in Chimayó. It costs considerably more than my Plastic Man comics, but we buy it anyway.

Near the end of our trek, we find a Korean restaurant with its door open. It's only eleven-thirty, but one sniff of the aromas sweeping out that door and I'm famished. My wife orders velvet chicken while I have Korean barbecue—each of us sharing with the other—and both dishes are delicious. We talk mostly about our kids, about how proud we are of the way they get along and about how they're developing—even Jared, if school can be discounted; he helps with his grandparents and complains little. We've really been lucky—three healthy tads—and we know it. Life's taken us a long way together.

After lunch I'm ready for a nap, but I settle for a strong cup of coffee at a nearby sidewalk cafe. The passing crowd seems older but not much different than two decades before, when we first came here: a few aging hippies, still wearing the same blouses and love beads; two young, mustached white men in Panama hats holding hands as they wander by; a harried Asian woman trying to corral three small children while she pushes a stroller containing an infant. Yvonne grins and raises her eyebrows; she has firsthand experience in chasing after older kids while another squirms in a stroller.

Almost everyone appears more affluent than I remember, and many wear clothes with labels exposed. A black man and a white woman, about the same vintage as us, take a nearby table and immediately launch a loud discussion about where "Jomo"—their son?—should attend college. "New College will help him sharpen his social consciousness," the woman points out, but the man is unmoved. "San Francisco State was good enough for us, baby. It's good enough for him."

"What about Saint Mary's? It's good," the woman counters.

This time the man grins. "Baby, no way we can afford a private college. Besides, State's good," he points out, and one of his large hands covers hers.

Yvonne and I pay our bill and depart, a little embarrassed at having shared another couple's world, if only for a moment.

I'm not ready to let this day go, so I suggest that we drive to Berkeley, park north of campus and wander over to Telegraph Avenue. We find a parking place surprisingly close to the university, then stroll hand in hand past all the new buildings and old groves, past monuments to the football teams of 1898 and 1899 and log benches donated in 1921 by a lumber company.

"I really love this old campus," I smile.

Yvonne squeezes my hand. "I do too."

Most male students seem to be wearing bright, baggy shorts, T-shirts, and baseball caps, bills in back. Girls in skintight bicycling shorts arrest my attention more than once. "Eyes forward," chides my wife. "Just looking," I assure her. We do pass an occasional cluster of torn blue jeans, dyed black hair, and multiple earrings, and a few muscular young men in bright warm-up suits, but those baggy shorts and skintights seem to dominate undergrad styles. Far more of the students we see are Asian than when I began work on my graduate degrees way back when.

As we pass the library, a memory makes me laugh. "Did I ever tell you that when I started college classes, I couldn't figure out why they kept calling the teachers 'doctor'? I figured they had to be physicians, and I couldn't understand why a sawbones might be teaching freshman composition at a college unless maybe it was a hobby."

"You told me, but it's a great story."

"And now, like the old boy says, 'I are one.'"

"You are one," she smiles.

"Listen, let's go to the bookstore, then hustle home for a nap."

"Let's," Yvonne agrees.

We walk under Sather Gate, past kiosks, and she says, "Look," pointing at a poster that says: "Kick the Curse! STOP THE SEXIST TYRANNY OF MENSTRUATION! If Amazons Didn't Have to Menstruate, Why Should You? Free Lecture Noon Saturday in the Women's Center."

"Well, we stopped it three times," my wife says, poking me.

We wander to the Student Union, then downstairs to the store's entry. In the rush of student traffic two middle-aged men emerge from the door and one stops. "Leroy?" he says. "Leroy Upton?"

Now I stop. He doesn't look familiar. "Yeah," I smile.

"Don't you recognize me? Armand Richard. Jeez, it's been at least twenty-five years."

He had been a year behind me at Bakersfield High. "Damn, Armand, how are you?" We shake hands.

"This is Bob Bevins—he's from Bakersfield too."

I don't recall the name, but Bob and I shake hands and I say, "Do you know my wife, Yvonne?"

"Just vaguely," Armand smiles and shakes hands with Yvonne.

Bob does the same thing, then he says to her cordially, "Didn't you use to go out with Floyd Henshaw?"

My wife's face goes ashen for an instant, then she smiles again, "Yes."

My heart has turned to coal.

"God, I haven't seen old Floyd forever," grins Armand. "Have you, Leroy?"

"I saw him at Travis Plumley's place a couple of months ago. He's doing fine. What're you up to now, Armand?" I quickly change the subject.

"I'm a job-placement specialist in San Jose. Bobby here teaches at the University of North Carolina. He's out for a visit, so I just brought him up to see a good school and to blow his money."

"I've got three daughters at home," Bob chuckles, "and they'll love these 'Go Bears' sweatshirts."

Armand pokes his shoulder. "Ahhh, he bought that stuff for himself."

We finally exchange addresses and bid one another good-bye, then Yvonne and I enter the bookstore, but the day is no longer as bright for me.

Later, driving silently back toward Mill Valley, my mind wanders from one repugnant memory to the next. Why the hell did I have to go to the bookstore? By the time I actually entered it, I could no longer remember what I'd wanted to buy. But I remembered Floyd. And Suzie.

As we cross the bridge, my wife asks, "What's wrong, hon'?"

"Oh," I lie, "it's just a little headache." It's really a big heartache.

After we enter our house, I notice a note in Suzie's handwriting next to the telephone: "Dr. Nakamura—please call back."

37

"I swear, your mother she drives me nuts sometimes," Pop said once we were in the car. "Hell, you'd think there's a damn war on or somethin', the way she's carryin' on."

Mom had been too upset to drive to the draft board's office, where I'd be picked up for the trip that would lead to two years in the army. "It's probably just because I'm an only child that she worries so much."

"I s'pose so. But when you let your feelin's go like she does, you just give yourself away to other folks. I surely hope you never turn thata-way."

I had no intention of losing control of my feelings. "Why didn't you two ever have any more kids?"

Pop appeared to search one large hand for a moment, then he explained, "Well, you heard that story before. You was born sideways—a breach birth, they called it—and they had to use these instrument deals to help you get out, and that tore her up real bad. She couldn't have no more babies."

"Oh." I'd never heard it put quite that way before.

He parked the car across the street from the draft board's office, where a group of young men were assembling next to a collection of cheap suitcases. I would soon add a stained cardboard wonder with worn metal edges to that assortment. My father opened the trunk, pulled it out, then glanced at me strangely for an instant, a look like the one in a photo of him holding me when I was an infant. He blinked, then said, "Don't worry, I'm not fixin' to embarrass you by walkin' over there and makin' a fuss or nothin'."

Across the way, two tearful mothers were clinging to abashed sons while other young men averted their eyes or smirked.

He put the small case down in front of me and extended his large right hand. I took it, and as we shook he cleared his throat and said, "You just do your damndest, give a good jump for your money, and you'll do real good. I know you to be a good worker, Leroy, and I seen you play enough football to know you can take care of yourself. Ol' Hubby he used to say you was the best young buck he ever worked with."

It had been just a few months since Pop had been one of Mr. Hobbs's pallbearers. Neither of us said anything, but we exchanged a look we would show no one else. This was about as intimate an exchange as I'd ever had with my father, and I could only nod my head and say, "I appreciate that, Pop."

"In this life you're a-gonna lose damn near ever'thing—your friends, your folks, whatever. If you just expect life to be tough, you damn sure won't be disappointed, and you might appreciate the good stuff more."

"Yes, sir."

I was about the same size as he was, and I had his sharp features. We stood there, looking like two versions of the same man: him in boots, western-cut jeans, and a western shirt, me in stylish slacks, a bright sport shirt, and loafers.

"I never been in the service, so I ain't got no advice for you 'cept to work hard. I sure hope you'll think about that college deal while you're in. I'd be real proud for you to go whenever you get discharged. Me and your momma we could help you out with it some."

"I know, Pop. I'll go when I get out."

"Your ol' high school coach I seen him downtown the other day, and he told me he still thinks you might could get a football scholarship, and you always got real good grades."

"I'll see if I can't play some while I'm in the army." I felt like we'd been standing there a long, long time, so I picked up the suitcase and smiled. "I'd better be getting over there."

"Yeah." He extended that hand one more time and I took it. If he'd moved toward me I'd have hugged him, but he didn't.

Once I crossed the street, I recognized a few other inductees—all a little older than me, since I had volunteered for the draft, while most of them had simply run out of luck. One, a former all-city halfback named Ron Hall, hailed me. He had just graduated from Fresno State, where he'd been a grid standout, but now he had two years to give to Uncle Sam. "I sure hope I get a chance to play a little ball," he confided. "A guy at State said life's really easy for ballplayers."

"I hope I can, too."

"You'll make it if they let you. Listen, Upton, I've been wondering why you didn't go on to college and play?"

I didn't want to admit that I'd received no scholarship offers, but what I told him was true. "I just didn't feel ready. I don't know what I want to do with my life, and I guess I don't want to waste the chance."

The bus that carried us to the induction center in Fresno stopped at every small town along the way to fetch a few reluctant recruits in each, mostly farm boys looking awkward and a little awed. Many were Mexicans and Blacks . . . with a few Filipinos, too. I noticed everybody who wasn't obviously white. At Pixley, a thick Hispanic with the unfinished features I identified with mental retardation lumbered aboard. I poked Hall, saying, "Look at that guy."

The bus driver called, "Are you Chavez?"

There was a long pause.

"Hey! Are you Chavez?"

Finally, another Latino draftee called, *"Como se llama, hombre?"*

The big kid looked up, then mumbled, *"Me llamo Rodrigo Chavez."*

"He's Chavez, *pinche.* Close that fuckin' door. It's gettin' hot in here."

When we finally arrived at the induction center, a corporal handed us small bottles, told us to pee in them, and sent us behind a partition. "Don't any of you boys drink that," he called. "I got first dibs on it." We all laughed.

"Hey, guy," said the Chicano who had answered for Chavez, "gimme your bottle. I drunk a buncha beers this mornin'. I'll piss for all of us." Hall and I grinned and handed him ours too.

An hour later, our physical examinations completed, we stood on a yellow line taped to the floor while a slim black sergeant explained, "After I takes roll, you mens will be sworn in. You will be billeted in Fresno tonight and shipped to Fort Ord tomorrow after we process the mens from up north. You will be issued meal tickets and Specialist Four Lynch here will escort you to the Hotel Sequoia. Any questions?"

There were none, so he looked at his clipboard and called, "Amundsen?"

"Here."

"Here, who?"

"Here, Sergeant!"

"That's better."

"Banducci?"

"Here, Sergeant!"

"Brown?"

"Here, sir!"

"Sir! I'm not no mothahfuckin' officer, nigger. I works for my money! Here, Sergeant!"

"Here, Sergeant!"

"Chavez?"

After a moment, the sergeant repeated himself: "Chavez? Where the fuck is Chavez?"

"*No está aquí*," I heard one Mexican kid whisper to another.

"What's that? No talkin' that Mes'can shit in the ranks."

"He ain't here, Sergeant," said the guy who'd peed in all the bottles.

"Not here? Where the fuck is the mothahfuckah?"

Some rapid Spanish was exchanged, then the urinater said, "He never been to Fresno before, so he went for a walk. He's what you call it retarded, so"—the urinater shrugged—"maybe he got lost."

"Sheee-it. Went for a mothahfuckin' walk. Who watchin' him, *Specialist Four Lynch?* I done foretold you the mothahfuckah a re-tard." The black man's voice elevated an octave when he said, "Now you done *lost* the mothahfuckin' mothahfuckah!"

"Welcome to the army," Hall whispered to me.

38

"Well, what I was afraid of happened," Ted tells me. "Your mother was a terror last night."

Because we took her home? Maybe it's because we didn't allow her to stay home with her family? But I say only, "Yes."

"Being home for Thanksgiving seems to have triggered something . . . I can't tell you exactly what. But I'm coming to suspect that something awful must've happened to her in the night at some point in her life. She becomes another person after dark, and the visit home caused some real agitation. The psych techs tell me she really kept them busy."

He hesitates, then says, "Listen, Leroy, I'd be grateful if you'd hold off on visiting for a few days, okay?"

"Okay." I don't like blame being assigned to a happy family gathering, but I swallow my resentment.

The psychiatrist seems to anticipate my objection. "I'm sure she had a great time, and that it was good for her, but she's just very fragile, and these things are so complex. I hope you all had a good time. Marie's asleep now, by the way—she was up most of the night."

What can I say? "Keep me posted, Ted."

"No problem, and check with Gino if you have any questions. Are you okay? Do you need a tranquilizer?"

"I'm okay."

By the following week, my father seems to return to the state he was in before his last small stroke, except that he can no longer walk without help, so he spends much time in a newly rented wheelchair and, to the delight of Trish, who's back on duty now that Mom's gone, a hospital bed. His appetite remains robust, and he smiles as easily as ever.

I find smiling more difficult, however, and so does Yvonne. Poor Pop is being shredded one piece at a time.

Another week passes with my mother remaining at Ross Hospital. Unspoken tension hangs between Yvonne and me, for it is clear that my wife does not intend to have both of my parents with us at once—at least not in their present conditions.

I do not visit the hospital during that long interval, though I speak on the telephone with Dr. Nakamura or a nurse daily, and I learn that it has proved more difficult to reverse Mom's sleep cycle again than they'd anticipated. Otherwise, she is much improved, beginning to participate in group-therapy sessions and being at least somewhat social with other patients.

I speak with her over the telephone, too, and our good conversations lead me to think that perhaps, just perhaps, we *might* be able to bring her home, give her another try.

On the eleventh day after her Thanksgiving visit, Ted calls. "Leroy, your mother is ready to be released. Our health resource specialist, Cynthia, has found a bed for her at Crestview Convalescent Hospital right in Mill Valley—not far from where you live. If you're in agreement, I'll have her transferred."

My heart suddenly drops. Yvonne is at work and I need to consult with her, to ask if I might possibly avoid condemning my mother to a nursing home. We have plenty of room, I rationalize, and surely we could retain Alberta to work with her now, in her improved condition. I have rehearsed these arguments but have not tested them. To bring Mom home today, on my own, might cost me more in the long run than I'm willing to pay.

"Leroy? Are you there?"

"Yeah."

"Listen, you're not stuck with Crestview. You can move her anywhere anytime—tomorrow . . . today, if you want—but I recommend this facility. I do a good deal of work there, and I can vouch for the care. So does Jim Cox. Ask him. It's really a nice place—as nice as it can be, anyway."

In the family room, Trish is feeding Pop. The television is on and a game-show host is bellowing, "Ten *thousand* dollars! Ten *thousand* dollars!"

Finally, I sigh, "It's not where, Ted, it's what. I just can't feel right about a nursing home . . ."

"Don't do this to yourself, Leroy, or *you're* going to end up in Ross Hospital. Everyone seems to have created some stereotype about these places and the kind of people who leave family members there. Your mother is *sick*. This is a *hospital*. She needs the care offered there. Don't torture yourself."

"Okay. Okay. Can I pick her up and take her over?"

"Don't," he advises. "This'll be easier if an ambulance takes her and you meet her there at . . . say . . . three. If you drive her over, that car of yours is going to want to veer home, and she's not *ready* for home yet. This is a *necessary* next therapeutic step, not a life sentence for her. Besides"—his tone lightens—"this is all on Medicare. No charge."

"Right," I say. "No charge."

I wander outside, breathing deeply, sucking air into my lungs as I contemplate this turn of events—my mother in a nursing home. The greenery surrounding our house—the rhododendrons, the azaleas, the ferns, the towering firs and the oaks—all drips condensed mist, and the soil emits a fecund aroma. But I feel barren, as though something in me is parching.

"Hey, Roy!" I hear from up the hill. A moment later Bill Brody slouches down the path. "How're you doing?"

"Okay."

"You sound low. Your dad . . . ?"

"My mother this time."

He grasps one of my arms and says, "I'm real sorry to hear that. I know what you must be going through."

I find myself wondering if he really can know, then I remember his brother. "How's Ben doing?"

"Not good. I've been flying back to New York on weekends to see him, that's why I haven't been around. His cancer's metastasized. Can you believe it? Forty-four years old, with his own law firm, three kids, a great wife, and he's a dead man." Bill is smiling but gazing at the ground, and his eyes are damp.

This time I grasp his arm. "Life's a fucking piece of work, Bill," I say.

He smiles sadly. "You can say that again."

I meet the ambulance at Crestview and am immediately ushered into an office, where I read and sign several sets of papers. Then an older man introduces himself as "The Ombudsman"—you can hear the capital letters when he says it—and he delivers a lengthy, more than a little officious explanation of his duties and of my mother's rights. When he finishes, the chief nurse introduces herself, shows me my mother's chart, and discusses each drug with me—a virtual repeat of my earlier conversation with Ted Nakamura. But I sense the importance of this ritual, so I endure it.

Finally, I'm able to visit my mother's large room and find her asleep in one of four beds; two others are also occupied. A young black woman, whose identity tag reads "Carolina—Licensed Vocational Nurse," enters the room, so I ask if my mother is supposed to be sleeping during the day.

"I haven't read her chart yet," she replies, "but usually when people first move in we let 'em rest. A move can be real hard for older folks. You want me to wake her up?"

"No, it's okay. Aren't there any private rooms here? Cost is no object."

"No, but there're some doubles. These folks don't need to be alone, Mr. Upton. It make 'em real sad."

I hadn't thought of that, but had instead been responding to my own sense of wanting the best for my mother, so I say no more about it. "I've got to leave now, anyway," I tell the LVN. This timing is bad for me because I have an emergency hiring-committee meeting to attend at the college, and it doesn't promise to be over until after eight. "One of my sons'll be in to visit Mom later."

"Visit anytime. There's no special hours, but we start gettin' folks ready for bed about eight."

"Okay. I'll pass the word to the family."

That evening, after the meeting but before returning home for dinner, I am seated next to Mom in her room when, from the hall, I hear "Uhhhn! Uhhhn! Uhhhn!"—inchoate, desperate howls. "That's one I told you about," says my mother. "How long do I have to stay in *this* hospital? When can I come home?"

"When the doctor says you're ready," I explain, but it feels to me as though she's imprisoned here, with no say, no freedom. I can understand her frustration because I share it.

"The *doctor* . . ." she says and looks away.

Across the room two old women lie as though comatose, both folded like pale, broken statues, their mouths agape. They do not move. I cannot see any evidence that they are breathing.

Crestview is busy at this hour. I hear television sets and voices echoing in the halls. Many visitors are seated in lounges or rooms, some pushing wheelchaired residents through the hallways, and many of the visitors seem to be old friends. I jump when from the hall I hear a woman's high-pitched voice screeching: "Helllllp! Helllllp!"

"That's another one," my mother says.

I try to change the subject. "The kids are all going to be home next week."

For a moment she smiles. "Oh, I wish *I* could go home."

"Just keep improving and you can, Mom."

"Improving from what? Why am I here? I don't feel sick . . ."

How do I tell her? "You had a breakdown, Mom. I told you about it before."

"I *did*? I don't remember that."

"Don't you remember Thanksgiving dinner?"

"When? Was I there?"

"Do you remember when you were living with Yvonne and me?"

"*Living* with you? Of course not. I have my own home. Where's Earl?"

"He lives with us, Mom."

"Earl does?" Her eyes wander, then she says, "Oh, that's right. We did move away, didn't we?"

"Yes."

"And Jared has purple hair, doesn't he? I hate that bit."

I am shocked by her sudden recollection. "He did. Now he's peroxided it. He's a blond."

"Oh, I like that better. And Mitch, my handyman?"

Another pleasant shock. Her memory seems suddenly to have turned on. "He's fine. Wasn't he in to see you earlier?"

"Mitchell? I . . . don't . . . know," she appears suddenly dazed, then she smiles. "He was such a chubby baby. How old is he now?"

"Twenty."

One hand flutters to Mom's face. "He *is*. My, how fast he's grown up. He was the *cutest* baby."

"Yes, he was."

"Won't Suzie graduate soon?"

Once more I am stunned. My mother has not been able to keep the kids and their activities straight for a long, long time.

"And Yvonne?" Mom adds. "Is she still working?"

"Yep."

"I don't see how those young gals like her do it—work, raise a family. Huh?" She shakes her head in wonder.

My wife is purposely staying away from Mom's room, not wanting to once again trigger that angry paranoia. Despite her pleasant behavior at Thanksgiving, everyone in the family is a little frightened about how Grandma might act. I, however, find this place—not my mother—frightening.

As if on cue, those howls erupt once more, "Uhhhn! Uhhhn! Uhhhn!" A moment later the high-pitched "Helllllp!" echoes through the hall. A new voice chimes in, "When's lunch? I'm hungry." Across the room, those two women remain motionless, mouths gaping like caverns. A large young man in jeans and a plaid shirt nods as he passes the doorway while pushing an equally large old man in a wheelchair.

"Did you ever see that movie, *The Snake Pit*?" Mom asks. "The one that starred Olivia de Havilland?"

"No."

"No, you were too little. Well, that's what this place is like, a snake pit."

I can only nod. A few weeks before, she had sat snarling in our house, largely unaware of her surroundings. Now she seems cogent and sensitive, but she is here in this . . . madhouse.

"And they've got me tied up like a prisoner." I notice then that a restraining belt holds her in her wheelchair.

"I . . . I guess that's so you won't fall . . . break a hip," I explain, but I'm not certain I believe it. Mom is sharper than she's been in months, maybe years, calmer; yet *now* is she restrained.

"I can't even go to the bathroom without asking for help."

"I'll take care of that."

Once more the hall echoes with those deep howls: "Uhhhn! Uhhhn! Uhhhn!"

"There're people at dinner who just shake and shake, and the nurses have to feed them. There's some others that cuss. It's awful, all those *old* people. I'm going to eat in my room."

"That's good."

"Hellllp! Hellllp!" The cries are desperate, as though rape or murder is occurring in the hall.

"You know what's wrong with her?" Mom asks.

I shake my head.

Mom's own face has hardened. "I *hate* it here. I can't even think straight, all these crazy people."

Gutted by guilt, I say nothing. Since Dr. Nakamura seems to be sold on this convalescent hospital, I determine to telephone Jim Cox as soon as I return home. Surely Mom need not stay in a place like this.

A youthful nurse's aide dips into the room, calling, "How are you, sweetie?" Her dulcet tone troubles me.

"I'm fine, except for this belt."

"Oh, do you have to potty?"

Mom's face tightens. "No, I don't have to *potty*."

The aide seems to miss her tone. "All right, sweetie, just ring me if you do."

A moment later, I notice Carolina walking past in the hall, so I hail her.

"Somethin' wrong, Mr. Upton?" she asks.

"No, nothing serious. I just wonder about that restraining belt. Why does my mother have to wear that? It forces her to stay in a wheelchair, so she doesn't get any exercise at all. That can't be good for her."

"Well, when she came in, you know, we didn't know how steady she was. Those belts are mostly to keep patients from fallin', not to control 'em. If you stop at the office they'll give you a form to sign that makes the family responsible if she do fall, and she won't have to wear one anymore."

"That's all there is to it? Thanks." At least I can do that much for her, and I do.

As soon as I return home, I dial Dr. Cox. "Jim, I just visited my mom. She's much better."

"Yes, she is. I saw her too."

"How much longer do you think she'll need to stay in the nursing home?"

He hesitates, then answers, "Feeling guilty?"

"Guilty as hell."

He sighs. "Well, her mental condition is chronic, Roy. It can be controlled but not cured. It will ebb and flow. I take it that it's ebbing right now."

"She's better than I can remember her in . . . well, maybe years, but she's stuck there."

"Okay, but she might be worse tomorrow."

Tomorrow? I find that hard to accept. "Jim, that place really is awful."

"It's the best in the county."

He hasn't understood me. "I don't mean the care, I mean the patients."

"At least sixty percent of the people in convalescent hospitals are there for dementia—that's a hard fact. They *are* distressing places because they're where we—our society—put people we can't deal with anymore."

"Or won't."

"Or won't," he agrees.

"So what can I do?"

"You can do anything you want, Roy, but do you think Yvonne and the kids can or should put up with the constant threat of her regressing and exploding at home? There's no easy answer to this one, buddy."

"Isn't there some other level of care?"

"We could try a residential-care facility, but let me talk to Ted Nakamura. And listen, don't get too sanguine, and don't, don't, don't let guilt get to you. You're doing the right thing."

"Yeah," I say with no conviction. Across the family room, my father, what remains of him, sits in profile. He is vigorously chewing something, and a stalactite of drool hangs from his chin.

39

At 5:36 A.M. Yvonne calls me: "Roy, hon', can you give your dad a shower? He's had an accident." Yvonne guides Pop, his eyes dull as clods, into our bathroom, and I see that his bottom is smeared with feces.

"Sure, I'll give Pop a hand. Got any coffee?" I ask my wife.

"Oh, I might." She kisses me.

While my father stands in the steamy shower, I sip from the mug my wife has handed me. Yesterday morning, she and I had coupled in this very shower, now my father stands mutely while I take the nozzle from its holder and spray his butt, soap him once more, then rinse again, carefully flushing his nooks and crannies.

After completing our ritual cleansing of the family jewels and his rear, then washing the bits of feces that collect on the shower's floor into the drain, I say, "You ready to get out, Pop?"

His voice rumbles, barely understandable, ". . . my license."

He creeps slowly as a stalking cat, gripping the towel rack, although I ask him not to. "Pop, you'll pull that off the wall if you slip. It won't hold you. Hold on to the grab bar." He ignores me, and I know that his grip is so tight that the struggle to force him to release the towel rack might pull it from the wall, so I sigh and vigorously dry him with a large towel.

Finally I hand him the towel and say, "Dry your own balls, Pop. I'm not touching those nasty devils." This line, as always, elicits a grin . . . a slow one this day.

I diaper him, pull a clean T-shirt and undershorts on him, then help him climb into a sweatshirt, sweatpants, and slippers. Finally I plop him into his wheelchair and push him out to the family room,where a steaming bowl of oatmeal and a cup of coffee await him.

"Thanks, hon'," Yvonne says after I've seated my father and helped him get started on his breakfast.

She is sitting at the dining room table, exploring the multiple-listings book and not looking at me, but I stare at her, irrationally disturbed at the implication of her "thanks." It sounds as though she considers my help exceptional. Fatigued indignation begins swelling in my throat, but I turn away: I'm too stressed. There is nothing to be gained by expressing this, but there is plenty to be lost.

Instead I veer back into the hall and walk to our bedroom, undress, then slip into the shower, where hot water on the back of my neck melts the remaining cobwebs as well as my indignation: Ahhhhhh.

A tap on the shower's opaque glass door startles me, and I turn to see the olive image of Yvonne's body through the steamed barrier. "Want company?" she asks.

"Sure do," I say, immediately aroused.

She slides into the spray and we slide into one another, mouths together while the water pulses over us.

Long after she has departed, I lie on our bed clothed only in shorts, mind wandering. What had Suzie said? Grandma always talks about all her boyfriends and how she got stuck with Grandpa. And I had laughingly replied that she said that because she really hadn't had many. Then Suzie, too sharp for my good, had observed, "Mom must've had plenty, then, because she never talks about any"—and I had felt that familiar stab.

"No," Yvonne had smiled, "Dad was not my first boyfriend, and yes, that is ancient history. My life started after Dad and I were married."

That was all she'd said, and as Suzie seemed to consider it, her expression became the one that always reminds me of Floyd. In truth, Yvonne rarely discusses with the kids anything that occurred before we were married, and I suspect that I'm responsible for that. Several years ago, there was a terrible exchange between us . . .

"You asked me before why I didn't like you kissing my navel," Yvonne had said. "Remember, you made fun of me?"

I did remember, because by then I had kissed her everywhere else, but when my mouth strayed to her belly button, no matter how excited she was, she'd always jerked away, saying, "No!"

I merely nodded.

My wife's face had suddenly gone bloodless, and she'd continued staring fixedly ahead. "I can't stand for you to do that because that's where my father used to kiss me from the time I was . . . I don't know . . . *little,* maybe three, before he'd pull my pants down and do . . . other . . . things."

"Your *father*?" I'd gasped. That was beyond my imagining.

"Sometimes with my mother when I got older," she'd choked. "The only love I ever got from them was sexual. I thought that's all there was. I guess I thought the only thing about me people might love was . . . just . . . sex. And it became addictive."

"Jesus!" I'd replied, still stunned.

"But, Roy, then I met you, and you loved me and let me love myself."

I came at that moment as close to weeping as I had since childhood, and not for myself.

Later, though, after I'd composed myself enough to say something, Yvonne began a sentence, "When I was dating . . ." but I cut her off: "I don't want to hear about who you *dated.*" "Dating" her always meant screwing as far as I was concerned.

She stopped, frozen for a second, her eyes searching me, then she merely nodded and walked away. I was immediately sorry that I'd failed her trust, but I couldn't bring myself to explain why I didn't want to hear about her dates. It was just too painful.

Although I believed her to have been true to me, I had for years felt somehow violated by her earlier promiscuity; somehow my own was different. I had also taken perverse pride in my own marital fidelity, and had been, or at least seemed to be, the only member of my department at the college during the so-called sexual revolution who didn't line up coeds for favors. Not that opportunities hadn't persistently presented themselves. But I'd always resisted.

Then, just months before our fifteenth wedding anniversary, I took a group of students to Eugene, Oregon, for a recreational society conference. Normally Yvonne would have accompanied me, but this time she remained home because both Suzie and Mitch had social events scheduled. No big thing—I'd escorted troops of students solo more than once before.

But this time was different. There was a reentry student, an English woman my age, on the trip. Her name was Beryl, and she was the divorced mother of three teenagers. As sometimes happens, we gravitated to one another while the younger students frolicked, enjoying their antics, and I used her as my shield from randy coeds. But one evening we consumed too much stout at a pub after seeing a folk music performance on the University of Oregon campus, and I ended up in bed with her. It was that simple—me feeling at the time as though I had to finish what I had allowed to begin. Basically, that's what I recall about that first evening with Beryl, that and the unique conformities of her body: fuller that Yvonne's, hairier, less expert but desperately responsive.

And I remember in exquisite, haunting detail the four nights that followed. I remember the shower I took with Beryl one day, the lather and the easy familiarity we had so suddenly developed. Most of all, I remember the bus trip back to Marin and my certain knowledge that I had to discontinue what I had allowed to begin—or give in to it completely. For me there could be no middle ground.

But it didn't end that easily. There were tears and telephone calls and desperate pleas from Beryl, who said she loved me, that she would be content with just being my mistress. By then I was so consumed by guilt that I was inured to her appeals. She left the area to finish college in Long Beach, and I'm not certain that I didn't drive her away. No matter, for I had failed the wife, the friend, the lover who trusted me, although as far as I know, Yvonne never learned of my indiscretion. And, of course, I had failed the vulnerable Beryl too. And I had certainly failed myself.

Those failures ended my illusions of . . . what? . . . virtue, I guess. Yvonne need not know what I did—her life has been difficult enough without me adding that—but I know, and I am not a forgiving man. I have not slipped again, and I doubt that I ever will now that I have acknowledged my own weakness.

The bedroom door opens: Yvonne, fresh and sweet in jeans and a sweatshirt. She is carrying a mug of coffee. "Hey, lover," she grins, "still in bed? Want some coffee?"

Still broiling, I don't like that word "lover" that she often gasps while having sex, that I'm sure she has gasped to others, but I say only, "Sure."

When she hands it to me, I wring myself free from painful thoughts, grasp her wrist, and pull her close. We're here together and that, not those memories, is reality. So are my feelings: "I love you, babe," I say, then I gently kiss each of her eyelids. "Without you I wouldn't be alive." My voice catches as I say it.

Slowly she places her coffee mug on the table next to the bed, then leans over and kisses me on the mouth, the chin, the neck. "Oh, Roy," she murmurs, "I love you so much. I love where we've come together, our family, our lives. You're my breath."

I *know* she hasn't said that to anyone else.

That evening I have just enterd the house, returning from my evening walk with Pepper—so crippled that he can no longer lift his leg—when the telephone rings. I unhook my old dog's leash, then pick up the receiver. "Hello, this is Upton's," I say.

"Roy, that bitch's tryin' to take everything I got." The voice is scratchy and weak, but I know it's Jess Soto.

40

"Dad, can I, like, talk to you?" asks Jared, too subdued.

I immediately wonder what disaster he'll report. "Sure." His mother is in the kitchen preparing a lunch for him to take to school.

"Well . . . ah . . . " His voice is uncharacteristically tentative, so I know something important is up. "There's this girl named Maya at school and she's, like, . . . ah . . . pregnant, and her parents've, like, thrown her out. Could she, like, stay with us till she, like, gets it together?" His eyes scan the floor near my feet.

I've come to understanding that the number of "likes" he inserts in a sentence is often a gauge to the seriousness of the subject: Am I about to become a grandfather? "First of all, yeah. We won't leave her on the street. Things're tight around here right now, but we can squeeze her in."

"Huh?"

" 'Yes' is the answer."

"*Radical!*"

I put my hand on one of his shoulders. "What's she going to do about her pregnancy, have the baby?"

"I don't know, like, maybe get an abortion."

"Who's the father?"

He gets my drift. "I didn't do it, Dad," he quickly replies. "I mean, like, I balled her and stuff, but so did Tracy and lotsa other dudes. Now they, like, *ignore* her."

I look at the boy in front of me, half his head shaved, the other half bleached blond, his clothes a stylish pastiche of rips and patches, two earrings in one ear, the very cipher of peer pressure: he'd smear himself with feces and walk on his hands if his friends suggested it. Yet he's not without principles. I'm genuinely proud of him. He's certainly more responsible with Maya than I was all those years ago with Cherry and some others.

"We'll help her," I say. "She can certainly eat and sleep here, but you've got to leave her alone while she's here. You get my meaning—*no screwing*, pal, no taking advantage."

His face jolts at my language. For a moment he cannot reply, then he does. "Hey, Dad, I, like ..."

"And if you're not using condoms in your various sexual adventures, start using them. I'll buy you all you need. Don't be dipping into the community well without a rubber. AIDS is real. Herpes is real. Chlamydia is real. And so is pregnancy. I don't want you hurt, and I don't want you hurting anybody else."

"Time to go, Jared," Yvonne calls from the other room. "Please put the garbage out."

"Dad, thanks," and to my surprise he hugs me hurriedly. "Mom said you'd, like, say yes. But I really didn't do it, though, like, get her pregnant, I mean."

"Good. I'll buy you some condoms today."

"I got some."

"Use 'em, then."

As Jared lugs garbage out the side door without complaint, Yvonne slides next to me. "Hello, Grandpa," she smiles.

I'm not amused. "I'll call the school," I tell her, "see what I can find out about Maya ... what's her last name?"

"Hansen."

"And I'll call Bill Isola and see what's legal and what's not."

She is strangely unaffected by this latest news, smiling as she comments, "It's a good thing we've got these little distractions to keep us from relaxing."

"Right," I say, then I kiss her. Our daughter was due home last night for a long weekend. "Where's Suzie?" I ask. "Did she come in?"

"Oh, she drove in about midnight. I had coffee with her this morning. She and Steve—he's home too, strange coincidence—already headed for Muir Beach. She'll be back for dinner."

"Nice of her to come home for a visit."

Again my wife smiles. "Jealous?" she asks.

"A little."

"A lot, you mean." She kisses my cheek.

After an early-afternoon class and a brief meeting at school, I climb off my bike and swing into the plush lobby of the convalescent hospital to visit my mother. Before the door closes behind me, I hear those now familiar howls. "Uhhhn! Uhhhn! Uhhhn!" No wonder Mom—and others, especially the ones who have no visitors and no hope—hate it here.

Outside my mother's door, I take a deep breath—how will she be today?—then plunge in. She sits silhouetted against the window, and for a moment I am grasped by the deep realization that I am her son, that I once lived in her body, that her heart pumped life into me. She clothed me and fed me and taught me to read. Being her son has now moved me far beyond mere acceptance of all her largesse. Her illness is mine because we are flesh of flesh, and our mutual suffering is at last alerting me to what I have had and what I will soon lose. My face begins drooping in the presence of this small woman, the shadow of tears; "*Quit blubberin'!*" echoes through me, and I steel myself, swallow hard, but what I swallow knots in my heart.

Then she notices me and smiles from her wheelchair. "Oh, Leroy. Where've you been?"

"Mostly working, Mom."

"It's been *months* since I've seen you."

"Uhhhn! Uhhhn! Uhhhn!" echoes from up the hall.

"I was here yesterday." I can imagine why a day in this place would seem endless.

"You *were*?"

"Yes." Across the room those two unmoving, gaping women still lie on their beds.

"What day is this?"

"Friday."

"It *is*? I can't seem to keep track of time anymore, not in this place." My mother's eyes are bright and alert. She gazes away from me out the open window toward a sunny garden. "When I was little, maybe seven or eight, we had an old fig tree in the backyard and I used to go there, under the branches—they hung way down to the ground like a tent—and that place . . ." she is groping for a word ". . . that place where . . ." still groping, ". . . you know, where the branches come together?"

"The fork? The crotch?"

"Yes, the fork. Well, it was low and wide, so I'd climb in there, and it was my . . . my . . . my hiding place. I felt safe there. Nothing could hurt me."

"Your sanctuary?"

"My sanctuary, yes."

"That's nice, Mom." I've never heard this tale before and am pleased. She has not been sharing many pleasant memories lately.

"You know why I went there?"

"No?"

"So I couldn't hear my mother and father scream at each other."

"Oh."

Just then a voice, soft and yearning, from one of the supine women fills the room: "George, please come get me. Please come get me, George. Pleeease." The woman's eyes are open. Then she closes them and falls silent. But I am tugged by the realization that there once was a George for this poor woman, that she loved as Yvonne and I do, and that Yvonne may one day be lying in that same bed calling my name.

"What did that woman say?" Mom asks.

"She was just calling someone."

"Oh, did I ever tell you about when my folks opened that little café near Taft?"

I vaguely remember her having mentioned it when I was a kid. "Not really."

"Well, Daddy already had that store in Old River, and somehow he opened a little place by Taft and sold barbecue sandwiches to the oil workers. It was just a hole in the wall and it had one of those . . . those things that go around with meat on them . . ."

"A rotisserie?"

"Yes, a rotisserie. And we made sandwiches and Momma cooked homemade pies. And coffee. All of us kids worked there, but we sure had fun. My brother, Joe, was the dishwasher, and that darn Charlotte—she was only about twelve—she'd sit at the end of the counter with lipstick on and a dirty neck and she'd flirt with the oil workers and truck drivers." Mom begins giggling, a sound I've not heard for a long time. "She was supposed to help clean up, but she didn't do a darn thing . . . with that dirty neck," she falls silent momentarily, still grinning.

My fond memories of Mother's playful younger sister, dead for years now, make me laugh too. She was indeed a character.

"But I was the one who had the boyfriends, not Charlotte, and so did Momma. She'd sneak away every once in a while and leave us in charge—I think she'd go dancing with a boyfriend—then Charlotte and Joe would eat all the pie and make themselves sick." She is still chuckling.

This is a side of her family's life I've never heard. "What'd Grandpa think of all that?"

"Oh, he was *so* jealous." She is still giggling. "But he wouldn't leave that store where he was making money. He'd never take Momma dancing himself."

I'm amazed at how innocent Mom appears to be. My assumption about what transpires when men and women sneak off is, I suspect, not the same as hers.

"What happened to the café?"

"Oh"—she gestures as though throwing something away—"Daddy got disgusted and closed it. He made Momma stay home after that. I think he was just jealous. Anyway, she never had any more fun. He wouldn't ever take her dancing."

"Huh," I nod. `

"How long do I have to stay here?" she asks.

"I don't know, Mom. I really don't."

I glumly pump my bicycle home and enter a house filled with laughter: Mitch is on the phone, and his deep guffaws seem to shake the walls. Jared stands next to him, urging, "And, like, tell her about Mrs. Winston. She, like, *farted* in study hall, then tried to move her chair so we'd think it wasn't really a fart, but Tracy he goes real loud, 'Good fart!' so she goes, 'Get to the office!' Tracy goes, 'Why me? You're the one that farted.' It was, like, *real* rude."

I look in on my father, who's napping, search the house for my wife, but don't find her, and finally return to the family room, where the boys are still laughing. "Who were you talking to?" I ask.

"Hi, Pop," Mitchell calls. "Just poor little shy Suzie and Steve over at his house. We were . . . ah . . . discussing some of our old high school teachers."

"So I gathered. What're you two up to?"

"Mitch's gonna, like, take me to the next Renaissance Faire, so we're, like, planning my costume. I'm gonna go as a fool."

"Typecasting," winks his older brother.

Jared makes a rough pass at him, and they wrestle briefly, laughing.

"How 'bout you, Mitch? What's your costume?"

"He's, like, going as a fairy," grins Jared. "Typecasting."

Mitchell fakes a punch at him, then says, "A smith."

Well, he's certainly got the build for it. It's good to see the boys in the house enjoying one another. We don't have enough moments like these anymore.

"What're you three up to?" demands my wife, who has entered from the deck. She gazes at us—her menfolk, or all but one of them, anyway—just as I had gazed at the two boys.

"No good," I reply.

"I can believe that."

41

A great galaxy of birds rose suddenly in front of us, a moving cylinder, a tornado's feathered funnel that darkened then lightened then darkened once more as the fliers turned, swerved, and turned again. Wow! The shimmering shape sucked into a cumulus mass, dense as death, then veered into a transparent wave.

After almost driving into a ditch, my father pulled our car off the road. "Jesus," he gasped, "I never *seen* so damn many birds. Just when you get to thinkin' you know this ol' Valley, it shows you somethin' else." He shook his head.

"Me neither, but I'll bet this is the way it used to look all the time before us white people got here . . . a bazillion birds and rabbits and coyotes and bears . . . before we slaughtered most of 'em."

"Ya reckon?"

Millions of those birds—almost a solid mass—were swooping low like slow liquid into a vast spiral close to plowed fields. Suddenly a thin plume began pulling upward, a few deranged but seductive fliers, and the mass abruptly followed: compelled, compelled.

My dad and I remained stunned by what we were watching. Rain had fallen the afternoon before, and the agricultural fields through which we were passing were thoroughly puddled. Ahead and to the right of us, a small stream was marked by the warbonnet profile of tules—yellowish reeds twenty feet tall. Pop and I had decided to take a ride that morning, the final day of my furlough, swing out to Button-willow, then up to Wasco and Shafter, look around. We had not antici-pated anything like this avian explosion.

Other drivers also pulled over, and a tall guy walked up next to us. "What the hell is it?" he asked. "What're they doin'?"

"They're dancing," I replied, and he gazed at me for a moment, his head tilting like a dog hearing a siren.

"What're they *really* doing?" he insisted.

My father eyed him, then said, "My boy says they're dancin'."

The tall guy blinked at Pop, then wandered back to his own pickup shaking his head.

Pop grinned at me. *"Dancin'."* He poked my shoulder. "Sometimes I wonder 'bout you, boy."

He was going to say more, but a lady interrupted, asking, "What in the world are they?"

"They look like blackbirds to me," I said.

"Yep," Pop agreed.

Above, the birds were pulling into another plastic, sloping shape, moving in several directions: vast, a spreading amoeba, and it dawned on me that they were more *it* than *they*. Those fliers seemed incapable of *not* winging together, possessed by community like the cells of a jellyfish.

"I think they're not individuals anymore, Pop; they're a single . . . an *organism* . . . doing a dance."

"A *organism*?" He grinned and shook his head.

Ahead of us, a young guy who was chewing tobacco and spitting rapidly said, "I sure wisht I had me a shotgun."

Pop and I grinned at one another after hearing him.

Suddenly the fliers were over us, all but obscuring the sun, and I realized how incomprehensibly large this organism was, greater than any building I'd ever seen, a mile of birds high above in all directions. No shotgun could carry that high, no gun could dent that feathered density. Then they were moving away: flattened to a swerving, pliable plane, pinching thickly in the middle, splaying on the ends as they moved toward the low western mountains.

Some of the other drivers returned to their cars and motored away, but we remained, watching that incredible company of birds grow smaller against the faded fall sky, smaller. Just before they disappeared, the birds generated a tower that seemed to rise quickly, then it imploded into a series of slopes, became a shadowy, curving band, and was gone beyond the horizon.

"I never seen nothin' like that before in my whole damn life," my father admitted. "It looked like a tornada."

I could only shake my head and smile. I felt like some great secret had been revealed to me. I was thinking about the fingerprint in the pottery shard I'd found on that trip with Mr. Avila, about my connection to the person who'd made that mark. Maybe our existence was really a kind of communion, like those birds . . . dancing. When I get back from the army, I told myself, I'll definitely go to college.

"Well," my father said, as we returned to the car, "there's a hell of a lot to this ol' California, I'll tell you that much. It's always somethin' new out here. You recollect what ol' Hubby used to say? 'They call it all pussy, but it's always new to me.'"

I had to laugh, then I added, "But he'd say 'see' at the end of it."

"Yeah, I reckon he would. Ol' Hubby . . ."

"He was a good guy."

"Yeah he was, and the nastiest fart-knocker I ever knew. But I still miss him. There ain't a whole lot in this world bettern'n good friends." He paused, then added, "You knew Miz Hobbs died?"

This was a sudden shock. "No. I'm sorry to hear that. She was real nice to me. How old was she?"

"Miz Hobbs? Oh, 'bout twenty years older'n me, so that's early seventies. Their oldest boy, Willard, he's near my age. Her and Hubby was sure pals. He talked pussy all the time—and I b'lieve he really did do his share a screwin' when he'uz a young buck—but I one day asked him, 'You gettin' any strange stuff?' and he said, 'Yeah, I am, at home.' I knew him real good and he never done nothin' without Momma—he always called her that—and Momma done ever'thing with him:

dances, fishin', ball games . . . you name it. Ol' Momma she give as good as she took . . . and then sóme. That's what a man and a woman *can* be. They can be pards."

I knew what he felt he had missed, and probably what my mother felt she had too. They did very little together that I knew about, and appeared mismated. How they ever got together was a mystery to me, although I understood by then that heat had led to more than one strange union.

"Yessir," my father said, almost to himself as we turned east toward Wasco, where Hubby and Momma had lived, "when you get down to it, it's kin and pards that count. When you're dead, that's all that really matters. Money and bein' a big shot don't amount to shit."

"Maybe we're like those birds, Pop, all connected in our lives, but we just don't know it."

He turned and studied me. "Sometimes, Leroy, I think you're 'bout half smart," he finally said. Then he added, grinning, "For a kid that's half prune picker, anyways."

The next day I flew back to Fort Riley, Kansas.

42

The day starts badly.

My father has an appointment for a recheck at Jim Cox's office, but when I try to awaken him, there's little response. I hoist him into a sitting position, but he lists to one side and appears dazed. Yvonne props him up while I try to dress him. Finally I give up and telephone Jim at home, catch him at breakfast. Half an hour later he drops by on the way to the office. He examines Pop carefully, then, as usual, speaks to my dad. "Well, it sure does look like you might've had another little stroke, Mr. Upton."

Pop does not respond, but I'm grateful that Jim still talks *to*, not merely *about*, him. My father leans to the left, a thick strand of saliva forming on his chin like unblown glass. I wipe it with my handkerchief. Trish and Suzie hover at the doorway.

Jim turns toward me, and we walk into the hall with Suzie. Trish reluctantly remains with my father, though she clearly yearns to be part of the medical consultation. "Roy, you heard what I told your father. I'm sure he's had another small stroke. Like I told you the last time, there's no point in subjecting him to tests or a hospital stay. He's too frail and we can't reverse the damage, so what's the point? He's better off with you at home for as long as you folks can manage. Don't kill *yourselves* trying to do this, though. You're starting to look like an ulcer waiting to happen."

He pauses and searches my face, his eyebrows up—a do-you-understand look. "I mean it, Roy. You're starting to look pretty damned ragged. You keep an eye on him, Suz'."

He puts a hand on my shoulder, saying, "Roy, I want you and Yvonne to be realistic. Your dad is a tough guy. A *really* tough guy. A lesser man would've been dead a long time ago. In fact, he may be too damned tough for his own good . . . and for yours." He shakes his head.

"But," he adds, his voice lower, "in the shape Earl's in, any little thing might carry him off. He might be in the midst of a series of strokes that'll finish him right now. It's hard to know. He's already amazed me at the stuff he's bounced back from. But at some point he'll lose."

"Like all of us," I say. "It's beginning to seem like he's always been like this and always will be."

"He won't."

"I know, Jim. I know."

"We both know," says Suzie. "Poor Gramps."

I put my arm around her and she snuggles against me.

When I arrive at Crestview later that afternoon, Mom is standing in the hall with an aging black lady, conversing animatedly. She smiles when she sees me. "Ella, have you met my son, Leroy?"

I am genuinely pleased to meet Ella and to know that Mom may have initiated—or at least responded to—human contact.

"Why, no." The other woman smiles as we shake hands, revealing only three upper teeth—each ringed with gold.

"This is Suzie's father," Mom explains, and I am briefly stopped by her words. Then she turns toward me. "Suzie came to visit me this morning. She's *so* cute. She brought that Steve with her."

"Oh, really."

"Suzie's going to graduate soon, isn't she?"

"Yeah," I nod.

"My granddaughter is going to graduate from college soon," she tells Ella, then she adds, "I think that Steve's nuts about her."

"Could be." I'll let that subject slide.

"What's that Steve do for a living?"

"Steve? He's in college, Mom. He's your doctor's son. You've known him since he was a little kid. He was around our house when he and Suzie were in grade school. Remember the boy who had to wear leg braces?"

"He's *that* little pest?"

"Sure. He'll be starting medical school soon at Stanford."

"Huh," she snorts, and I can see *that* Steve, who has always seemed to me to be an infinitely pleasant kid, has somehow displeased my mother. But then, in-laws—even potential in-laws—have never fared well with her. Fortunately she changes the subject: "Ella and I were just talking about how some of these old gals steal your stuff."

"They steals my teeth," says Ella. She is serious, so I don't laugh.

"And that Hildegard that uses a walker, well, I caught her looking in my closet," Mom reports. "*German,* you know," she adds, nodding emphatically.

"Oh, *she* steal," nods the other woman. " 'Nother lady tell me that too."

"Nothing's safe here. When I had a home of my own, everything was safe," Mom says to her new friend.

"Yes," the other lady replies.

"I was moved, you know. After forty-four years they moved me from my home, and now I have to live in this place."

I swallow painfully.

"My son has a large home, but I guess there's no room in it for his mother." Her tone is laden with undisguised irony.

Across the hall, I see a woman about Mom's age carefully spooning food into the mouth of a man strapped into a wheelchair. I have seen her with him every day, and I assume she is his spouse, faithful to the end. There are several couples like that, one person living in Crestview while the spouse visits every day, sometimes all day—feeding, caring for the other: There are heroes in this world. The woman notices me staring at her across the hall, smiles and nods, then goes on about her business.

"Uhhhhhn! Uhhhhhn! Uhhhhhn!" echoes up the hall.

"That fool again," says Ella.

"That poor man can't help it, Ella," my mother explains. "Somebody probably put *him* in this place, too."

"He upset me."

"Yes, I can certainly understand that," Mother says, patting her new friend's shoulder.

"You're here because you've been sick, Mom," I say quietly. In fact, she is certainly acting well enough to come home.

"Oh, I have?" she says, her tone mildly accusing, then she turns to face Ella once more. "I . . ."

"Helllllp! Helllllp! Helllllp!"

"That's the one that bothers me, that screecher." Mom shakes her head. "I *hate* it when people yell. I was just telling Ella about when I was a little girl I went to a school way out in the oil fields when Momma and Daddy had a little store in a company camp. It was a one-room school. It seemed like all the other kids used to take flowers for the teacher, but we lived in a big canvas tent then, and there weren't any flowers out there at all.

"Well, on the way to school I used to pass a little house that was just surrounded by flowers, and I'd see an old lady out in the yard all the time, working on her garden.

"Every single day I'd walk by that yard, and that old woman was always there. One day, though, she wasn't, so I stopped and I picked three or four flowers real fast and stuffed them in my lunch bag. I just turned to leave and darned if the woman didn't come out, and she screeched at me just like this one does."

"My, *my*," clucks Ella, the pale palm of one hand against a cheek.

Mother's eyes are wide, and her hands are active as she talks. "Well, I was so scared that I just stood there, you know, while she sort of hobbled toward me on a cane like a . . . a . . . witch. Finally, I took off like a jackrabbit. I threw those flowers away and I never looked back. All day, I waited for the sheriff to come and arrest me, and for the rest of the year I never walked by that woman's house again; I always went the long way. I can still hear her screeching."

"My, *my*, my . . ."

And I am also thinking my, *my*, my, because I haven't heard Mom tell many stories until recently.

"Uhhhhhn! Uhhhhhn!"

"That fool again," Ella shakes her head.

"Helllllp!"

On my bicycle ride home, I simply acknowledge that Mom does not belong in that place. Belly troubled, I arrive home and park my bike in the garage, then walk around the house, exploring what remains of the garden in this season.

"Hey, Roy!" I hear a voice and glance up the hill to see my neighbor Bill striding down the path, dressed in golf shirt, faded jeans, and sockless moccasins. "How's it going?" he calls, coming toward me.

"Okay. How's Ben?"

He drops his eyes. "He's just barely hanging on. I was there last week, and he didn't even recognize me."

"I'm sure sorry, Bill." What else can I say?

"Thanks," he nods.

"How about you and Twila?"

He smiles. "We're okay. Next weekend she's involved with a paint-in down at the Garden Club, for the Women's Peace Caucus. I thought maybe you and Yvonne might be interested."

"A *paint-in*? What's that?"

"Well," he explains, "they're going to paint a giant mural of American atrocities—a hundred feet long on a single sheet of paper—you know, everything: slavery, stealing land from the Indians, beating up Mexico, invading Europe, framing Geronimo Pratt, bombing Panama, torturing children in El Salvador, murdering peasants in Guatemala . . . the whole picture."

"That's a constructive project," I say, hoping my face doesn't betray the fact that I can't take this latest trendy political nonsense seriously. "Tell her that the land where the Garden Club is built used to be the site of a Miwok village. In fact, this whole valley was Miwok land—your place and mine. Instead of painting a mural, maybe we ought to just clear out, book flights to Europe, and go back to wherever we came from." I grin tightly.

"Jeez, you're really on edge, Leroy. They're *just* painting a mural."

Maybe I am on edge. "We agree on that, Bill. That's all they're doing."

A few minutes later, feeling guilty over my response to Bill, I enter the family room in time to hear Jared say into the telephone, "Yeah, she, like, *got* herself pregnant, man."

After a moment he says, "Righteous, dude. I go, 'How come you, like, told me that?' She goes, 'I, like, couldn't help it.' I go, 'That's, like, a *lie*, man.' She goes, 'I couldn't, like, help it.' I go, 'Like, fuck it, man,' and she, like, starts cryin'."

I am, to say the least, both intrigued and disturbed by what I'm hearing. A few minutes later, my son is off the telephone, and he calls pleasantly, "Hey, Dad. Maya, like, doesn't have to move in with us. She's back home."

"That's good. Listen," I say, "I couldn't help overhearing your conversation. How could a girl get *herself* pregnant?"

Jared stops, his face grave. "Well, this girl, Jennifer, she, like, *let* Tracy do her. She *wanted* him to."

"Oh, so you don't think Tracy had a part in it?"

"She, like, wanted him to, Dad. She, like, went down on him, and he, like, did her, and now she says it's, like, *his* fault."

"You don't think he's involved?"

"And Tracy's, like, grounded again, too, but not for that," Jared adds. "Guess what he did."

I shudder to think what Tracy might've done.

Jared grins. "He, like, got this bumper sticker that says SHIT HAPPENS! and stuck it on the laxative shelf at the drugstore, but the manager, like, narc'ed on him, and the cops called his mom."

"Tracy better hope that's the worst trouble he's in."

I shake my head. Ah, youth.

43

Increasingly troubled by the sense that I'm not spending enough time with my mother, yet also burdened by the responsibility to visit daily, I ride my bicycle home the next day with therapeutic desperation, pumping harder and harder. Few cars disturb my reverie, and the smells of trees and earth and grass comfort me. I soon forget Mom's situation, concentrating on hawks gliding overhead, on the frantic dash of a squirrel as I pass a wooded gully. By the time I wheel into our driveway, I'm refreshed.

Yvonne's car is home—she's early—and down the street I see Trish pushing Pop in his wheelchair, his afternoon walk. In the house, I find my wife reading a contract and sipping tea at the dining room table. I slip into the room and kiss her shoulder, her neck, her ear. "How about a nap?" I ask.

She feigns indignation. "Is sex all you can think about? How about some intelligent conversation?"

"Circumference equals Pi R-squared. Let's smooch."

"You silver-tongued devil," she laughs. "You've talked me into it."

"Meet you in the bedroom after a quick shower."

She smiles, "See you there." My bicycling shorts are bulging, and her eyes glance there for a moment. Then she runs her tongue across her lips.

An hour later, spent, I'm cuddling her, comforted by the certainty of her warm body, knowing that as much as I love sex with Yvonne, I love loving her even more. Holding her has become necessary for me. She is drifting toward sleep, and I try to slip out of bed, but the sheets are so tangled that I'm trapped.

"What?" my wife asks drowsily.

"I'm stuck. We'll have to call for help. I can just hear Jared: 'Get the hose, Mitch! Get the newspaper! Mom and Pop're like hung up!'"

She laughs drowsily as I unwind myself from bedding, then kiss one of her nipples—she jumps and smiles. "Listen," I say brightly, "I think Mom's about ready to come home."

For a long moment she says nothing. Then she sighs. "Where will Pop go?"

I have no answer.

Disturbed, I stroll into the kitchen and find Suzie, her head buried in the open refrigerator. I notice that she wears skintight Lycra shorts and a cut-off sweatshirt that reveals a tan tummy and even a shot of her breasts when she bends forward; I wish I *could* tell her what not to wear—this is too alluring a costume. She hears me coming and announces, "Trish and Grandpa are in his room. Don't you guys keep *anything* good to eat in here?"

"Sorry, Grandma," I reply, "but we're fresh out of Twinkies."

She raises one eyebrow and squints—another expression that reminds me of Floyd Henshaw—and growls: "*Don't* call me Grandma. I don't complain *all* the time."

"Okay, okay. I'm going to have a cup of tea. Want one?"

"Sure. Where's Mom?"

"Resting."

She looks at me with a wry smile, then says, "You know, for years and years I thought you and Mom were the best-rested adults I knew, those naps you take almost every day. Then I grew up and I realized you might be the most horny instead."

Her choice of words shocks me, and I do not immediately reply. After a few moments of fiddling with tea bags and cups, I smile. "Those two things aren't necessarily in conflict, pumpkin. Since you ask, the specifics are personal, but a healthy sex life involves a lot more than just exchanging pleasure. There's bonding, there's comfort, and deep, deep intimacy; but if you're not lucky, it can just be lust, desperation, even domination and exploitation."

Now she is shocked. I've never before spoken so frankly of sex to her. "That's what I like about you, Dad," she grins. "You can turn any subject, even a pleasantly dirty one, into a lecture. You were a coach too long." This is an enduring complaint of the kids—that I slip into lectures too easily.

"Anybody making tea?" Yvonne has emerged from our bedroom. Her cheeks are rosy, her eyes cloudy. In that dim light she looks as delicious as she did twenty-five years ago, when we began sleeping together, or twenty-five minutes ago, when we most recently had. "Come 'ere," I say, then I wrap my arms around her and kiss first one eye, then the other, touching each lid with my tongue.

"Ahem! There's a *child* present," says Suzie.

Still arching to my kisses, Yvonne murmurs, "Yes, the child who came home from her date with Steve looking like she'd been in a tornado, I seem to recall."

"Oops," says our daughter. "Let's have tea and talk about something else."

"I kind of like talking about this," I say.

Suzie grins. *"Yep. Bet ya do, Tex."*

The three of us plop in front of the fireplace in the family room, Suzie snuggling in the middle. "This is fun," she says, "just like when I was little." She giggles, then adds, "Before you had those two awful *boys.*"

Yvonne musses our daughter's hair, and I, seeing them snuggle briefly, am again struck with how similar they are, how playful, how lovely. After a moment, Suzie's face turns pensive and she asks, "Mom? Dad?"

"Uh-oh," I sotto voce to Yvonne, "she needs money."

After another giggle, Suzie says, "Well, sort of. What would you think if I went on to graduate school?"

Yvonne and I exchange a deep look: we both know the financial implications of this, but we also know that it's the logical extension of what we have both preached and exemplified: education, education, education. "I think I'd end up in debtors' prison," I reply with a smile. I am, as always, it seems, proud of her.

"Would it really be hard for you?"

"No. Maybe inconvenient . . . no condo in Maui for a while."

Our kids know they will be given the opportunity to attend public colleges—like the ones Yvonne and I graduated from, not only because we can afford them but because we also believe that they are as good as or even better than expensive private institutions and that they reflect this state's diverse society.

My own academic career began at Bakersfield Junior College, then San Jose State. I nickel-and-dimed an M.A. at Cal while teaching and coaching at a secondary school in San Rafael, then finished my doctorate at Cal while doing the same thing at College of Marin. Yvonne completed her bachelor's degree while raising the kids; she commuted to San Francisco State two days a week for five years. Then she completed her M.B.A. there, too.

"We'll certainly help, won't we, babe?" I say to my wife.

Yvonne's look tells me we can once more defer our own small dreams, take a second mortgage if necessary, and I know my daughter well enough to assume that she intends to help pay her way through school. Although we live in this affluent community, we have always let the kids know there are distinct limits to our financial capabilities. We're a long way from poor, though. My wife's part-time real estate job contributes irregularly—though occasionally well indeed—to our income, so our combined earnings have elevated us into the upper middle class. In this town, though, that makes us low average.

Yvonne gives Suzie a proud hug and says, "You'd surely win a fellowship or assistantship, wouldn't you?"

"That's what Dr. Crowley says. He thinks I can get a fellowship in the geomorphology program at UCLA."

"Even if you don't, you go ahead and pursue it. We'll work something out. Mitch'll be going away next year," Yvonne says, "but he doesn't know where yet. Maybe UC–Davis, maybe Cal Poly, or maybe even Oregon State. He wants a small-town campus with a computer science major and a good track-and-field program. He'll probably win an athletic grant-in-aid of some kind, and I'm certain his grades will earn him at least a partial academic scholarship."

Intrigued and a little puffed with parental pride, I ask Suzie, "Would you take a master's or work straight through for a Ph.D.?"

"Ph.D."

"That's what I was going to suggest. Except for community college teaching . . . and slick M.B.A.'s in real estate . . . the master's is almost a dead degree anymore."

"Dr. Crowley told me the same thing."

Yvonne rises, shrugs her shoulders in that way that always titillates me, then says to our daughter, "Well, Dr. Upton, give me a hand in the kitchen. Your father remains an unregenerate male who won't cook."

"Can't cook. I buy the neckbone and beans, though," I add quickly.

Yvonne laughs, "That's not all you do with the beans."

"No farting, Dad," warns Suzie with a heavy scowl.

"Pull my finger," I urge, extending a digit in her direction.

She recoils, "Get *real*! Hey, look what the cat dragged in." She is grinning because she sees Mitch striding up the front walk, home from a long day at school.

A moment later, her brother enters the family room, stops, and says, "Ah, the old maid's still here. When're you getting married, anyway?"—one of Grandma's complaints turned into a joke.

"Soon as you do," Suzie replies and they hug.

Suzie and Mitch are joshing, walking toward the deck, where Pepper, wagging that big tail, awaits them. I gaze at the two kids, struck as I so often am with an almost abstract pride in the young woman and young man we have raised.

"Hey, Dad," I hear Jared call up the hallway—when did he come home?—"can you, like, come back here? Grandpa, like, fell down. Trish, like, can't get him up."

44

Since his last stroke, Pop can no longer walk at all, and he can no longer talk clearly; he can't feed himself, and he can't even sit up without help. I find myself wondering how much he wants to remain alive in this condition. He does eat, of course, and seems to enjoy a back rub or head scratch or hug. But looking at him I see only a ruin. I have changed his diaper this morning, hoisted him into his wheelchair, and pushed him to the family room, where hot cereal and coffee, as usual, await.

Once I've got Pop bibbed and have spooned some cereal into his mouth, I hurry into the kitchen, pour myself a second cup of coffee. Yvonne joins me there; she is ready for work. I put down my cup and hug her. She grasps me more desperately than usual, kisses my neck and cheek, then sighs, "I'm so sorry for Pop." As we glance at him, he seems to be trying to scoop up one of the blossoms printed on his long bib with his awkwardly grasped spoon.

"We both are, poor guy." I pause. "We both are."

From the hallway I can hear Jared's atonal voice crooning: "*Gonna get me a gun and kill all the whiteys I seee-eee. Gonna get me a gun and kill all the whiteys I seee-eee...*"

My wife and I exchange quick grins. "Is that the future Johnny Mathis?" I ask.

Yvonne shakes her head and chuckles. Thank God for comic relief.

"Hey, Jared," I say when he bops into the kitchen, "I hate to shock you, but you *are* a whitey."

He glances at me with all the interest of a boy who's just been told the Earth is round, notes that I'm grinning, and grins back at me. "*Gonna get me a gun and kill all the whiteys I seee-eee...,*" he is once more crooning as he leaves.

Trish, another whitey, soon arrives, so I'm free to help Suzie and Mitch load her car. Those two are off for UC–Santa Cruz for a couple of days, then he'll ride a bus home. A few minutes later, I'm stuffing gear into my bicycle's panniers when the telephone rings. I lift the receiver and hear, "Is that Mr. Upton?"

"Yes."

"This is Mavis, the duty nurse at Crestview. I don't want to alarm you, but your mother's heartbeat was irregular last night, so I called Dr. Cox. We've moved her to the medical wing."

"Is Dr. Cox there?"

"We called you and called you last night." She seems to be admonishing me.

"So what?" I snap. I hadn't heard the phone, but why call me at all? What the hell could I have done? "Is *Dr. Cox* there?" with some heat.

"Yes, yes, he is," she stammers.

Several seconds later, Jim Cox says, "Roy, your mother's had an episode of arrhythmia. I wish I could tell you why, but anyway I think it's settling down now. I've got her on oxygen as a precaution and I've altered her medication slightly..."

"Jim," I interrupt, "how serious is this? Is it life-threatening?"

"I don't think so, but with someone as old and fragile as she is, anything *could* be. She's a little incoherent, so it could be a little stroke too. Don't take for granted that she'll just breeze through, but she probably will."

"Okay, I'll be right over."

After we hang up, I phone the college and tell the secretary I have to miss my first class and why, then quickly finish packing my gear. My father, propped up with pillows, slumps in his chair as I say good-bye. Just as I turn for the door, the telephone rings once more, and I quickly answer, fearing it may be Jim Cox with more bad news.

"Roy," sobs Jess Soto, "that bitch is *killin'* me."

My own tension breaks and I feel like weeping too. I have nothing to give him.

Jim is no longer at Crestview when I arrive, but a young woman named Ruby is now the duty nurse, and she leads me into a wing where all the rooms are doubles appointed with hospital beds, and where the walls have spigots for oxygen, wires to monitor heart rates, and various metallic appliances. The other bed in my mother's room is empty, and she lies in restless sleep. On the wall, as at the nursing station we have passed, my mother's heart rate pulses across a screen. "She's resting now," Ruby mutters, then stands there.

"Thanks," I say and, after a few moments, she gets the message, leaving me alone with my mother. I kiss Mom's brow, stroke her thin white hair. "Mom? It's me, Leroy." She stirs, her eyes still closed, and her lips are working, but at first I hear nothing. Then I seem to enter a conversation in progress.

"*So* jealous of poor shy little Leroy Clark . . . just a married bachelor, that Earl . . . that drinking bit . . . tomcatting . . . my home . . . *terrible* father . . . beer on his breath . . . that roughhousing bit . . . poor shy little Leroy Clark . . . that Earl . . ."

"Mom? Mom?" I call.

"Is that you, Daddy?" she frowns.

"It's me, Mom, Leroy." I continue stroking her hair.

"Oh, I didn't do anything, Daddy. I didn't. No, I didn't. No."

I am fascinated but also embarrassed; these are not things I need to hear. "Mom, I've gotta go to work, but I'll be back right after class."

She suddenly smiles: "*So* handsome, Leroy Clark . . . *so* popular . . . *so* well dressed . . . girls from the finest families . . . doctors . . . lawyers . . . the country club." Her face suddenly hardens. "That football bit . . . broke his nose . . . that Yvonne . . . common . . . trashy . . . something nasty going on . . . got her in trouble . . . so sorry for Leroy Clark . . . children break your heart."

I am thinking that parents can break your heart too. I don't want to hear any more, so I give Ruby my office number, then depart for College of Marin.

When I return late that afternoon, Mom is still somnolent but no longer muttering. Her color is good and, as I stand in the doorway, dinner is wheeled in. "All right, Marie," says Carolina, grinning at me, "time to wake up for dinner." She tugs gently at one of Mom's arms.

"Don't," moans my mother.

"Come on, Marie," Carolina continues urging.

"*Don't*," Mom snaps.

Carolina grins at me. "Ouuuhhheey!" she says. "This woman can act *ugly*. She put you through some changes. Come on, Marie, we got chili beans and corn bread, your favorite."

"Don't! Don't! *Don't!*"

"That's the way," urges Carolina, who has pulled my mother into a sitting position.

Finally Mom's eyes open and she demands, "Oh, why are you *doing* this?" A moment later, to my astonishment, she says, "What's for dinner? I'm starving."

I would not have persisted in the fight to awaken her, I know, but would have allowed her to sleep. This pleasant nurse is not burdened by a son's guilt when Mom resists, so she has gently, tenaciously completed her task.

"Mom?" I call.

"Leroy? Oh, you're here. Are you eating with me?" She has already begun spooning chili into her mouth. Carolina departs.

"I'll eat at home, but I'll keep you company for awhile."

"Is poor shy little Suzie coming to visit me today?"

"She had to go back to college today, Mom. Mitch went with her."

Her face looks troubled. "Is he going to school there too?"

"Just a visit, Mom."

Suddenly she looks around herself and asks, "What room is this? Your room or my room?"

Before I can answer, Jim Cox calls from the doorway, "Hi, Roy," then enters. "Hello, Mrs. Upton." He carries a chart. "Well, it looks like that cardiac irregularity has steadied today. How do you feel?"

Mom's mouth is full of chili and corn bread, but she mushes, "Fine."

"She looks fine, doesn't she, Roy?"

"Except for not having any appetite," I say. We both chuckle.

"What?" asks my mother.

"Well, I've got a couple of other patients to visit, so I'll be back in a few minutes after you've finished eating." He raises his eyebrows at me, so I walk into the hall with him.

"She is looking a lot better, isn't she?" he asks.

"You're the doctor."

"I appreciate that vote of confidence," he smiles. "She is. I don't think she had a stroke, even a small one—those symptoms were just confusion, I think. But I'm afraid that this episode might've undone her sleep cycle—she didn't really wake up all day, and she looks mighty alert to me now. I just talked to Ted Nakamura. He thinks this kind of upset might've reversed the cycle again, and if it has . . . well, it'll be a problem."

I can only shrug. "I hadn't even thought about that."

"When she's been through a possible life-and-death situation, that kind of stuff is secondary, but it won't seem secondary to the staff here. And you certainly can't take her home if that sleep cycle's reversed."

45

My first full day back after being discharged from the army was dark and ominous, but I felt great. I was lounging in my parents' small house that afternoon when J.D. pounded on the front screen door and hollered, "Miz Upton! Can Leroy come out 'n' play?"—just as he had when we were in grade school.

I jumped to my feet. "Hey, pardner!" He slid in, and we shook hands and pounded one another's backs. "How you doin'?"

"Fine and dandy. You look great, Roy. I seen ol' Earl down at the pool hall just now and he said you was home, so I thought I'd stop by."

"How's your wife?"

"Real good."

"And that new baby."

"Purty. Looks just like the mailman, same mustache and ever'thing. The older one's cute too, but mean like her momma. She looks like ol' Floyd."

We were guffawing at that one when my mother looked in from the kitchen, calling, "Who is it? Oh, hello, J.D."

"Hi, Miz Upton," he nodded and almost bowed.

My old pal slouched to the couch across the room from me. Mom, as usual, joined us. There were few private conversations in our house.

"So," he asked me, "did you play some ball while you was overseas?"

"Yeah. It was fun."

"Well," he said, "you guys had a pretty good team back in high school. You see any of 'em yet—Plumley, Soto, Tommy, them guys?"

"Naw, how's everyone doing?"

"Well, Soto finally married ol' Marge; he'd been after her since ninth grade. And your ol' girlfriend Lahoma, her and Tommy got a kid now. Tommy he's workin' with me out at Shell Oil," J.D. said.

"Lahoma's *such* a nice girl," my mother observed, and she cast her eyes at me.

Lahoma's name did stop me for a minute. I had been surprised when I'd learned last year that she'd returned to the Bakersfield area after college, and that she'd married my ex-teammate.

"Ol' Tommy's dad's real sore that he never became a doctor like him, but he's on his way to bein' a boss for the Shell, I'll tell ya that much. He's a smart sucker, and he graduated Stanford."

"He's a good head," I said.

J.D. scratched his chin. "Let's see . . . Jimbo's due out of the county road camp pretty soon. Ol' Floyd's finished his Navy Reserve hitch. And Bill Mack's still away at college . . . where? . . . at Nevada, I think. Soto and Marge they live out in west Bakersfield and he works at . . . ah . . . Getty Oil, I think. Oh, yeah, your buddy Plumley's still workin' for a well-pullin' outfit, but he's finishing J.C. at night. His wife, Juanita Martinez—what a dish she is!—she works at some real estate office. And guess what, ol' Plumley says he's gonna transfer to UCLA and, after that, go to law school."

"No lie? Crazy Plumley going to go to law school? I always figured he'd *need* a lawyer, not *be* one."

"He's making all A's is what I hear." J.D. shrugged.

This is counterintuitive information. "Are we talking about the same Travis Plumley? Juanita must be doing his homework," I grinned.

Mom interjected, "Billy's Mack's dating that Trumaine girl when he's home."

"Who?" I thought I recognized the name.

"Yvonne Trumaine, that cute little gal that works down at the drugstore," my mother explained. "She has the *cutest* figure. You knew her cousin, Larry."

"You mean that gorgeous dish I saw in there this morning? *She's* Larry Trumaine's cousin? She sure got all the looks in that family," I said. "And Bill's going with her. Boy, has his luck ever changed."

That morning I'd nearly walked into an aisle full of lotions because I was staring at a shapely, dark-skinned girl with a magical smile who stood behind a counter during my shopping trip to the drugstore. In fact, she had eventually waited on me, and when she leaned forward to fetch me an old-fashioned shaving brush from a glass display case, her scoop-necked blouse fell forward, offering a glimpse of her breasts. At that moment, she looked up, noted my line of vision, and demurely stood up, but her eyes flashed angrily at me.

As a result, I'd wandered home excited by her beauty and disturbed by my own none-too-subtle performance.

J.D. raised his eyebrows at me as he said, "Old Bill's goin' out with Yvonne Trumaine? Huh. Don't he *know* about her?"

That whetted Mom's curiosity. "What about her?"

J.D. gave me that look again, then replied, "Oh, nothin'. Feel like goin' for a ride, Roy? I can show you how the town's changed since you been gone."

"Sure."

"Do you have to go?" Mom said.

"I don't have to, Mom, but I want to." I stood and walked to her, then rubbed her back. "J.D. and I won't be gone long."

"None of that drinking bit."

"Right."

Wind jerked and tugged J.D.'s car as we toured old haunts. "What about that Trumaine chick?" I asked.

"Let's just say I heard from more than one guy that she's a damn good piece. She puts out."

"No lie?"

"No lie. Hey, speakin' of that, your ol' galfriend Cherry's got out of town . . . up in the Bay Area now, I hear. Got a good job."

We drank in an oil-field bar that afternoon, as the sky continued darkening, and I finally had to convince J.D. to take me back home before my mom called the sheriff. Walking out to his car, though, we could tell that those gusts were still strengthening, and my skin was peppered by tiny stings made by coarse dust. To the west, an orange light glowed high in the sky, but the low horizon had deepened to brown. One old man passed us as we climbed into my pal's car and said, "Looks a lot like a damn Oklahoma black blizzard to me, boys."

We pointed south toward home—the car increasingly jostled by that wind and visibility lessening with each moment until suddenly a curtain descended. Dust closed in so thick it choked light, and I saw ghostly tumbleweeds bouncing in front of us, those and the eerie coral color of other autos' lights moving in our direction. "This is gettin' to be one rough son of a bitch," grunted J.D. "Good thing I'm drunk so I can drive 'er," he laughed, as his car was buffeted about like a punching bag.

In a matter of moments, it seemed to me, I couldn't see a car length in front of us. "How the hell can you drive?" I asked.

"Radar and beer."

A few minutes later, however, radar and beer failed the driver, and he eased onto the road's shoulder. "This really is one rough son of a bitch," he repeated.

Eerie openings in the dust would suddenly offer us twenty, maybe fifty, yards of visibility, but whenever J.D. prepared to drive again, the storm would once more seal us. Even within the vehicle, everything smelled like fresh soil. It was like being trapped in a cave, and a hint of dread began to rise in me. To the west, I could see no sign of the sun, and once, while I searched for it, a vast, pale tumbleweed suddenly sprang against the car window like a wraith, causing both of us to jump.

"Shit!" rasped J.D.

When I was finally dropped off late that evening, my mother embraced me. "Thank God you're home," she gasped.

My father was sitting at the dining room table grinning. "Well, how'd you like that little breeze we had, boy?"

"Not bad," I grinned back.

"He could've been *killed*," my mother said. "I've been worried *sick*."

"By a little wind?" Pop chuckled. Then he said to me, "Hell, Leroy, me and your uncle Clyde never had to come to California for dust storms. We coulda just stayed home. This ol' San Joaquin Valley ain't all that different from Oklahoma, I can tell you that much."

"I guess not."

"You know how we used to gauge wind back home? We'd tie us a thick loggin' chain to a big ol' tree and if that chain blew straight out, it'uz a breeze. If that chain whupped around like a pissed-off bull snake, there'uz a wind. If the tree and chain was gone, there'uz a gust." He laughed and so did I.

"It's not funny, Earl," my mother said. "Leroy could've been *killed*."

My father winked at me and grinned.

46

"Hey, slugger," I call when Mitch wanders yawning into the kitchen. "How was Santa Cruz?"

He grins sleepily. "Got any coffee?"

"A little. Not going to tell me about your visit? Must've been a hot one."

Mitchell stretches, his heavy muscles bunching, then pulling long. "It was *excellent*. If they had a track program I'd transfer there. I could sit around and watch banana slugs chase the hippies. That campus is *so* beautiful, Pop." He is pouring himself coffee, into which he splashes non-dairy creamer.

"So your big sister showed you a good time?"

"Oh, yeah. She fixed me up with one of her roommates."

"Cute?"

"Well, you know Dolly Parton, the singer who's married to a businessman?"

I nod.

"Well, this gal looked a lot like the businessman," he grins. "Same mustache and everything."

We both laugh, then wander to our favorite spot outside, but find it too chilly. It has rained during the night, so there are puddles on the deck and steam rises from the woods behind us.

Yvonne joins us. She's not going to her office today, so she wears jeans and a sweatshirt, and carries a cup of coffee. "Hello, boys," she calls, then she sits on the arm of my chair and kisses my forehead.

"Hi, Mom," says Mitch. "Suzie says for you to send money."

"What a shock," Yvonne replies. "Are we going to buy our tree today?"

"Sure," I reply. The approach of Christmas has not been much on my mind.

Just then, Jared staggers in. He's been at the food coloring again, and his hair is a multicolored disaster. "Are we, like, gonna buy our tree today?"

"Yep," I reply.

Our older son looks dreamy for an instant, then focuses his eyes and says, "You know what I miss most now that Grandma and Grandpa live up here?" he asks.

"What?"

"Going down to Bakersfield. Christmas at their house was always the coolest."

Yes, it was, and I am swept with nostalgia. For nearly twenty-five years we had seemed to live without change: my folks were always there, and I felt like Yvonne and I were moving within time, unaware of aging, although our kids were growing up; everything else seemed static and certain and comforting. My folks were well then, Pop laconic but droll, Mom pleasant even to Yvonne.

During those years we would drive our loaded station wagon south on old Highway 99 the day before Christmas, slowing in patches of tule fog that were sometimes so thick that we'd have to be caravaned by Highway Patrol officers—the kids loved it. I'd recite the history of towns through which we passed or talk about football games I'd played in them, the kids would be openly bored while Yvonne, bless her, feigned interest.

Usually, we'd swing into the driveway at my parents' small house in the early-evening darkness—the living room and kitchen would be lit—and pile out of the car. Mom always met the excited kids on the porch with hugs, but Pop was rarely home. She'd telephone Art's Place, the pool hall and beer bar where he then conducted business, and he'd soon appear, shake my hand, give Yvonne a long hug, then turn his attention to those bouncing, giggling bundles. All his reticence quickly melted in the presence of the kids. "Where'd you find all these rascals at, Leroy? I b'lieve they're red Indians."

"None of that roughhousing, Earl," Mom would warn, then she'd turn toward me, raise her eyebrows secretly, and hiss, "I hate that drinking bit."

By then Pop was entangled with all three kids. I was always amazed and delighted that he was so much more relaxed and affectionate with them than he'd been with me.

"Little shy Suzie *hates* that wrestling bit," Mom invariably added.

Little shy Suzie, of course, led the wrestling, climbing her tall grandpa like a telephone pole, and Pop held her overhead with one hand while she giggled and writhed and the boys tugged at his legs.

My folks usually set up a small tree on a table in a corner of the living room, and by the time our presents were piled beneath it, they reached from the floor to the tree and spread in all directions. Pop and I would spend half the night assembling Santa Claus presents, sipping Tom and Jerrys and chuckling at the "simple assembly instructions," then sleepily enjoy the elation on the kids' faces the next morning when they opened the gifts.

During those years Yvonne and I would socialize in the evenings with the Plumleys and the Sotos, leaving our kids with Grandma and Grandpa while we partied. This went on up until a couple of years ago, but those Christmases now seem distant and much too soon past. Good times gone, but at least we had them.

I even recall things as simple as once more greeting my folks' neighbors—the Hillises and Pruetts and Thorps and Purvises—those good, hardworking people who had struggled west to realize some measure of the California Dream, and whose small houses and pickup trucks with campers were monuments to their success. "Leroy, are you a-gainin' or a-losin'?" Mrs. Purvis always inquired, and I never knew exactly what she was referring to. Mrs. Hillis used to cross her arms over her chest, place an open palm on one cheek, and cluck, "My, my! Are them young-uns of yours ever growin' . . . jest like milkweeds."

And grouchy Mr. Thorp always seemed to find an excuse to point out, "School don't teach you ever'thang, Leroy."

I'd always think *no shit,* but would say, "Yessir, that's a fact."

My dad would chuckle, "Ol' Thorp just talks to hear his damn head rattle. If he couldn't grouch, he'd just have to shut up, I reckon. He's been tellin' me he's fixin' to move back to Texas now that he's retired, says California's full of earthquakes and beatniks, but he ain't moved a damn step in that direction and he won't. He'll talk my nuts off about it, though."

I felt I could go to any of those neighbors for anything—they would treat me like their own son. Yvonne and I have many friends in Mill Valley, but none like that; the Great Depression had tempered and amalgamated them. Now most of those good neighbors are dead, and grouchy Mr. Thorp sits drooling and witless in a Bakersfield nursing home—he never got back to Texas. Every time we visit our hometown, we seem to learn that another of them is gone, and obituaries in the *Bakersfield Californian* are heavily weighted with people from Oklahoma, Texas, Arkansas, and Missouri, folks my parents' age whose children are Californians scattered throughout the state, throughout the society.

Only now, with my own mother and father sliding toward their graves, do I admit that the world has always been changing and that I chose not to notice. Recognizing their dotage, however, I admit that I am aging, too, waiting for that first shovelful of earth to hit my face so I can perhaps merge with the people who gave me life. The depth of distress that I keep hidden within myself is a cipher for the love I am unable to express to them. When I try, I can only hint at how profoundly I am involved: to do more would cause me to blubber.

"Dad?" Jared says, snapping me blinking out of my reverie, "Can you, like, give Grandpa a shower? He's, like, had an accident." Ironically, a country singer is crooning from the radio: "*Here in the reeeal world . . . ,*" and I have to chuckle as I wheel my father toward the large shower in the master bedroom . . . the real world, indeed.

That afternoon—Alberta in to watch Pop—the boys, Yvonne, and I drive north to the Petaluma area, where at a Christmas tree farm Mitch and Jared jostle and wrestle one another until they finally agree on just the right fir. We cut it, pay, then lash it to the car's roof for the drive home. As we had prearranged, I removed my bicycle from the car's roof rack before we tied the tree on. I climb into my cycling gear, kiss my wife, and climb onto my bike. The boys have agreed to visit Mom at the nursing home, so I can have the afternoon for the long ride back to Mill Valley.

I pedal a back road—through green, nearly unsettled Chileno Valley, over a hump of the Coast Range toward the rural cheese factory in northern Marin County, through verdant ranchland to Lake Nicasio, breathing cool, clear air, seeing dairy cattle grazing fresh greenery from early rains. This region of rolling, grassy hills—splotched and creased with live oaks so dark that they appear almost black—is often as emerald as Ireland during winter and spring.

Finally, twenty miles or so into the ride, I whiz down a steep hill into San Geronimo Valley, turn left at the golf course, then pump through sparsely settled country toward Fairfax. On a lark, I swing off the main road to ride through rustic Woodacre. There is no business district here, just a store or two and a post office in the overgrown, wooded community. I've always liked the beauty and unpretentiousness of this place, with its potters and painters and self-published poets living next door to custodians who can't afford prices in Ross or San Anselmo or Mill Valley.

A pleasant hour and a half later, I finally wheel my bicycle into our driveway and halt. I immediately notice Yvonne searching from the kitchen window. Behind her I see the profile of my father slumped in his wheelchair. I wave at my wife, and before I can put my bike in the garage she hurries out the front door, her face grave.

"What's wrong?" I ask, thinking of my mother.

"Travis just called," she chokes out, tears spilling from her eyes. "Jess killed himself."

47

Telephone calls to and from Travis in Bakersfield fill the evening: Will I be a pallbearer? he asks. Yes. Will we bring the kids down for the funeral? No. Jess's brother, Lou, calls to let me know the family wants no flowers, but prefers donations to a Catholic social services program; he is shaken and says little more. It is a tense, terrible night.

Travis phones back and he's pissed. "Juanita and I just had a bad one," he sputters. "She wants me to call that goddamn Marge and give her some sympathy. She'll shit a green brick before I do that. Marge better hope her life doesn't depend on me ever kissin' up to her."

"That's two of us," I snap, on edge myself. "I don't know exactly what went on between 'em, but I know what happened to him when she pulled the marriage apart."

"You damn rights," grunts Travis.

Unable to sleep, I replay and replay the past: when I was a senior in high school, the football coach decided to film our games, then critique our performance the following week in a classroom session. Viewing those shaky movies, however, I soon realized that the action on the screen never captured the contest I had experienced; no, that reality was internal and intense, too private to be captured by a camera. I began to believe that "objective" reality was an illusion; the past actually consisted less of facts listed in our history books and more of those internal experiences. When I said something to that effect to Jess Soto, he'd shaken his head and said, "You know what, Upton? You really are a dip-shit."

And now I am living these events, privately yearning for the erasure of memory . . . or the erasure of some haunting memories, anyway.

I look in on my father several times, then try to read, to watch television, and am tempted to break open the brandy. Jess is dead beyond all theory. Nothing I can do changes that.

In the morning Yvonne gives me a back rub, but even that doesn't help. Finally, she has to go to her office and Trish arrives to care for my father. Feeling wrung out, I telephone the convalescent hospital to check on my mother's condition—she seems to be improving.

After another call to Travis—apropos of nothing, I just need to talk— I drive to Crestview, where I find my mother sitting in a wheelchair in her new room. "Hi, Mom."

She looks up, eyes vague, and at first seems not to see me, then demands, "Leroy? Where've you been? You *never* come to see me."

"I was here day before yesterday." The delicious smell of barbecue fills the air and I'm immediately hungry.

"It's been *longer* than that."

"No."

"When can I go home? I hate it here. They won't let me go back to bed."

I sigh. The white-clad nurses and institutional feeling of this place have brought Jess's death back to my thoughts. I shouldn't have come. "How's the food?" I ask, making talk.

"It's not bad—except they have too much turkey. I hate it. And they give me Jell-O. I hate that too. Can I lie down?"

"Well, they cook for lots of people . . ." I can't develop interest in this topic, but it suddenly occurs to me that I hear no shouts, no grunts. Except for the drone from distant television sets—many patients leave theirs on all day—this place is unnaturally quiet.

"At home I could lie down anytime I wanted. Here I have to *ask,* and they *still* won't let me."

"Doctor's orders," I say.

"The *doctor*," she snaps.

"Oh, Marie," calls a voice, and I turn as a pretty brown woman in a white uniform prances into the room. "Are you ready for the barbecue? Is this your son?"

"Yes, this is Leroy. Leroy, this is Raenae. She's a new nurse. It *is* Raenae, isn't it?"

"You *know* it's Raenae. Your momma talks about you all the time. She says you're a professor."

I don't think of myself as a professor, but I smile and say, "I teach P.E. at College of Marin."

"Oh, P.E. was my *worst* subject. I better not talk to you," she chuckles.

"Leroy got all A's," Mom asserts—not exactly the truth.

"She sure likes to *brag* on you."

"And Suzie gets all A's too," adds my mother.

"She brags on Suzie too." Raenae pats Mom's shoulder and grins at her. "It's real nice meetin' you, Leroy," the attractive woman says, moving toward the doorway. "See if you can get her to come to the barbecue," she urges.

Suddenly my mother is smiling. "You know, Leroy, Raenae and that other colored gal took me to breakfast on this . . . this *bicycle*"—she nods at the wheelchair—"and they put me right next to a biddy who cusses all the time. Those *characters*!" She is actually laughing.

I smile.

"That gal cusses a blue streak, and *nasty* . . ." She shakes her head. "Those colored gals know I hate that cussing bit, so they just tease me." She is still grinning. "Why do they do that?"

"Because they like you, Mom."

"Is my name Upton?"

"Your married name is, yes."

"Well, how is it spelled? Somebody asked me and I couldn't remember."

"U-P-T-O-N."

"Will you write that down?"

"Sure."

"I must be nuts or something," she observes pleasantly. "Is it Thanksgiving?"

247

"Thanksgiving? That was a while back, Mom. Remember, Suzie was home?"

"Oh, Christmas is coming. I need some money so I can buy a turkey and groceries. Everyone will be coming over, you know."

"Okay, Mom."

She is smiling, apparently planning the meal she will never cook, and I can't help remembering when she ruled the kitchen. I am gazing at her when my eyes begin to fog and the corners of my mouth begin tugging downward—*Quit blubberin'!*

After a second I steel my face. I had intended to tell her about Jess, but now I can't.

Just then Raenae's dark face pops into the doorway. "Marie, you comin' to eat? We got a place all set for you. You, too, Leroy."

"Oh, *barbecue*," says my mother. "I hate it."

"She'll be there in a minute, Raenae," I tell the nurse.

The brown woman smiles. "Good."

"Ohhh, I just *hate* barbecue," Mom says.

"You used to love barbecue."

"They don't know how to make it up here"—her chin thrusts forward—"not like down in Bakersfield."

"You haven't had any up here."

"Ohhh . . ."

The lounge has been decorated with bunting to give it an outdoor feeling, and Raenae seats us at a long table with other patients. Immediately, a large man who sits across from Mom in a wheelchair turns to me and announces, "Wilford, he used to carry a roll a money big enough to burn a wet dog with."

I smile and nod, "You don't say."

"Hell of a guy, Wilford. He could damn sure whup a man."

"What'd he say?" asks my mother.

"Here you are, Marie." Raenae puts a paper plate with beans, potato salad, green salad, and a hamburger smothered in barbecue sauce in front of my mother.

"Ohhh, I can't eat *all* that."

"Eat as much as you can," Raenae smiles.

"You didn't tell me it was so *cold* here," my mother says.

"Cold?" says a lady wearing a dressing gown who sits to Mom's left. "Cold? Hah! I'd like to have a cold beer to go with this food." The woman, who wears makeup—a rarity here—smiles at me, then winks and says, "But I'll take what I can get. Thank God for small favors is what I always say."

"What'd she say?" asks Mom.

The man, who has been chewing vigorously, says, "In nineteen and thirty-three me and Wilford and the wife we taken us a place in Arkansas, but by nineteen and thirty-four we was flat busted. My wife she taken it rough, and she never did forgive me, and Wilford he never had that big roll no more either. That's when we all decided to come out here. Finally, the wife she taken off with Wilford and left me in Modesto. I got his dog and he had to buy the wife dentures," he grins triumphantly.

The lady in the dressing gown has been following this monologue, and now she bursts into laughter, "Ha! Ha-ha-ha! That's a good one, Bert. You were lucky to get rid of her. My first husband was like that: as long as things were going good, he was all sweetness, but let a little trouble start and *Oh Boy!*" She rolls her eyes. "You and me shoulda hooked up, Bert."

"Damn rights."

"Are you married, honey?" she asks me.

"Yes."

"With children?"

"Three."

My mother tugs at my sleeve, her mouth full of beans and potato salad. "What'd she say?"

"She asked if I was married."

"I don't like hamburger," Mom says, but she carefully cuts a piece from the charred patty, then gobbles it.

"You're sure eating it, though, aren't you, kid?" observes the woman in a dressing gown.

"What'd she say?"

"Wilford he never ate a thing but beefsteak back when he was totin' that roll," the man announced. "Drank ready-made whiskey too."

Behind us, I sight a young man about the age of my older son feeding a woman my age who slumps in a wheelchair. I am shocked, and Raenae notices me staring. She silently mouths, "Alzheimer's." I nod, realizing how close I might be to my mother's position . . . or my dad's.

"What is it you do for a living, honey?" the woman on Mom's left asks me.

"I'm a teacher," I answer absently, still watching that woman being fed by the young man I assume to be her son.

"Isn't that nice. It's steady work."

Mom swallows, then says, "My son's a professor."

"And so handsome, too," the woman adds.

Raenae returns to the table and brings a glass of ice tea to my mother. "You want some, Leroy?" she asks. "There's lots of food, too."

"No thanks, Raenae. It sure looks good, though."

"Here," says my mother, "you eat this. I hate it." She extends the quarter of a patty that remains.

I can't resist laughing. "No," I say, "you seem to be choking it down."

She is engulfing another spoonful of beans, so does not immediately answer. Then she says, "They can't cook beans up here either."

"Yeah, I can see that," laughs the other woman.

Back in her room, Mom immediately goes to the toilet, then emerges and complains, "Why'd I have to go to a *barbecue*? It was terrible. They can't cook barbecue up here."

"You cleaned your plate." Despite my heavy mood, I have to chuckle.

She plops on her bed and adds, "Who was that Wilford fellow you kept talking about?"

"That wasn't me. That was your old pal Bert, and I don't have a clue who Wilford is."

Raenae wheels another lady into the room and calls to Mom: "Did *you* ever put away some groceries, Marie."

"I hated it."

"Uh-huh," she chuckles. "You should've tried some, Leroy."

"I didn't want to spoil my supper."

"Darn," says Mom, "I've got to go to the bathroom again," and she hurries past the open door and closes it. She is in and out of her wheelchair, and seems mostly to use it as a vehicle.

"It was good seeing folks having fun at the barbecue," I comment.

Raenae nods. "Yeah, your Momma seemed to really enjoy it, but she sure was actin' up this mornin'."

"Was she?"

"She can be real strange, real . . . *ugly.*"

"Yeah, I've noticed."

"Bet you have. But she seemed to enjoy the barbecue." Raenae chuckles. "She livens up when you're here."

"I'm gonna come by tomorrow and pick Mom up for lunch, give her a try at a restaurant."

"Oh, that's nice. She'll do real good."

"Everyone at the lunch seemed . . . ah, lively," I comment.

"Those're the lucky ones," explains Raenae. "The real sick people, the sad ones, they eat in another dinin' room."

Something else hangs on my mind, so I add, "Seeing that younger woman at the barbecue made me think about how short life really is . . . how soon I might be in a home like this one."

Raenae looks at me a moment, then smiles, and says, "It just make me want to appreciate my momma and daddy more. My momma passed two years ago—cancer. She was forty-three. I just miss her and miss her every day."

"Oh, I'm sorry," I say, and I am, but I'm also sorry that my own view has been so self-centered.

"She's with God now," the young woman explains matter-of-factly, "but I still miss her."

I give my mother an extra hug and kiss before leaving.

48

The next day after my morning class I again visit Crestview. At the nurses' station I find twenty or so people in wheelchairs, folks who cannot help themselves, being assembled like a wagon train fearing attack. All are freshly cleaned and dressed, but there is little joy; these are not the alert seniors who attended yesterday's barbecue. Most of these faces are slack, and some are devastated. All wear restraining belts. One man, natty in a wool tweed cap, repeats over and over, "*Yo tengo hambre. Yo tengo hambre.*" A gray-haired lady, also expensively dressed, turns toward me as I wend my way through the crowd. "Won't you *pleeease* help me?" she whines. "I'll give you money. Please. I'll give you money." When I don't respond, she turns toward a man sitting blank-faced next to her and, again, whines, "Won't you *pleeease* help me? I'll give you money."

"Bastards!"

I turn and spy a woman with a nearly unlined, cherubic face and white hair tinted pink, her eyes wild; she is gazing at the ceiling. "Dirty bastards!" she spouts.

"Don't mind Dr. Mayweather," grins a hefty red-haired nurse. "She's not talking about you." She turns toward the cursing woman and soothes her, "Now, now, Florence. Lunch is almost ready." The nurse then asks me, "Are you taking Marie out today?"

"Right. We're going to try eating in a restaurant."

"Oh, that's nice. She really *is* better." Her nod is confidential and knowing.

But in it I feel that accusatory message: she doesn't belong here anymore. "Yes," I say, letting it pass.

I pick up the logbook at the nurses' station and sign my mother out. Someone tugs at my shirt. Turning, I face a tiny, misshapen woman, her body curled like a comma into her wheelchair. Although her hair is only slightly splashed with gray, her face is deeply creased and her tongue lolls from her mouth. With one clawlike hand, she is pulling at my shirt. I smile uncomfortably at her.

I am surrounded by wheelchairs. "How many patients are this debilitated?" I ask the nurse.

"Oh," she breathes deeply and looks away for a moment, "I'd say half or a little more. Your mom is actually one of the best. It seems like ninety percent are incapacitated when we've got everyone assembled like this for lunch," she smiles. Spying my mother standing in her doorway down the hall, she calls, "Marie! I've got your good-looking son cornered here," then she winks at me.

I smile and nod, but I'm thinking that this is an upscale establishment, yet no amount of money has protected these people from the ravages of age. My dad had always hated what he called big shots and Mom had seemed to admire them. But deterioration levels everyone. "Uhhhhhn!" cries a man's voice right behind me, and I jump. "Uhhhhhn! Uhhhhhn!"

The pleasant nurse smiles and nods toward the man. "That's only Mr. Leach. Those sounds are spontaneous. He can't help himself."

Behind me, I hear "Helllllp!"—the shrill screech of a tropical bird—"Helllllp!" I do not turn around. Instead I slalom through the wheelchairs toward my mother's room but, as I pass a doorway, my eyes meet those of an aging man who is spooning food into a woman's mouth, then wiping her chin when much of the pureed mess drools out. I hesitate, and he says to me, "We've got some swell memories together."

My mouth works, but nothing comes out. Tears well again—*Quit blubberin'!*—so I nod and hurry on.

My mother and I walk hand in hand toward the front door, Mom chatting nervously—"Where're we going? I sure hope they've got tacos. Food in this place is lousy." Near the entrance, another aged man in a wheelchair, a man whose face looks like a rabbinical stereotype, winks and gives me a thumbs-up. "Some arrangement, isn't it, kiddo?" he remarks—apropos of nothing, except life itself, I guess.

I return the gesture, but it does not reflect my tumbling emotions.

Despite my depression, our lunch at Denny's is unremarkable. Mom is, as far as I can tell, normal except for her reluctance to remain awake during the day, and part of me, at least, feels she no longer belongs in Crestview, just as I recognize that my father probably does. But we won't put him in there under any circumstances; he is too intimate a part of our home now. So our only option is to care for both of them, but this small, white-haired woman has everyone in my family frightened.

"I've got some bad news, Mom."

"Your father . . . ?" Her face is suddenly stricken.

"No. Jess Soto died."

She puts down her fork. "Jessie? What happened?"

"I don't know, Mom." It's not worth going into.

"Poor Jessie . . . and his family," she says, her eyes dampening. "Earl and I have to send flowers."

I drive home after returning my mother to the convalescent hospital, and I am unable to distinguish the guilt I feel for leaving her there from my grief over Jess's death.

Yvonne is home when I enter the house. "Trish had an emergency," she tells me. "She'll be back tomorrow. I'm just about to change your dad."

I kiss her. "I'll do it," I say, grateful for the task.

"I got time off for the funeral," she tells me softly.

"Good," I choke. "I couldn't go without you."

She wraps her arms around me, "I'm so sorry for poor Jess." This is like being held by my mother when I was little, and we remain silent for a long time. Finally, she kisses my cheek and releases me. "Did you call Marge yet?" she asks.

"No. Listen, can we talk about my mom?"

"Roy," Yvonne says softly, "you know we don't need any more stress right now."

I have more to say, but I swallow it and wander to my dad's room. Pop lies with open eyes, trying to coordinate his movements so he can roll onto his side. He has recovered from his most recent stroke, but another little piece of him is missing. I am no longer convinced that his toughness is an asset, yet I don't want to lose him . . . or anyone else. My face again begins crumbling, and I clear my throat to tighten myself; I seem to be suspended on the far, far edge of whatever control I retain over my emotions.

After several seconds, I call, "Hi, Pop. Time to get up." I grasp his hands and half lift, half pull him to his feet, his body swooping left until I manage to brace him, then I place his hands on the grab bar and hold him for a moment. "Have you got it, Pop?"

He cannot answer, but seems secure there, bent forward and puffing while I support him with one hand. Quickly, I pull his sweatpants down, remove his warm, soaking diaper—its aroma gagging me—then replace it with another. My father increasingly has difficulty downing fluids, so his urine is dense and foul. I hold my breath while changing him.

Pop's shirt and pants are wet too, so, sweatpants still bunched around his knees, I work his hands loose from the wall support, one of my arms under his shoulders. When I try to ease him back toward his bed, his body becomes stiff and panicky, one of his gnarled hands shoots forward with surprising speed and clasps that bar, almost upsetting both of us.

Now I puff, "Dammit, Pop, *please* don't do that. I won't let you fall." I must wrestle each finger free one at a time while holding his other hand, and he giggles—not a humorous laugh but about the only expression left to him. That finished, I once more walk him backwards those few steps, his movements ponderous and taut, his breath fast. Before we reach the bed, he stops shuffling his feet and his legs stiffen; he begins to slowly, rigidly collapse backwards.

I have bent to move the soiled diaper so we won't step on it, and I sense his hands slowly slipping from mine, his weight pulling away—he is listing, inflexible as a felled tree. Our hands snap apart, and I grab at him while I'm trying to rise from my awkward stance, but he slowly spins out of my grasp and thumps onto the carpeted floor—his eyes suddenly wide.

"Shit!" I gasp. I should have anticipated this.

In quick panic myself, I see my father lying there puffing, his face gaunt with fear. "Jesus, I'm *sorry,* Pop. I'm sorry," and suddenly I once more feel like bawling—*What the hell's wrong with me?*—and I violently blink away what could become tears, screwing a cap as tightly as possible on myself.

Then I grasp him beneath his armpits and strain to heft him to his feet. He is even more rigid than before, so it is like righting a thick pole, but eventually I manage to place him on his bed, lay him down, and cover him. I pull the metal restrainer bar up on the bed's side and slink guiltily toward the kitchen, realizing that my back is painful—I have strained it trying to arrest my father's fall, or perhaps by horsing him up with such desperate haste after his spill.

But that's the least of my injuries, so I veer quickly to the bathroom in our bedroom, lock myself in, and stand gazing out the window, puffing as my father had at the grab bar, but not weeping, not *blubbering.*

So much seems to be going wrong.

49

"We saw you play against Fresno J.C. last Saturday, Roy," said Travis.

"Boy, that one little spade sure de-cleated you on the kickoff, knocked you ass over teakettle."

That had been our final football game of the season, so he, his wife, Juanita, and I were sitting at the table in the student union at Bakersfield Junior College drinking coffee. "Hey," I said, "that guy wasn't little, he was just short . . . all muscle."

Travis, who had always loved to rag me, wouldn't let go that easily. "Little sawed-off turd. Me, I'd've turned him every which way but loose!"

Juanita shook her head, and said to me, "Does the term 'white trash' mean anything to you? I sure should've listened when my mother warned me about marrying an Okie."

We all laughed. All three of us were working part-time and plugging away at associate degrees. Well before four, when the next class started, the Plumleys departed for the library so he could look something up. I stood to leave when I saw the girl Floyd and J.D. had told me about— Yvonne, who worked at the drugstore near my parents' house.

She was sitting alone, finishing a snack, it appeared, and so pretty.

The stories I had heard didn't jibe with her appearance. What had J.D. asked Floyd? "How'd she like that big tool a yours?"

"Loved it," Floyd had said with a knowing nod. "And I mean *really* loved it."

I began to tingle where it mattered, so I approached Yvonne Trumaine and asked, "Is this seat taken?"

"No," she smiled up at me, a dazzling slice of white in that olive-skinned face. I couldn't imagine those delicious lips engulfing Floyd's tool. In fact, I really couldn't imagine any of the lewd stories I'd heard about her, but I sure wanted to find out.

"I'm Leroy Upton," I said as I sat down, "Floyd Henshaw's friend."

"I know who you are, Leroy," she said pleasantly. "I've been watching you play football. You're good."

"Thanks. And you're Larry Trumaine's cousin?"

She nodded.

"You're prettier than him."

Yvonne laughed, "I *hope* so. At least I don't shave."

"Where'd you go to high school?"

"I graduated from BHS."

"Me too," I said.

"I know. I read that in a football program. You were two years ahead of me. You're an army veteran and a PE major. You weigh 218 pounds. You're six feet three and a half. You were all-league and all-city in high school, and you played for the Fourth Armored Division when you were in the army. Right?"

This time I grinned. "Right," I said. "You know all about me, but I don't know about you. Listen, Yvonne, I've got a class coming up, but I wondered if maybe you'd like to go out . . . maybe even tonight, have a hamburger, maybe see a movie? My class is over at six-forty," I added hopefully.

She seemed genuinely surprised and pleased. "Mine too. I was going to study with girlfriends in the library . . ."

"Please," I turned on the little-boy charm.

"Okay," she grinned, and for a moment she looked like the prettiest fourteen-year-old I'd ever seen, except she wasn't fourteen. Neither of us was.

We met at the Student Union after class and walked to my car. "Hungry?" I asked as we drove off campus.

"Sure," she beamed, sitting so close her body's warmth excited me.

We motored to Andre's Drive-In, where I bought us each a burger, fries, and a large root beer. We talked, laughing more than necessary, but I found her as interesting as she was pretty. She lived in an apartment with three other girls, although her parents resided in town; that seemed odd to me. She had two older sisters, both of them married and living out of the area. Apparently her family didn't endorse her educational ambition, so she was working her way through school, putting in forty hours a week at that drugstore where I'd first seen her. She didn't seem to enjoy discussing her family, so I quickly changed the subject. Yvonne was majoring in language arts and hoped to become a secondary-school teacher.

When I told her where I lived—with my folks while I saved money for college—she laughed and said I was from the rich part of town. I could only grin, because our neighborhood was many things, but it was not an enclave of the wealthy.

"That's close," I chuckled. We were sitting in my undistinguished '49 Chevy, but she owned no car. She was not part of the affluent, high-profile, songleader clique that I'd been screwing my way through. Yvonne had always been nicely dressed when I'd seen her, but it suddenly dawned on me that she varied only two or three outfits over and over again. Maybe I was relatively rich.

She excused herself to use the ladies' room, and I noticed that, on a notebook she'd brought from school, she had written "Mrs. Leroy Upton" and "Mrs. Yvonne Upton." I'd known gals to do that before in my dating career, but never before we'd actually been out together. I was, as always, flattered, but couldn't help chuckling. In a place where so many married young, and so many adults expected early marriages, there had to be a little desperation at work in that doodling.

When we finished eating, I drove us to the 99 Drive-In Theater. A cowboy epic was playing, and I pulled the speaker into the car and adjusted it, then turned toward Yvonne. "I'm real glad we could get together," I said, and I meant it because I was enjoying her company. "You want anything from the snack bar?"

"No thanks." She was closer to me now, and her eyes had taken on a soft focus that young gals used to invite a kiss, so I figured what the hell, and put one arm around her, and kissed her softly, then not so softly, and she kissed back. I hadn't bothered to turn on the speaker.

A few minutes later, and I perceived one of her hands exploring my fly—I was being felt up. A moment later I had her blouse unbuttoned and was kissing, then sucking, a breast. "Ohhh," she groaned. "Ohhh, I *want* you," and she deftly freed my erection, then straddled me. "I *want* you. Ohhh lover! Ohhh God! Ahhh! Ahhhhhh!"

After several minutes, she gasped, "Thank you. Oh, thank you." Dazed by the sex, I was also nonplussed. I'd never heard *that* before. Thank you?

When I at last started the car to drive us home, I was spent but still churning; the sex, the repeated sex, had been rapturous and varied, but also strangely . . . what? . . . almost detached, like she was enjoying it, but it gave no clue to who or even where she was. I almost felt guilty . . . or maybe seduced. I stopped in front of the small apartment house in East Bakersfield where she lived and kissed her once more.

"Will I see you again?" she asked, and I heard something like resignation in her voice.

Everything Floyd had said turned out to be true. She was great sex . . . the best I'd ever enjoyed. But I was disturbed, too, because I liked Yvonne now that I'd spent some time with her, and I wanted to know her better. I wanted to know why she did what she did—a bright, beautiful girl like her didn't need to put out to find dates; that baffled me. On the other hand, I definitely wanted more sex with her. A couple more dates couldn't hurt. No way a guy could ever get serious about a pushover like her, that much was certain.

"How about meeting me for lunch tomorrow at the cafeteria?" I asked.

"Really?" Her face suddenly illuminated. She seemed genuinely surprised.

"Really." She kissed me, we kissed, and kissed again, and kissed again. . . .

When I finally drove away, despite the action, I actually remembered the girl as much as . . . no, more than . . . the sex, and I wondered what she remembered.

That night my sleep was uneasy.

50

Under a sky the color of an old nickel, Yvonne and I plunge down Interstate 5 on a trip I never imagined we'd be taking. To our right are damp, barren hills dotted with occasional wild-looking cattle; close to the road on our left, the straight, concrete channel of this state's longest stream, the California Aqueduct, directs billions of gallons of the northern water south. Beyond that treeless channel, are startling, varied shades of green highlighting the grids of cultivated fields; in low places, patches of ground fog linger like memories.

"Jess is the first one," I finally sigh.

"There's a first for everything," says Yvonne. "Somebody had to be the first one to die, but it didn't have to be so soon or so sad."

"He always said he'd piss in my grave."

"He was wrong." Like me, she is staring ahead. "Did you call Marge?"

"No."

"I wish you had."

The freeway dips, and suddenly we are engulfed in a pool of that fog, thick as oatmeal. I slow the car and turn on the headlights. Then we are out of it, soggy fields and barren hills once more visible.

"We're apt to see some people at the funeral we haven't seen for a long, long time," my wife observes. "Maybe some we'd rather not see."

"Right." I understand what she is saying and am discomforted by it. This will not be one of our usual visits home to a few special friends but will instead be a public event. We are driving toward our pasts, and I know I am apt to be in the company of men who once . . . *knew* my wife, and some women I *knew* too. Nonetheless, we continue south through flat land—garnished by pools of rainwater, by ghostly rows of palm trees and those stretches of lingering fog—extending to the distant, snowy Sierra Nevada, all magnified by the air's rain-washed clarity.

Three hours later, in a familiar old building, eerie echoes and the pungent smoke of incense surround us. I have not been inside Our Lady of Guadalupe Church since the day Jess and Marge Soto were married. It is smaller than I remember, and strangely unadorned despite bleeding statues and stained-glass windows. The pews are stark wooden benches. I am seated with other pallbearers near the casket at the front of the church. Across the aisle from us Marge and the children huddle weeping; Jess's three sisters and two brothers sit one row behind them.

In front of the large congregation, an aging priest is slowly chanting a funeral Mass, and I am transfixed. The medieval trappings of Catholicism have always intrigued me, although its medieval political positions haven't. But this is an experience beyond politics, the ancient ritual comforting.

After reading from a large red Bible held by a small girl, the old priest faces us and begins a homily. "I first met Jesús Joaquín Soto forty years ago when he was attending Guadalupe School. His mother and father, Luz and Joaquín, were my parishioners, and I buried them from this church. I confirmed Jess, watched him graduate from high school, and I married him to Margery here. I baptized their children, gave them First Communion, and I confirmed them." His voice is strong, his pronunciation flavored with Spanish.

He sighs audibly, then continues: "Now I have given him extreme unction and I am saying Requiem Mass for him. Doing those things is what it means to be a priest.

"I would remind you that I am also a man, and Jess Soto was my friend. I knew him as a tough young athlete and as a hardworking husband and devoted father, and recently I knew him as a sick, tortured man. Some of you will wonder why one who took his own life is being granted a funeral Mass in this church."

I'm shocked that he brings this up, but the old man's tone is pugnacious and he thrusts his chest forward as though challenging those who might disagree with him.

"Jess Soto did not commit suicide. No, he was killed by the madness that consumed him. He was a victim not a perpetrator.

"I would remind you, also, that Our Lord's message in the New Testament is one of forgiveness and love. He can forgive us even when we cannot forgive ourselves. He tells us we must follow his lead, that we human beings are at our best when we forgive . . . but not necessarily forget, for there should be scars to remind us that we are flawed. We are at our meanest when we perpetuate hate or carry grudges. Have you ever noticed how many people can't forgive others because of the guilt *they* feel? Forgiveness isn't easy, but it's not supposed to be. God knows all, so only he can judge. We can't. Only he understands motives and pressures that we cannot begin to fathom.

"Today our brother Jess is no longer with us, but be assured that his flaws are forgiven and that he is with our Savior. Jess's suffering is at last done, his illness is spent. He is praying for us.

"Now we must pray for his family—for his wife, Margery, his children, Jason and Caitlin, for his brothers and sisters, for Salvador and Luis, for Dolores and Maria and Isabel. And we must give thanks for having known him. Our Jess is secure with God." There is undisguised grief in the old man's voice.

A chorus of sobs has slowly increased during the homily, and now it fills the hall as the priest returns to the altar and once more begins the ritual prayers for the dead.

I poke Travis, who sits next to me, and hiss, "What's that about suicide?"

"Catholics believe suicide represents final despair, so people who do it are damned. It's the worst sin."

Later we pallbearers stand, wearing white gloves and white boutonnieres, on both sides of our friend's coffin next to an open grave. We are east of Bakersfield on barren river bluffs, an area where we used to hunt for jackrabbits, where we'd parked with our girlfriends. Now it's a manicured cemetery with grass like a putting green and a large pink-marble mausoleum nestled among oleanders. The sky has turned a clear slate blue and a brisk wind whips us, cleansing the air. Snowcapped mountains loom in the distance east, south, and west.

Marge and the kids slump on folding chairs beneath a canopy that shudders in the gusts. Jess's sisters and brothers are under the canopy too. Holy water is sprinkled over the coffin, hitting Travis and me without making me feel much holier. After a final incantation, the priest walks to Marge and the kids, embraces each of them, whispers something, and moves on to Jess's brothers and sisters. Everyone begins filing by.

Travis and I exchange embraces with Isabel, Maria, and Dolly, with Sal and Lou, who says, "You're coming by, aren't you?"

"Damn rights," Travis responds.

A moment later we hug Jason and Caity.

Finally, we find our wives and drive to Lou's large home, a tense, silent trip.

"You know," Yvonne says just before we arrive, "we don't go to church, but that service was really comforting. It wasn't like the empty, intellectual ones we've attended up north . . . people reading from Emerson and playing Beatles' songs. I felt like healing was really in progress."

"That's what keeps me going to Mass," Juanita admits from the backseat. "Accessing the . . . the *sacred* . . . that's what it's all about. Those rituals reach right into me."

51

Later I wander the large backyard of Lou Soto's refurbished Victorian house on Oleander Street, my hand wrapped around the neck of a beer bottle. Within the house family and friends are milling, eating, commiserating, trying to recover from the funeral they have just attended. I have no appetite.

Out here large trees, mostly cottonwoods, elms, and oaks, tower over the neighborhood, and, at the far end of the yard, an old barn has been restored too. A century or more ago, Bakersfield's mercantile elite built mansions in this neighborhood, and in those days the only brown skins seen around here worked in that barn. When Lou, Jess's younger brother, moved here, he invited Yvonne and me to inspect what he called his "new old house." A lifelong bachelor who owned his own real estate office, Lou was delighted to show us the vast round room, the parquet floors, the gleaming maple trim, the stained-glass windows. "Not too bad . . . for a Mexican," he'd winked.

I'm in the backyard now because I don't want to talk with Marge. As far as I know, none of Jess's buddies have comforted her, and I cannot bring myself to even speak to her: she drove my friend crazy with her ambition and insensitivity, and I cannot offer her pardon.

Eventually—as I knew would happen—Yvonne finds me wandering through the garden and confronts me: "Roy, I know how you must feel, but no one is more crushed by Jess's death than Marge. She needs *our* support, not just mine. It's time for you to stop this and go talk to her."

I gaze over her shoulder toward the fancy red barn with its white trim. "I can't do that right now, babe."

To my astonishment, she reaches up and grabs my chin, forcing me to face her. "Don't *judge* her, Roy. *Don't judge her,*" Yvonne's voice sizzles. "You haven't the *right*. You're a better man than that. I've never known you to be small. You don't know what really went on between them and neither do I." She begins to sputter, her chin quivers, then she spins away from me and rushes into the house, one hand covering her face.

I remain in the yard, pissed off at myself at how I just handled that, but still unable to swallow my turmoil and go to comfort Marge. Finally, I sit on a bench in a cluster of birch trees. A large bald-headed man lurches out of the back door and walks directly toward me. He has a bushy gray mustache and looks uncomfortable in a suit and tie. I try to recognize him but fail; whoever he is, he isn't in very good shape. I stand as he stops and smiles. "Don't remember me, do you?"

I can only grin and say, "No."

"You never were very smart, Upton. I'm Ernie, Ernie Smith."

Now my grin broadens. Ernie Smith and I had played football against one another throughout high school, bumping heads more than once, and we'd partied together a few times too. "Ernie, how the hell're you doing?" It's been close to thirty years since we've seen one another, before I went in the army, certainly.

"Good, Roy, real good. I've got a pipe business over in Taft. And you? What're you up to?"

"I'm a teacher up in the Bay Area now."

He pats my back, saying, "No shit? Up with all the queers?" He winks, then steps back and examines me. "Hey, you're getting gray-headed and uglier, but damned if you don't look like you could still play."

"Rather have my hair turn gray than have it turn loose," I respond with a smile.

He guffaws, "You've got something there." Then his voice lowers. "Too bad about Jess, huh? He sure was a good guy. He could hit pretty damn good, too, I remember. He clocked me a couple of times."

"He could play ball," is all I can say.

"You and Jess sure played good on old Cherry," he laughs.

I grin.

"Oh," Ernie perks up, "speaking of pussy, you know who I saw in the house—and looking good as hell too—remember that Yvonne Trumaine?" He raises his eyebrows and licks his lips. "Man, I remember when she was *everybody's* steady stuff."

An icicle slides into my heart. "Yvonne's my wife, Ernie."

He staggers back a step, then stutters, "*No shit?* Oh, I'm sorry, Roy." He hunches slightly like he's expecting to be hit.

"I'm not sorry, but get the fuck away from me while you can." My sadness is quickly churning into rage. I step toward him, my body ready.

Ernie mutters, "Jesus, Leroy, I . . . ," then he scrambles back toward the house.

After a moment I follow him. My beer bottle is empty and so is my heart. I am shaking. If I'd listened to Yvonne, I wouldn't have had that encounter with Ernie. My wife was right, I'm in no position to judge Marge or anyone else.

I slide into the crowded kitchen looking for Jess's widow, but not certain what I can say, and nearly walk into the old priest, who is eating a barbecued chicken leg and holding a goblet of wine. "Oh, Father Manuel," I say. I need to forget what has just happened, and talking to the priest might accomplish that.

"Jess would love this gathering, wouldn't he, Leroy? You're *Doctor* Upton now, I understand."

"I finally finished my Ph.D." Anger still boils in me, and I have trouble controlling my voice.

"Congratulations," says Father Manuel, apparently assuming it is sorrow that is causing me to choke. "And be comforted because I'm sure Jess *does* love this party in some mysterious, unimaginable way."

"Yes."

Gesturing with the chicken leg, the priest smiles. "When he was a youngster, Jess was an altar boy, and I remember two things about him best of all: he used to sneak drinks of altar wine until I told him it was blessed and would turn to poison if he drank it"—he chuckles at the memory—"and he loved to serve funerals because the families always gave him tips. I thought about that when Luis was tipping the boys and girls who served today." He smiles and adds, "Luis was a *malcriado,* never an altar boy."

I sigh, not ready for humorous anecdotes about the friend I have just helped bury. "I really appreciated what you said about Jess not being responsible for his suicide."

"Yes, well, it's true. Poor Jess had been ill for a number of years."

Ill for a number of *years*? "What exactly do you mean by 'ill'?" I'm thinking "distraught," maybe, or "tormented," but not "ill."

"Of course, he'd been on medication—lithium, I think—and he was able to remain in control when he took it, but . . . " He shrugs sadly. "Jess was a very sensitive man, and change seemed to burden him—in fact, everything did—that's why he made Margery's life so difficult, not because he was bad."

"He made *her* life so difficult?"

"No one felt worse about it than he did when he'd realize what he was doing, but toward the end he lost all touch with reality."

"Are you saying he was *psychotic*?"

"Why, yes, *que lástima,* I am. You didn't know, Leroy? Well, I guess that's no surprise. We Latins keep those things *en la familia*—our private lives are private."

He lets that point hang there, and I think, Yeah, I've never mentioned to anyone what haunts me about the past, why I can't stand to even be around Floyd or J.D. There are things a guy can't talk about.

After another sip of wine, the priest continues. "It's a wonder to me that Margery hung on so long—struggling to get an education so she could support the family—but he stopped taking his medication and she finally had to think of herself and the children and separate from him." The priest's tone is matter-of-fact, as though all this is common knowledge. "I counseled them both and urged him back to professional care, but it wasn't enough. He was a good man, Leroy, a decent one, but he was like all of us—flawed."

"Yes," I say, a second icicle piercing me, "like all of us." I am thinking about my dead friend who could not talk about his problems, and about what I've silently allowed to haunt me.

52

Across the room, Marge sits at a card table amid a cluster of women, one of whom is my wife. I begin weaving my way through people like a running back avoiding tacklers, slipping past this cluster, then that one—nodding to some acquaintances. Then I am next to the table. "Marge," I say, blinking and having to clear my throat.

She rises slowly, as in a dream, her eyes on my shoulder, not my face. "Yes?" Her voice is faint.

As soon as she stands, I scoop her into my arms, kiss her cheek, and say, "I'm so, so sorry about Jess . . . and about how I've behaved." My eyes are warming and I blink again, hard. "You guys are family, mine and Yvonne's. We love you." Tears have spilled from my eyes, then I feel my wife's arm over my shoulders, her cheek against mine; she is holding us both, and we are all weeping. "I don't care what people say about blood being thicker than water, love is thicker than blood . . . love is what we choose."

Marge sobs, "I thought you blamed me."

"Marge, I blame *me*," I reply. "You were the one who fought the battle. I pretended there wasn't one."

Some people circle us now like a football huddle, and I see Travis across the room. "Hey," I call, "get over here." He does, and without even glancing at me he embraces Marge. I can't hear what he says, but it is intense, and it causes him, too, to spill sobless tears.

Yvonne and I grasp him, then Juanita joins the huddle, all of us in tears, but beginning to smile now. "Listen up," Travis says, "I gotta say this. With our folks dyin' and all, we *are* one another's families. We *chose* one another when it was easy, so now we've gotta stick together when it's hard. That's what it means. That's what the hell it all means." More are joining the huddle: more people, more words, more tears. Everyone seems to be watching now.

"Amen," says Yvonne.

Then I see another face beyond the far edge of the cluster around us, looking almost frightened: Floyd Henshaw. My belly lurches and my fists close. I squeeze my eyes shut, but when I open them he still hovers there as though he wants to join us but knows he can't. Our eyes meet; Floyd nods, then quickly retreats.

My middle is still tight, my mouth coppery, and I feel a vast catheter pulling painfully out of my core: I need to *hurt* him. I squeeze my eyes shut once more, remembering Father Manuel's homily, and say to myself, No, this has to end, this *must* end. But that fury or intensity or whatever it is doesn't dissipate—a seething scar remains where the catheter had been.

Glancing at my face, Yvonne says, "Hon'?" Her voice is concerned. "Are you okay?"

"Yeah." I'm not, but I intend to be.

Father Manuel was right. "Excuse me a minute," I say, then I disengage myself, and thrust through the onlookers like a man walking against a gale.

Floyd has shuffled away, not quite fleeing, but moving steadily. I manage to catch him near the kitchen door and grab his arm. "Hey," I say.

He flinches, but does not back off. "Yeah," he grunts as he turns to face me.

"Good to see you, Floyd. Times like this, it's real important to be with old friends."

He blinks and seems to stagger back a step, then grins and extends his hand, and we shake. "You damn rights," he says. "Damn good, Roy. *Damn* good." Then without thought I hug him—the first time our bodies have touched since I'd pummeled him so badly all those years ago.

"Tell me how ol' J.D.'s doing," I ask a moment later, one hand on his shoulder. "Tell him I said hello, that I miss his scrawny ass."

Two hours later as my wife and I speed north toward home, I am pulsating over the events of the day when Yvonne says, "I saw you with Floyd today, Leroy."

That icicle again stabs my heart, but I nod, breathe deeply, and thrust the old pain away.

She continues, "There's something that I've been wanting to tell you, something really difficult . . . I haven't known how to start. It's about Suzie . . . " She pauses and seems to gulp.

I don't want to hear what's coming next, but know I have to if I'm ever going to escape what I've been doing to myself. I take a deep breath and brace myself as though to lift a great weight.

"I hate to even think about the time before we were married, let alone to talk about it," my wife says, "but your mother's been telling everyone, even the kids, that you're not Suzie's father."

"I know."

"Sometimes I think even you wonder about it." She pauses, seems to wait, but I say nothing.

When she again begins to speak, though, I interrupt. "I just know I love you and I love Suzie. You don't have to say any more."

"Yes, I do. I have to say it for *me*. Your mother's story isn't true. It's not even *possible*. I was out of control then, but not stupid. I knew how to protect myself."

And this stabs me because it reveals what I already know and hate, that she was aware of what she was doing . . . behavior that just doesn't match with the woman I know and love. But I can't let myself slip back toward the madness. I cinch my soul, and simply nod again; if she has to say it, then I have to hear it: for better or for worse.

"Then, Roy, I met you, and somehow everything was different. I wanted your baby. Suzie's yours. She's *ours*."

I find myself choking back tears as I struggle to respond: What can I say? "I think I loved you from the start—despite the sex, not because of it. I wanted you because . . . because . . . I sensed who you really are in that girl you used to be." I can hardly control the steering wheel.

"I was falling down a steep slope, Roy, and you saved me . . ."

"No, we saved each other."

The landscape is almost colorless in the faint winter light. A few wispy patches of ground fog still sit like cotton in low places on the land east of us. The sky has turned metallic.

"About your folks," she says, "we can work it out—or at least we can try. Together we can deal with anything. We really can. If your mom's better, we can try bringing her home."

"We can even deal with *not* bringing her home," I say. "I hate it, but I know she's in the right place. Let's take care of Pop, and when he dies we'll see about Mom. But thanks for being willing to try . . ."

This stretch of I-5 is straight, flat, and, today, eerily empty, so we are zooming north at seventy miles an hour. To our left, damp arroyos crease onto treeless hills. On our right, that familiar agricultural grid-work spreads as far as I can see, puddles shimmering here and there.

Half a mile or so later, almost choking on what should be easy words, I croak, "Yvonne, I love you. I hope you know that all the way down to your boots . . . to your toes . . . to your *toenails*. I've no regrets about us, except maybe that we didn't meet a lot sooner." I turn and smile at her, trying to lighten this heavy conversation. This tension should have been broken twenty or more years ago, but I couldn't; in fact, I can just barely talk about it now, so I lift her hand and kiss its palm, because I do indeed wish we'd met before all the things we'd rather not remember in both our lives had happened.

My eyes remain on the road ahead, and I see those faded, crooked letters, L-O-V-E, on my fingers curled over the steering wheel. A large truck tractor pulling a chrome dairy-tank trailer appears in the rear-view mirror, then gradually passes in the left lane, the long, shining cylinder sliding by. The rig suddenly lurches in front of us—too close— and that dangerous lane change grasps my attention. Before us, the oval, mirrored back of the tank reflects our green Honda.

On the curved surface, our image seems not to move while the empty road—narrow in front of us, broadening behind—flees past. We are framed there by swerved, surrealistic colors—brown hills curve on one side, green fields curve on the other, while faded gray encircles us above. For several moments, I watch us in that large mirror hurrying toward our own funerals, so inconsequential in the great scheme.

My left hand remains on the steering wheel, those faded letters from my past in front of me, and that tanker slowly, slowly pulls away. Our image becomes smaller. Around it, I notice sky and landscape again, but my attention remains on the shining, convex oval, on our car reflected in it. The road becomes a dark line, the moving land and sky churning colors. And I sit, lost in this world, next to a woman who has embodied for me what those fading letters on my left hand only intimate. Yvonne is my dearest friend, my pard, and soon we'll both be dead forever: no one will know we ever lived.

But that's wrong. We'll have known, and our loved ones will have known. I realize that I am one of those lucky people who is exactly where he wants to be with exactly the person he most needs, and if our old mistakes were necessary to get us here, I accept them even as I abhor them. For Yvonne and me, and all the rest of us suspended between birth and death, love really *is* what matters . . . thicker than blood or anything else.

I take my wife's hand and once more kiss its palm, then say, "God, I'm so grateful you're in my life . . ."